THE CHINESE BEVERLY HILLS

A Jack Liffey Mystery

THE CHINESE BEVERLY HILLS

A Jack Liffey Mystery

John Shannon

MP PUBLISHING

THE CHINESE BEVERLY HILLS
Published in 2014 by
MP Publishing
12 Strathallan Crescent, Douglas, Isle of Man IM2 4NR British Isles
mppublishingusa.com

Library of Congress Cataloging-in-Publication Data
Shannon, John, 1943
    Chinese Beverly Hills : a Jack Liffey
mystery / John Shannon.
        p. cm.
        ISBN 978-1849822442
        Series : Jack Liffey Mysteries
1. Liffey, Jack (Fictitious character) --Fiction 2. Private investigators
--California --Los Angeles --Fiction. 3. Chinese Americans --California
--Los Angeles --Fiction. 4. Missing children --Fiction. 5. Mystery Fiction.
I. Title.

PS3569.H3358 C34 2013
813.6 --dc23

Cover design by Claire Bateman
ISBN 978-1-84982-244-2
9 8 7 6 5 4 3 2
Also available in eBook.

A nod and a wink to my nephew Jim Harrison, *il miglior fabbro.*

We are all cripples, every one of us, more or less.
　　—Dostoyevsky, *Notes from the Underground*

People who are powerless make an open theater of violence.
　　—Don DeLillo, *Mao II*

ONE

No Human Being is Exempt from Panic

The sliding door of Firehawk-15 walloped open and they were both yanked outward by a gasp of the fire below. The Sheepshead Fire was crowning up into the canopy of ponderosa pines only a few hundred feet beneath their helicopter. Despite all his experience, Tony Piscatelli was shocked that the chopper had filled instantly with pounding heat and the smell of woodsmoke. The firefront in the San Bernardino Mountains east of Pasadena looked a terrifying mile wide as it advanced along the slope.

They'd been told there were fifty inexperienced volunteers down there, men from the minimum-security Wayside Honor Rancho Jail. The prisoners had mainly been chopping brush for firebreaks on the safe flanks of the fire, but the blaze had unexpectedly turned south and then back over a ridge into unburned fuel, threatening to trap the amateur groundpounders.

The two Forest Service smokejumpers took hold of each other's shoulders in the doorway and waited for the jump to find the civvies and lead them to safety over Trophy Saddle. They had their go from Chopper 10, the little control fire chopper above them.

Their bigger Sikorsky, on loan from L.A. County Fire, hammered into the turbulence and then orbited a burned-over safety zone. The firefighters tested their harnesses and made their final preparations to fast-rope down. A gigantic column of smoke billowed off the firefront, a red glow pulsing deep within the black.

"Hook up," Piscatelli shouted over the firestorm, slapping his jumpmate's shoulder. His stomach clenched up in nausea, as always.

"Hooked," Jerry Routt shouted back. They both tugged on the Sky Genie rig to make sure all was tight. They'd been fire service hotshots for fifteen and ten years, respectively, trained at first to work in disciplined groups of twenty men, but now the equation had been reversed. They were the elite of the elite, pulled aside to be smokejumpers because they'd shown they had initiative and daring.

Piscatelli tossed out a drift streamer, judging the air currents by the blue smoke flare. The firestorm yanked the streamer toward the burn column, and it tumbled end over end as it fell at an angle. Piscatelli touched his throat mike for the pilot. "Get us farther south, away from the firefront, man. Take us to one hundred, but find another LZ. You'll find a burnover at eight o'clock. Send the burger meat later."

Lightning shot blindingly out of the smoke column, and thunder followed like ripping canvas, trailing off into a growl.

"The LZ! See it?" Piscatelli shouted to the pilot.

"Negatory," the pilot called. "Wait! Fer sure. Three hundred and descending. This place is total crazy winds, my doomed heroes. I'm having trouble holding it. Jump with God."

"Hold that thought!" Piscatelli shouted. He felt his gut tighten.

"I gotta piss so bad," Routt said, but then laughed.

"Ready to go?"

"Ready, Teddy."

"One hundred feet, pals," the pilot shouted.

"Ropes!"

They hurled their half-inch nylon lines out into the ripping crosswinds. Their body weight would take the ropes pretty much straight down.

"Three rope turns!"

"Three turns!"

They leaned into one another and Piscatelli gave his old reliable friend a shoulder punch.

"Rock and roll!"

They rappelled out of the chopper together. Horizons whirled and heaved as they did a controlled slide down toward the blackened LZ.

*

Jack Liffey heard the thumping of Gloria's cane upstairs, louder than absolutely necessary, a bit of a statement. It tracked approximately from bed to bathroom, a pause, back into the bedroom, then whacked the floor a couple of times in mute rage, and abruptly clattered across the room, hurled.

"Jack!"

Jack Liffey wanted to take her up a cold beer, but the doctor had insisted she cut back on the self-medication. He tried to think of something else that might cheer her up. With three broken ribs, a rebuilt hip joint, two internal organs taken out—a kidney and a ruptured spleen—and six months' forced leave from her job at the LAPD, not much qualified as cheer anymore. Not to mention the psychological afterburn of her bitter ordeal in Bakersfield, which had included sustained beatings and rape. She still wouldn't tell him word one about it, but he knew a lot of it indirectly.

He headed up the stairs, noisily enough to alert her that he was on the way. She was facing away from him on the bed, wearing only a skimpy *peignoir*, or whatever the hell it was called. He was tempted to caress her, but she hadn't let him touch her in the six weeks she'd been back.

"I'm here," he said.

"Why? Why would you want to be anywhere near me?"

No jokes, he told himself. "Because I care, and you could use some caring." God, what an idiot I sound, he thought. Hold tight. She's going to give you a blast, but she needs you to stay calm as ice.

"You must be insane, Jack. Who could care about a worthless mess?"

"You're one of the worthiest human beings I know. Can I get you something?"

"Like what? A plastic bowling trophy?"

"It's up to you, sweet."

"I am not sweet, and why is it up to me? Why is it *always* up to me? Can't you ever get your fucking mind around what *you* need?"

"I guess I need to look into that." Hold on, hold on—he braced himself against her big metaphorical thumb that was pressing against the metaphorical bruise he carried around from so many previous failures. She had an unerring instinct for taking advantage of advantage. A sharp cop.

Wounded dark eyes came around to him, and he tried desperately to appear kindly and patient; she burst into a fit of weeping. He rested his hand on her shoulder softly. She let him. After she collapsed onto the bed, she let him hold her, spooning her. But not for long.

"Go away now, Jack. I don't want to turn you permanently against me."

"There's no chance of that."

"Stop it. Go away."

"I'm right downstairs." Just hurl your cane again.

He headed down the creaky staircase in the old frame house in East L.A. He wished he could kill the two malicious, dimwitted cops who'd abused her, but she already had. They'd wanted payback for showing them up in their own town, doing their ostensible jobs like any real pro would, and probably costing them their last chance for promotion.

Downstairs he could hear the inconsolable sobbing, so unlike her iron strength that it broke his heart. He turned on the TV to drown out the sound. Dinner was still two hours away, nothing else to do. A chastened and worried Loco tottered in to visit, sensitive to the aura of grief that permeated the house. The dog avoided Gloria now. It was a half-coyote with its own problems, in remission from bone cancer after surgery and chemotherapy—procedures that Jack Liffey hadn't yet found a way to pay off. The dog had been altered by its ordeal; he was more affectionate now, at least when he felt like it, his eyes losing some of their wild yellow opaqueness. He settled heavily on Jack Liffey's feet.

An image finally coalesced after the old TV's slow warmup. Smoky and disoriented shots of a mountain wildfire from a news helicopter.

"...More than a hundred thousand acres have been burned as of two o'clock, but only two structures have been destroyed and no lives lost. Tom, can you hear me? Tom? I'm sorry, we're having trouble with voice contact with Chopper 11. More than a thousand firefighters are battling the Sheepshead Fire now, including personnel from the Forest Service, the Bureau of Land Management, and county and city fire departments. And fifty volunteers from the Wayside Honor Rancho, who are threatened by the fire's detour over San Dimas Pass."

The young, square-jawed announcer appeared harassed, at loose ends, pushing around papers in front of him as unobtrusively as he could.

"The National Weather Service says smoke from the fire has already spread across Nevada and Utah. California has only received about one-third as much moisture as normal this year, and average temperatures have been almost ten degrees above normal."

"Patrick…am I on?"

"Tom, are you with us? I think Tom is back. Any word on the rescue team?"

"Nothing here. We're heading for Beaver Flat, where the volunteers are reported to be headed. Their two buses were incinerated on the fire road about half an hour ago, but expert smokejumpers are dropping to their rescue. You can go to the fire command center in Riverside for direct information."

Jack Liffey dialed down the sound, and when he realized Gloria had stopped weeping, he muted it completely. Forest fires didn't grab his attention that much, much like police chases on TV. They were just part of the ecology of disaster in Southern California: earthquakes, mudslides, and shooting sprees. TV always showed the same images, the same details, the same ironies and tragedies.

All as meaningless as a bad toss of the dice. Unless, of course, the fire ever threatened his daughter Maeve, who was living in a fire zone far to the west in Topanga.

*

It had been a difficult hour for Maeve Liffey. Bunny had finally agreed to undress and pose for her on the broken-down sofa, and between quick sketch lines and brush strokes, Maeve had been sorely tempted to fly across the room and cover her ample body with kisses. But somehow she'd kept to professional conduct so as not to upset the complex relationship among the four UCLA coeds who lived in the rambling rented house in Topanga canyon not far above Malibu.

"Thanks so much, Bunny."

"You need a better space heater. Jesus, Maeve. Are you sure you can survive out here?"

"I'm okay. I'll look into a better heater if you'll pose some more."

Bunny didn't commit. She wrapped her bathrobe tight around herself and trotted the fifty feet back to the main house. A few weeks earlier Maeve had moved out to the old garage, cleared out a generation of trash and turned it into her studio and bedroom, freeing her room in the main house for a fourth student to cut down their rent. There was no kitchen or bathroom out here, but she didn't mind sharing the ones in the house and she could use the extra space for painting, an obsession that had overtaken her not long after starting her first classes at UCLA. She'd had no idea she had any artistic talent at all, but even with her tendency to self-doubt, she could see how good her work was rapidly getting. On the canvas, the dynamics of Bunny's body were right there to see. The possibility of a sudden nudge or shift, an eruption of movement—even a good cuddle.

Her ringtone cried out the hook from Melissa Etheridge's "I Want to Come Over." She had only the cell, like everyone else in her generation. The day of the landline was just about over.

"Hi, kid."

"Hello," Maeve said to the strange greeting. It was a woman, but an odd voice, brash and accented, Asian maybe.

"This Maeve Liffey? Daughter of Jack?"

"That's me." Already she was suspicious. Who would be calling her dad on her number?

"Hey, Tien Joubert here. You remember me from many years, girl? My English still crap, but it don't mean I'm stupid, I been to Sorbonne. Speak five language. I run whopping big import business now. Your dad miss a good thing."

Maeve knew who she was now. The woman had hired her father ten years earlier to find a missing girl in Orange County, but she'd also relentlessly seduced him at a vulnerable time in his life and helped destroy his relationship with a previous live-in. Maeve's protective instincts toward Gloria rose automatically.

"I remember you. You grabbed onto my dad at a bad time."

"I worth hundred million bucks, girl. I don't need no broke-down roundeye man. I got plenty men knocking day and night. I need help to find girl, and Jack's phone number no good. Somebody at the number say go chase my tail."

Maeve guessed she meant the phone number from his old condo in Culver City, which he hadn't used in at least eight years. She debated saying *go chase your tail*, but she knew her father was desperate for business, as always. Finding missing children had been his specialty since the aerospace business collapsed and no one needed technical writers anymore. He always said it paid better than delivering pizzas, just. "Give me your number and I'll have him call you." It was as far as she was willing to go, and she might let that promise lapse, too, after careful consideration of the particular *broke-down roundeye man* in question.

The woman gave her a number with the 714 Orange County area code.

"This missing girl isn't you, is it?" Maeve asked.

The woman laughed with a self-assured abandon that gave Maeve just a hint of what had attracted her father.

*

Routt struggled to control his animal terror—his inner lizard brain still had an instinctual fear of fire. Orange flame billowed over the ridge to the right. The roar was almost deafening, but the head of the fire was temporarily halted along the ridgeline while it sent its scouts spilling south to outflank them. It was hard sometimes not to read a cunning and malevolent will into a blaze.

At that moment Routt stumbled, astonishing himself. He never stumbled—never. He still held the California high school record in the 180 low hurdles.

He glanced down and froze in horror. What had tripped him was a girl's body, lying prone just inside the wash. There was an obvious gunshot wound in her forehead. Recent. She was small and young and Asian.

"Tony! Over here! Before it's too late."

"Jer, go-go!"

"No kidding! Gotta see this!"

Reluctantly, Piscatelli took a few steps back. He reacted to the body, but he was too disciplined to take the time to talk it over. "Okay, she's gone. Let's get out of here."

"This is a murder."

"We know where she is. Let's get to a safe zone."

Routt saw that the girl's right hand was clasped. He reached down and plucked a necklace from her stiff fingers, tucked it quickly into his pocket.

"J.R., *now!*"

Buds of fire bloomed over the ridge, blinding holes in the world too bright to look at. The whole ridgeline writhed with fire at once.

"Situation!" Piscatelli shouted.

Routt felt the gusts of overpowering wind sweeping toward the fire and knew the beast was declaring itself a firestorm. How hot did they get? He tried to recall. Maybe 1,600 degrees. Hot enough to ignite asphalt roads. He sighted a gravel wash to the left. It was below the trail by thirty feet, good for a possible flameover, though bad for chimney effect from below. But you only had what you had.

"*Left*," Routt shouted.

"Drop packs!" Piscatelli shouted over the roar.

That was it. Piscatelli was no pussy. Routt took a millisecond to glance at the clawing fists of fire coming straight for them. Their hundred-pound packs contained backfire torches and fusees and would be deadly in a flameover. Drop, indeed. Routt spun and hurled his pack as far as he could. They wouldn't even be able to get to the safe zone.

"Shake and bake! Now!"

He heard Piscatelli go on his radio, asking for an emergency bucket drop right on top of them.

Routt ran the extra yards to the wash and yanked the shelter packet out of his stomach pouch, tugged the red rings to pop it open. It unfolded, agonizingly slowly, and he flipped the head of the foil shelter away from the fire. The flame was in a personal rage at him, growling. He'd never seen anything like it. He yelled "Gone shelter!" to Piscatelli as he clambered inside the low foil sandwich of a tent, and once on his belly inside he folded out the floor panels underneath him. He'd never been quite this frightened, and it took him down a peg in his own estimation. But training stayed with him like instinct. He slipped his forearms inside the hold-downs and bucked his butt around to thrust the sides of the shelter away from his body to get air space. Head low, breathe low. Don't panic. It's *always* better inside.

Go away, fire, Routt begged. I'm not the kingfish. I'll make a bargain with you, Whoever. Don't tell on me and you can scorch me just a little.

"Pisky, how you doing! Pisky! Talk to me!" Routt bellowed.

The world was a freight train passing right over him. A tornado of wind whipped and punched at his shelter. Pinpoints of light glowed through the foil, a few burning hairlines along the folds. The heat was becoming unbearable, and he fought the urge to burst out of the shelter and run.

"Piss-s-s-sky! Talk! I ain't so good!"

No reply. Shit shit, Routt thought. This wasn't supposed to happen. "Pisky!"

Training said to keep talking. Fight the sense of being alone.

*

It was ostensibly a hunting lodge in northwest Indiana, at the center of thousands of wild prairie acres, but the Reik brothers used it mainly as a remote Camp David for conferences with opinion-makers, now and future. Later in the week it would be a private meeting with several Californians and one of their think tanks, ACP, the American Council for Prosperity.

For now, the brothers were alone with their mint juleps on the open verandah that overlooked the small lake and rangeland that the elder brother, Gustav, called the Kill Zone. The inner room behind them was lined with weaponry to play with.

"Andor," Gustav mused. "What was the happiest moment of your life? Your adult life, I mean. Forgetting the days of Dad."

Their father, Maximillian Reik, had been an abusive tyrant of the first water and had beaten their mother mercilessly as a kind of punctuation mark whenever he'd bested someone in a business deal. A first-generation immigrant from Central Europe, he had made the Reik fortune by marketing oilrig drill bits in West Texas in the 1930s. The sons had expanded the fortune a thousandfold in the 1980s, first with refineries and pipelines and then by latching the Reik empire to the new technology of hydraulic fracturing—fracking—shooting superheated toxic chemicals at high pressure into the earth to break up layers of shale and quadruple the output of an oil or gas field. Halliburton and Schlumberger were bigger names than Reik Industries, but not by much.

"Oh, yes, let's forget Daddy. The happiest moment of my life, huh? Maybe I haven't had it yet. Nobody's assassinated that nigger president."

Gustav sighed. The middle-aged brothers agreed substantially on all things political, but Andor just couldn't stay civil about it. Gustav was on opera and ballet boards in Manhattan and knew how to moderate his speech. "Has the Californian arrived?"

"You mean the giant garden gnome or the Jewboy?"

"He's not a Jewboy, Ad. Seth is a good Protestant name. He's keeping his little teakettle brewing for us."

"Fuck California," Andor said. "It's just homos and Volvos."

*

Jack Liffey flipped through the channels, but the only stations not on some version of the Sheepshead Fire were Judge Somebody and an infomercial. He flipped past a poker game featuring several solemn-looking teens in hoodies. Did people actually watch poker on TV? What was next? Watching haircuts?

He flipped back to the fire—at least disasters were one of the few events ever broadcast live, like barricaded suspects and football games. The big San Gabriel Mountains fire seemed to be turning back on all the newsmen and firefighters and setting off a general panic of panel trucks and fire engines reversing down fire roads and men in yellow coats dashing madly down canyons.

Jack Liffey could certainly empathize, after his own experiences: a brushfire he'd been caught in, a monster mudslide, being thrown down an L.A. storm drain in a flash flood. Panic was just panic. Nobody was immune.

He turned the TV off just as the phone rang.

*

Maeve Liffey sat at the desk with her laptop, rarely used now because ordinary coursework had fallen away in the face of her tropical fever for painting.

She had a simple choice: phone her dad about Tien Joubert, or not. Back when he and Tien had first become acquainted, her father'd had a problem keeping his pants zipped, with some pretty bad consequences. But since then she'd had her own unruly sex life—a consuming passion for a Latino gangbanger that had left her pregnant, an abortion, and then an overwhelming infatuation with a rich and intellectual girlfriend. Now she felt she was pulling inward to let her psyche recover. She was powerfully drawn to Bunny, but could put that off.

It was Gloria she worried about, her dad's live-in, who was going through her own ordeal that neither of those hermetically isolated adults would talk about. Maeve had guessed that sex was off the table for Gloria right now, and her dad might just be vulnerable. Tien Joubert insisted she had all the suitors she needed. What to do?

After a moment, she picked up her iPhone and tapped an icon.

The icon was a picture of her dad.

*

Jack Liffey floundered and dug and then found the ringing handset at last under some tossed newspapers. He pushed the green button. Green is go, red is stop—it was about all he knew of even old-generation wireless phones. The speed dial was beyond him, as was everything to do with computers. "*Bueno*," he said. It made sense where he lived, but it often got him in trouble, having to deal with a flood of idiomatic Spanish coming back at him.

"Give it up, Dad. You can barely handle 'Grass-ee-ass'."

"The creaky old brain still has to try. To what do I owe the honor of a phone call from a young adult who's already detached herself from the fathership and is making her solo descent to the lunar surface?"

"Cut it out, Dad. I'll always be joined to you by a *huge* cable. I love my befuddled daddy to distraction."

He closed his eyes, almost on the edge of weeping at the abrupt affection. Gloria's maddened state has got to me, he thought. "Thanks, hon. I'll always be here for you."

"I know that. Tell me, who rescued *you* from the riots in South L.A.? I'll save you the trouble. *I* did, age fourteen. Do you need saving right now?"

"I'm fine. How are you doing at that huge campus? A place like UCLA can be pretty intimidating."

"I think I'm finding myself."

"You mean painting. That's great, I mean it. But you're still putting time into coursework, too, I hope. You have a tendency to focus down like a laser."

He heard the pause.

"I'm fine. Let's face it, Dad, there's always a little freshman slump, trying to adjust."

"It was sophomore slump in my day. Don't think I can't come over there and tan your ass if you're slacking off."

She laughed. "Dad, you never tanned my ass in my life. And these days it would be considered—well, never mind. My ass better remain my own business. Listen, tell me about Gloria. Is she up and around?"

"She's ambulatory. With a cane, but stairs are still beyond her."

As if overhearing the phone conversation, Gloria started bellowing in frustration, and he heard the cane pound hard across the floor and then thwack into the wall.

"Is she talking about it yet?" Maeve asked innocently.

Gloria went on cursing and drumming her feet for a while, but she didn't call his name. That had become the final, urgent signal.

"No," he said.

"You don't know what it's all about yet?"

"You'll have to ask her, hon. I know it was pretty bad."

"This is hard on you, too, isn't it?"

"She's in a bad way. When you know people are *really* in need, it's a lot easier to help them."

"Not everybody feels that way, Mr. Buddha. My generation doesn't use the word 'duty' very much."

Out in front of the house, a motorcycle ratcheted noisily past and someone shouted.

"Listen, Dad, I actually called you about something."

A chill went down his spine. Another pregnancy? She'd stopped a random bullet? She was dropping out of college? "Go on."

"Do you remember that Vietnamese woman named Tien Joubert?"

Is a bear Catholic, he thought, does the pope shit in the woods? The woman had turned his life upside down a decade back. "Yeah, hon, I do. I'm not into dementia yet. What's this about?" He could feel the reserve enter his voice, as if Maeve were about to suggest a special offer on term life insurance.

She told him about Tien's call and gave him the number. "Please tell Gloria I love her very much."

Funny the subject should boomerang right back to Gloria, but there it was. He knew exactly what Maeve meant: keep your pants zipped this time.

TWO
The Eisenhower Daydream

He counted to seven slowly between inhales to stave off hyper-ventilation. The keening outside was unbearable. Fire glinted through pinholes, wind slapped the silica and foil shelter. He was a religious man, Missouri Synod Lutheran, and he prayed for his partner and himself. He had to see his wife and children again.

"Our Father who art in Heaven…"

He forced his mind to use the four-fold garland, recite line by line and meditate on the words. Learn, thank, confess, accept.

"Why have You forsaken me?"

Something was starting to go wrong. Heat seared his back and buttocks. His consciousness had entered another place entirely by the time the bellowing outside began to relent.

He lay motionless in a new kind of space—probably between Earth and Heaven—in great pain for a long time. Every stir caused more pain. He heard a helicopter, maybe, and footsteps, voices.

"Over here, Bud." A man was suddenly very close. "You okay in there?"

He grunted.

"He's alive. Drop the litter."

He imagined he looked pretty bad if the guy wasn't even sure he was alive. The shelter was tugged, maybe cut, but he kept his eyes clamped shut in the new light. Not fire—daylight.

"Don't move, man. You're gonna make it. Guarantee." There was a pause, a light plucking at the back of his coat. "You've got first and second on your back. No third I can see."

Firefighters didn't lie to one another about that. He felt two fingers pressed to his neck for a pulse as a sweet voice began to sing to him in the distance. Angels?

"Pulse one-forty. You know I can't give you water yet. You hurting? Scale."

The state of shock was a step away, they both knew it, and shock could kill all by itself. "Ten. No morphine," he managed.

"I know."

It would mask signs the EMTs needed to see. The angelic song was swelling, approaching, and he could almost make out a hymn. "The other jumper?" Piscatelli managed.

"He didn't make it."

Blunt and direct was the code. "Quick?"

"Real quick."

"Why?" He wasn't sure what he was asking.

"Looks like he had something inside with him, can't tell now. It fired up. What's his name?"

"Jerry Routt."

Routt had known better than to carry anything flammable inside a fire shelter. He moved his lips, the words inward and inaudible, meant only for his dead comrade: "No more death or mourning or crying or pain, for the old order of things has passed away…"

*

"Here's Chop-Chop 'Bama."

Marly Tom grinned as he showed them his new poster on a sheet of foamcore, his characteristic wavery rendering of Obama's face, but with a wispy, dangly moustache and buckteeth, and the iconic coolie tunic with its filigreed buttonholes. The tip of an AK-47 could be seen poking up in his hand. Elsewhere in the country, posters might link Obama to socialism or Hitler or some local civil rights guy, but in Monterey Park, all right-thinking people knew that the Chinese were the real enemy.

At the bottom of the poster was the line: *Berieve. Or I keer you!*

His pals broke out in laughter and slapped his back. Once upon a time, the abandoned barber shop on a side street just off Garvey had been a busy headquarters for their parents' group, SAMP—Save American Monterey Park—but that war had been lost twenty years ago in the flood of Chinese immigration.

"Great work as usual!" Zook said.

"Maybe he is a black Chink," Captain Beef said. "Wasn't he born in India or something?"

The row of shops was owned by their patron, Seth Brinkerhoff, who gave them use of the blacked-out barbershop as their art studio, clubhouse, game room, and mancave. It was just about the last storefront in Monterey Park that had not become a Hong Kong restaurant or a Taiwanese bank.

The old working-class town they'd grown up in forty miles east of downtown Los Angeles was long gone, and Zook had felt betrayed and helpless for years. Almost everyone else from their high school had left, including the members of what had once been their motorcycle club, Satan's Commandos.

It was all due to the liberals and fags on the Westside, of course. The BMW-driving, wine-drinking, Chinese-buttkissers. They didn't have to live here, surrounded by gibberish mahjongg signs and rude shopkeepers who yelled you away if you didn't look Chink-a-dink.

Tony "Beef" Buffano turned suddenly on Zook, all three hundred pounds of him. "We can't let that nigger win, Z."

"Of course not. Calm down, Beef."

Marly Tom and Ed "Zook" Zukovich were the resident brains, and they didn't worry much about Beef's goofier outbursts. He had a good heart when you calmed him down, and you always loved the guys you went through football with.

"How about a midnight run to put up some of the posters?" Zook suggested.

"Goody!" Beef said.

Marly Tom smiled. "I'll print some up."

They whistled and belched and underarm-farted.

"I'll take that as a yes."

Zook looked around at the pathos of their prized Commando clubhouse, two of the old barber chairs ripped out at the roots and replaced by a rickety footie table and a few mismatched chairs. All they had to do for Seth in return for this largesse was run a few business errands and keep the Chinks and liberals nervous.

Zook's daydream was bigger. He wanted, some way, to reanimate the club and maybe even drive out the Chinese for good. As a member of the newly awakened intellectual avant-garde, he knew he appreciated the dangers of worldwide conspiracies like George Soros and the Trilateral Commission long before they were obvious to the unaroused public. The quality needed in every thinking man these days was the will to look at things unflinchingly.

*

"You're not really named Hardy Boys?" Gustav asked with a frown.

The enormous man had smacked open the French doors to the verandah like a force of nature. He was wearing a khaki bush shirt, khaki shorts, and knee socks, like some outsized South African leprechaun. He bellowed with laughter. "Hardi Boaz. Hardi is short for Gerhardus. With all respect, one white man to another." The man-mountain held out a frypan-sized hand and, uncharacteristically, Gustav took it. Andor followed him out into the Indiana night humidity, where Gustav had been reading.

Gustav was annoyed. He had retreated here to reread Ayn Rand, and was intent on finding out why it was crucial to decouple the rise in economic growth from median income. But that would have to wait now.

"The big South African is honored, sir. On behalf of the Border Guardians of California, thank you for your support."

Gustav knew that the man had been a mercenary of sorts in South Africa, and that after Mandela, he had moved on to America, unable to abide black rule. He ran a vigilante group east of San Diego who did what the Border Patrol couldn't—loosely, shoot first if you had any excuse. Nobody wanted innocent people hurt, of course, but if they turned out to be simple laborers crossing to *el Norte*, you could plant drugs on them or just bury them.

"Pleased t'meetchew, man. And the good man behind me. I think I am in the deep shit for charging in here like a gutshot rhino, eh. Sorry, a million pardons, hey. Yes, I will, thank you." He snatched a drink off the table where Andor had chosen to sit.

Gustav noticed the man had an odd way of not looking anyone in the eye. He was amused to see Andor's brows darken as his drink poured down this big clown's gullet. Gustav lifted his own julep.

"Can we do this gentleman the favor of the big gun?" Andor suggested.

"Why not?"

Andor went back into the house and Hardi Boaz sat down unbidden in the man's chair and stared out into the forest across the narrow lake. "You got Gooks out there?"

"You use that word?"

"Ja, sure. I work with guys from 'Nam and Iraq."

The usage had actually started in the Korean War, Gustav thought. He had a querulous urge to contradict this man, but the urge to enjoy his dynamism was stronger.

"*Magtig*, me, and my troopies run the border from San Diego to El Centro, I can tell you. Lock up the virgins and kiss my arse. We got the will, we got a nice hot desert on our side, we even got our own drones. You're not taking notes."

Gustav smiled, but there wasn't much humor in it. "I know what you've got. I paid for it. Have you ever had the pleasure of firing a Tyrannosaur?"

Andor was waiting behind them, holding a chunky-looking bolt-action rifle.

"No, sir. I knew a big-game chap who owned one." Boaz took the A-Square Hannibal .577 rifle and inspected it. "Jaysus. The only bore I seen bigger was on a battleship."

"Sometimes you have to stop a rhino, not just annoy it. We got some big twenty-point bucks out here, but let's not wait around. There's a two-hundred-pound solid salt block just left of the cottonwood. See if you can make a mess of it."

The big man opened the rifle bolt and inspected the cartridge the size of a small flashlight, then ran it home again. "May our enemies die soon, I say, and bloody hell."

Gustav noticed his brother watching the man with great anticipation, as if expecting him to grow a second nose. They had never seen anyone fire the Hannibal without being knocked flat or thrown back through the French doors. It had the heaviest recoil of any shoulder-fired weapon ever made, a 220-pound punch.

"And Hardi will have his fun along the way," Hardi Boaz added. He braced a bit, but not much, and sighted out over the breeze-rippled lake. The explosion was far too loud, and the big man rocked a little with the punch. The salt block had vanished in a white puff.

He put the butt of the rifle down at parade rest and sighed. "Ouch," he said without inflection. "I take it you two gentlemen are having your fun along the way, too. There's no recoil pad on this weapon. You got no bloody need to teach me no lessons."

"We have plenty of work for you, Mr. Boaz," Gustav said tonelessly.

*

She advanced on him and rubbed the material of his fraying sport coat between two fingers. "I get you good coat, Jackie, cashmere, good Italian design. Not this Target shit." She pronounced it Tar-zhay, as so many did, but in her case, he wasn't sure it was a joke. French had been Tien Joubert's first language after Vietnamese; then Mandarin, Cantonese, and only then English. "Good shoe, too. Ugh." She made a face. "Why you still dress like high school teacher?"

"In my job, it's good to be invisible."

He'd always enjoyed her artless candor, and he had enjoyed a lot more about her, too, as the pheromones gusting his way were reminding him. Her face was still striking, with the porcelain beauty of a doll. Amazingly, she still lived in the same big, crass, upper-middle-class house on an artificial basin full of yachts. The town in north Orange County insisted on spelling itself Huntington Harbour, so he insisted on pronouncing it *Har-BOOR*. The house was all blue carpets and glass and stainless-steel furniture, like a sixties daydream of a robot-servant future.

"You still handsome man. Maybe I come after you. No, no worry. I got men banging my door all day. I worth half the gold in Fort Knock. My English still crap, I know."

People running after money at her speed never had the time to learn much of anything that wasn't immediately useful, he thought.

He rarely joked with her because she had absolutely no reflection or irony. That generally required a slower life process.

"How you been, Jackie? Got woman that good for you? Got money? I try to phone that apartment and the phone no good."

"I haven't lived there for a long time, Tien. Can we sit down and relax a little? I'm having a hard time keeping up with you."

She laughed. "You always like that. I had to drag you into bed with me. But it was good, right? Even now, I got pretty tight body." She pressed her breasts as if to demonstrate. "You want to see?"

Quickly, he said, "I'll take your word. How about some tea? You used to love tea."

"You sit." She turned on her heel and glided gently to a doorway. "Lupeta, *háganos algún té, por favor.*"

Amazing. She'd learned a bit of her sixth or seventh language. He'd never managed even a second, though he'd tried hard with Spanish. He knew Tien was a bright woman, even if her intelligence shot off in odd directions. She was tough as nails with the shady characters who tended to hang around Asian import-export.

Out the wall of glass across her patio-dock, he could see that she'd replaced her little fringe-topped tootle-bug boat with a yacht the size of Kansas. He couldn't even see the top deck. Unfortunately, it destroyed the view, unless you got off on masses of white fiberglass.

She came back and settled into the blue easy chair opposite him. Thank heaven, he thought. She was entirely capable of settling abruptly onto his lap.

"You still have John Bull?" he asked—an affectionate English bulldog he'd liked.

"He die. He get old, blind, can't hear much. I take him out one last time, down street, to get his end in girl terrier. So he die happy."

"My dog got bone cancer and it cost a small fortune to keep him going. I don't know why I did it. I guess I'm sentimental."

"You ain't told me if you got good woman."

"Yes, Tien. I have a wonderful woman, an American Indian who works for the L.A. police. She's very clever and—" He tried to think what quality Tien might respect. "—indomitable. I live with her in East L.A. now."

She made a face. "With all the Mexicans and gangs."

"You people in Orange County are so scared of the part of L.A. away from the ocean. It's all fine." He needed to separate himself from Tien as much as he could.

"I scare of nothing, Jack. You know that."

"Good. I'm scared of all sorts of things. Why don't you tell me about this missing girl."

A hefty woman came in carrying a tray with all the tea accoutrements.

"*Gracias*, Lupita. *Allí. Lo verteré.*"

Tien leaned forward and poured out two cups of tea. He hated Chinese tea but he sipped anyway.

"The girl name Sabine Roh. She my niece—many time remove, you say. Complicated. In Vietnam her name would be Ng Suong, but her parents good sport, they good immigrant, you know—try hard to fit in. They turn name backward, like America, and make it more simple. Sabine conceive in refugee camp but born here, her mother three week off the boat. They go to Monterey Park right away, where all the rich hicks from Taiwan go."

"Hicks?"

She gave an unreadable shrug. "The Rohs from Vietnam like me, but Chinese inside. I tell you Sabine super-duper good girl as she grow up. Brownie stuff, Catholic Church two time a week, class president. She work for me in summer, learn business fast. Good and pretty, too. I love this girl so much."

"She have enemies?"

"Hah! In that town? That place still got white bums on motorcycles, bums in city council, bums in Chamber of Commerce. Lotta rich Chinese from Hong Kong and Taiwan move to the San Gabe Valley, but they funny. Not good guest. They never really put thank-you-USA flag up pole and salute Mickey Mouse. Put up big Chinese sign on every store. *Merde*! So stupid. That make round-eyes protest all the time: 'Gooks go home.' Ghost people there go nuts and demand English only. And something call *slow growth*—really mean no more Chink malls. And it all so unnecessary." She was talking so fast that her command of English seemed to degenerate before his eyes.

"Welcome to America, Tien. Hold off on the editorials and tell me about the girl."

Tien sipped her tea and took a deep breath. "You know my rule. You got to come out even-steven in life. Exact even is best—not on top, not on bottom. I loan money when people need it bad, don't ask for interest. When I want something, I get it. Big screen TV, first in line for iPhone. Friend at courthouse.

"This family, the Rohs, they save my old uncle after VCs take over. He was like father to me, donkey's age. They get him out of Vietnam to refugee camp in Thailand and then to USA. Plenty risk. Crazy commie kids with guns everywhere those days, you know."

Tien made a sour face. Practicality so thoroughly dominated her thinking that Jack Liffey had never told her he'd once had a political streak of his own. She'd never had much of an interest in dreams, only what you could grab right now.

"Boo for all that. I owe this guy Lan and his wife Qui. Owe big time."

She sat down and he waited, but she was lost in her head for the moment.

"How long has the girl been missing?" he asked finally.

"Sorry, Jackie. First you got to know. Sabby got flea in ear for years. She always want to be nun. They too Catholic, but Mom and Pop Roh say *no way José*, put foot down. So Sabby study to be lawyer. I bet she think one day when Mom and Dad gone to Heaven she get herself off to nun school. She one damn pretty girl, too. Could get guys like flies, just like me." She grinned. "Not so bad legs for old woman, huh?"

He had to glance. Yes, they went all the way up. "How long has the girl been missing?"

"Mr. Down-to-Business. At least until the tits come out. No, no— calm on you. You safe from me, Jackie. Maybe."

Something about his presence had pulled her hormone trigger. He couldn't believe she'd changed so little in ten years, and he wondered if inside he'd changed. But he could keep his pants zipped this time. It was harder, of course, with Gloria in full physical retreat.

"Want cookie, Mr. Business?"

"Sure." He disliked those, too, but anything was better than this tsunami of temptation thundering toward him.

Tien Joubert—the French surname came from an early and discarded husband—glided effortlessly around the glass coffee table, a remarkably small and delicate woman, and set two almond cookies on his plate, making sure to press a little against his leg.

"Sabine Roh gone for one week now, Jackie, ever since telling mom she go to meeting at St. Tom Aquine Church. She good girl, as I tell you. Never never lie to mom."

"People can be unpredictable, Tien."

"What you mean?"

She sat in her easy chair and he relaxed.

"They meet someone and emotion overwhelms all logic." This wasn't a very good subject to bring up, he realized. "You have no idea how many 'really good kids' I've looked for who'd gone off the rails. It happens."

"Not this little girl, believe me. Years and years she marinate herself in wholesome." Tien Joubert handed him all the necessary names and addresses and phone numbers on a sheet of her business letterhead. *Lucky International Commercial LLC*, it said, with a very classy logo.

"I'll find her."

"I just hope she not dead, like last one."

He'd met Tien on commission to find a similar girl who eventually turned out to have been murdered by a serial killer. He felt no guilt about it—she'd been dead before he showed up. But he hoped Sabine wasn't consigned to the same fate. She sounded like one of the kids the future needed.

Ever since the end of the long Eisenhower daydream in the 1950s, it had become a spooky hard rain out there for kids.

*

Maeve parked across Greenwood so the new scrape on the right side of the car wasn't visible from the house. She'd done it at a Hollywood disco one night with some friends, after two beers. It was only an old Toyota Echo, but it was still reliable and she hated to think of herself as unreliable.

Her dad's pickup was gone, but Gloria's little blue SUV was still tucked up the drive. According to her dad, Gloria could barely walk, but was elsewise okay. Maeve didn't really trust his upbeat tone. She'd lived with Gloria off and on since she was fourteen, and the woman had become her trusted auntie and backup mom.

She knocked softly, then finally let herself in with her own key. "Glor, it's only me!" she called. Maeve looked around briefly and then made her way to the staircase. "Gloria, you up there?"

"Where the fuck else would I be?" Then the anger caved in. "I'm so sorry, Maeve. Come on up and sue me for abuse."

Maeve pretended the outburst was all a joke and forced a laugh as she stepped into the bedroom. She was shocked by Gloria's looks. She'd lost a lot of weight and she was pretty disheveled. Gloria clung hard to a black cane as she sat up on the edge of the bed.

"Can I get you something? Can I brush your hair?"

"Be a princess and get me a beer. Two beers."

Maeve fetched her one bottled Indio from the fridge, and brought up one of her dad's ginger ales for herself. "Only one beer was cold," she lied.

Gloria smiled at the lie. Her cop radar still worked. "Don't worry, darling. I'm not really a lush. Jack just takes everything the doctors say too literally. What do they know?"

In the bathroom Maeve found the hairbrush. "Turn sideways." The woman usually kept her hair cop short, but the lustrous jet-black American Indian hair was growing out and tangling, flecked handsomely with gray. Maeve wished her own mouse-colored hair had some of this body.

"Ow." A snarl.

"Sorry. I'll be more careful."

"What brings you over to the poor side of town?"

"You probably want the truth, don't you?"

Gloria winced as Maeve caught another tangle. "You may as well not bullshit me. That forces me to change mode."

"I surrender. I came because I'm worried about my *Tía* Gloria, and I'm worried about the big picture with you and Dad. That's the truth."

Gloria thought for a few moments, then gulped a lot of her beer. "Do you always need things all figured out?"

"You know me. I'm full of concern and slow Zen."

"What the hell's that mean?"

Maeve realized there was going to be no lightness of mood just now. "I don't know, sorry. I care about you as much as my mom, Gloria. I care about my dad. I want everything in my whole world to be okay."

"I love you, too, hon. If you keep up this heavenly brushing for a while, I'll answer any question you ask as long as you agree to answer a few of mine."

Maeve reached to sip at the soft drink can, then went back to brushing. "A real women's truth time." She took a deep breath. "What happened to you up in Bakersfield?"

Gloria made a twisted face. "Sure, throw it all down on double zero on the first spin. Woman to woman, do you mind if I summarize a little? I'm hazy on details."

"Whatever, *Tiaíta*."

Gloria smiled at being called a slangy 'auntie', but then she frowned and retreated back inside herself. In fragments and phrases she told Maeve a little of the tale of two very rotten and very stupid cops who had cuffed her and spent an endless evening working out their drunken rage on her, the woman cop from "the big L.A." who had shown them up as incompetents. She'd been beaten a lot and then—she used the police term—sexually assaulted many times. There was a long break here. She had no memory of it, but she knew she'd managed to grab an ankle gun from one of them and shoot them both before they could kill her as they'd been promising all night.

"It was the powerlessness," Gloria said. "Those *pendejos*!" She shuddered. "I still feel it inside me, every day, every hour. It sends me to bad places."

Maeve kept brushing her hair mechanically, though her eyes burned. She let the brush sag for a while. "Awful. Awful," Maeve choked.

"Dig it," Gloria said harshly. "So let's get your mind off *Tía*. Truth time, remember?"

Maeve took a long drink of the ginger ale and nodded once.

"Where you at in your head now, girl? Cocks or cunts?"

Maeve wanted to protest that there was no reason to put it so vulgarly, but she didn't. "Both. Why do I have to choose a body part? I'd rather choose a whole person I'm fond of, whichever sex."

"That's no answer," Gloria said. "Trust me, you can't keep switching your feelings around."

"Have you ever loved a woman?" Maeve asked, and she started brushing Gloria's glossy hair again.

"I've never noticed feelings in that direction. But damn men, either. Your dad is one of three men I've let touch me. Total, three."

"You know, that wasn't really where my question was going. How are things with you and Dad?"

"You might make a cop someday. You get one turn and you pretend you get two." She tilted her head back into the brush. "Right now, I'm as dead as a stone inside, hon. I got no feelings at all. I got no what do you say... 'libido.' Your dad is the kindest man I've ever met and I really rely on him. It's spooky—I'm such a pain in the ass to him and he's so good to me. But that's the way it is right now."

"I figured there was another guy," Maeve said lightly. "Didn't you hint it to me?"

"Now you got me against the wall. Jack's your daddy." She seemed to consider, and then Maeve felt a tremor. "You want it all, you can't have it. We all want a white knight to ride out of the fog and fix up our whole life. Somebody cheerful that we got no history with, so we can think there's no problems between us and never will be. I may be a mess, but I had those dreams, too. The rest you just got to guess."

An old muscle car was revving on the street outside, but Maeve tuned it out. She was so tense she thought she might just freeze solid and keel over. "I want both you guys as perfect as a fifties sitcom."

"It's my turn—but first I get another beer. I'm sure it's cold by now."

"You sure?"

"Don't start. Just don't."

Maeve trudged downstairs. This visit wasn't working out as tidy as she had imagined. She trudged back up and handed Gloria the second and third of the bottles and had the fourth herself.

"Okay, stepdaughter. Neither of us is going to be self-righteous today, I hope. You know what your dad is worrying about the most? You. He worries you're goofing up at college."

Maeve let out a breath. "Can I appeal to your sense of mercy?" she evaded. "I'll do this again when I know more about what I'm doing. And next time I want to ask what it was like growing up a Native American, a real outsider. I was such a white, middle-class, clueless girl."

Gloria cocked her head, thinking. Maeve knew Gloria's childhood was *really* off limits.

"Yeah, some other time."

*

"That's a great one to take down."

They'd taped over the license plates and then taped the dome-light buttons in the door well of Marly's Oldsmobile Rocket 88 so the light wouldn't come on when they jumped out with their paint guns. Zook loved radical shit like tonight. The true thinking man loved action, despite what they said.

"You know why I love Chinks so much?" Marly Tom announced.

"Go for it."

"Because you can blindfold them with dental floss."

They spluttered and laughed.

"Let's hit it," Beef said. "I always hated that sign."

The car screeched to a stop just off Garvey, the main drag at two a.m. They jumped out and ran toward the stack of business signs promoting eight shops in the mini-mall. The bottom segment was just two huge Chinese letters. The next one up translated its Chinese to *BBQ Queen*.

There was a special animus affixed to this spot, since it used be their holy Dixie's Diner. They lined up like an execution squad, aiming the paintball rifles upward—a Tippman Custom 98, an Extreme Rage ER3, and a BT Omega. Marly Tom had reloaded the paintball shells with permanent oil paint.

A few cars were passing but nobody stopped to gawk.

"For white men with big dicks!" Beef shouted.

The pressure tanks of their guns were fully charged and they fired again and again until the bottom placard was unreadable.

"Up!"

They hit Prestigious Learning Center, then Café Happy and they were working on Da Zhen Asian Travel when they heard a siren, and discretion ruled. A few random shots disfigured the top signs.

"Out comes the Beef-phone!"

Beef always documented their mayhem with his cellphone camera. He shot two snaps and followed it up with a haw-haw bray.

As they trotted back to the car, they noticed a shadow up the side road, watching them.

"Hey, what's he want, looking at us?"

"Chrissakes, Beef, go ask him."

Instead Beef launched a quick series of shots and the shadow took off.

THREE
Better Living Through Chemistry

Not a pro, but at least somebody smart enough not to barbecue himself, he thought. The torcher had used the most common timer of all: a cigarette shoved into a book of matches. Walt Roski of the county's Fire Investigation Unit bent down to point out the shiny ash flakes to his trainee team of half a dozen recruits in white work suits.

He explained that the immediate fuel load had been bulked up with newspapers as his finger traced lines of accelerant sear, probably charcoal lighter. The team had been on the scene for half an hour studying the presumed heel of the fire in Sheepshead Canyon, and two of them were documenting everything with big digital cameras.

His cell phone called him away from the scene—the voice of he who must be obeyed—and Roski left the recruits to pound in posts and string off meter squares like an archeological dig. He was annoyed, but he knew a fed smokejumper had died the day before and another badly burned, and he was sure the call had to do with that.

He charted his course carefully along the fire roads. The main burn was flaring due east again, still only sixty percent contained, with the open end of the firebox above Monrovia six or seven miles away. He was perfectly safe here, but all the landmarks were altered and the burnout still smoldered in spots.

It saddened him to see big charred-off trees. A house could be rebuilt in a year, chaparral grew back in a season or two, but ponderosas and firs took a generation. Finally he came upon a half-dozen glum-looking men standing around—clearly desk jockeys, wearing ill-fitting firecoats over their J.C. Penney suits. A motionless bright yellow Jet Ranger rested nearby, a federal chopper, not county. The Shiny Shoes had dropped in from the sky.

"Gentlemen, Walt Roski. County Arson." He shook hands all around, not remembering a single name, except Kenya from a handsome black guy. He never did remember names unless he wrote them down. Bad trait for an investigator, but he was getting old and several varieties of rage from a bad divorce and other life calamities had burned through him, leaving his own ecosystem pretty charred.

A short man with Forest Service patches on his coat stalked toward him, an aging gamecock. You could feel the political buoyancy, an ass-kisser who'd risen through the bureaucracy like a turd in a toilet. He'd taken off his tie, but he still wore black wingtips that had no business up here.

"Gene Rockfelder, Region 5, Vallejo." He didn't offer Roski his hand. "Walter, they say you're very good. We'd like you to turn your attention over here."

"Nothing else on my plate just now," Roski replied tightly. The man using his first name already made him clench his teeth.

Roski followed him on foot in silence for over a minute. What he saw on the gravel wash was immediately self-evident and pained him deeply. The fire shelter had been knifed open to get a body out. The area should have been a safe zone. It was heavily graveled, and had probably been relatively clear of brush. But he saw that the gully heading down would have made quite a chimney.

"What we need you to look at is a breach in the shelter. We think something ignited inside. The man should have known better. He had more than fifty jumps."

"How many jumps you got?" Nothing was as infuriating as an office-bound cocksucker dissing a real firefighter.

The short man turned and stared hard at him. "Say what?"

"Thank you for your assistance, sir. I'll check the scene out."

Roski squatted down and studied what he could see of the tent floor, without touching anything. He'd seen a burned-out fire shelter only once before, but not as peeled back as this, and this was the new-generation design. He wondered if it might have an undiscovered flaw. With a ballpoint pen, he lifted a little flap of fabric. Yes, the inner foil and PVC appeared to have burned away before the outer Kevlar and foil.

All of a sudden, the red blob of a laser pointer was orbiting an irregular object on the shelter floor. "Right there, Walter." The light circled a mangled lump, like something rescued from the seabed.

"Don't do that," Roski said irritably.

"What?"

"You heard me. I know my job. It's amazing for a rube like me who's way out in the counties, but true."

"Nothing intended, Walter."

Roski stood back up in a true rage, not sure what was eating him really, but unable to stop. "Report me for insolence, Tiny Tim. I love getting flak."

"You must be on edge today. I'll let this go."

"You're just a buzzing noise in my head. Go away."

"Weeping Jesus."

"But first, have your Fed pals yellow tape this area before they square-dance all over it. I'll be back soon. Right now I'm staring a torcher square in the eye down at the heel of the fire. If you know what 'heel' means."

"Enjoy your short, unhappy tenure, cuz."

*

"We don't go to live in Ming-huong, no way," Mrs. Qui Roh told him with animation. "Sorry—that's Vietnamese for Chinatown. Chinatown all crammed full and mostly old Kuomintang people from 1950. You know, Chiang Kai-shek people. Monterey Park good for all Asians. We got one cousin live here before we come from camp in Galang Island—1987. We was boat people from Vietnam many years. Oh, that horrible camp, mister." She shook her head as if trying to clear it of all memories. "Bad soldiers. Beat men and take girls. We not speak of it no more."

Her husband, Mr. Quan Roh, sat in a low, stiff chair in the corner of the room, turned half away from the discussion as if frozen in a kind of disdain for the world he was trapped in. Roh's bustling and portly wife had been left to answer Jack Liffey's questions alone with her broken English. The house in the low hills overlooking Monterey Park was an amalgam of Asia and America, soft sofas and low black lacquer tables, big Chinese jars and IKEA bookcases.

"I really only need to know about your daughter," Jack Liffey said gently, sipping at a delicate, handleless cup of tea. "I hear Sabine is a very smart girl. Is she named after someone in the family?" He was very careful to use the present tense.

The woman waved both hands at him in horror. "No, no, Mr. Liff. Chinese people not do that. That big insult. Everybody got own name. Some people even got style name for later in life after the milk name wear out."

"What a great idea," Jack Liffey said. "I'm getting tired of Jack. Could you tell me about Sabine?"

"I got it all. Friends. Photos. High school diploma. Acceptance letter to Williams. But I tell you anything you want, too." He took the fat manila envelope that she stabbed at him.

Williams. Just about the top of the heap these days. Even Maeve hadn't had an acceptance there, though she could have gone to Harvard, Stanford, Amherst, or several others if she'd had a rich uncle. "I'm sorry I have to ask this: Would anyone in town here be angry at Sabine?"

Mr. Roh stirred himself for the first time since barely acknowledging Jack Liffey's presence twenty minutes earlier. "*Thong miao*," he blurted out, glancing over fiercely. He appeared to smile, fleetingly, then subsided and turned away again.

Jack Liffey pretty much knew what the expression meant, from deep in his Vietnam memory box. He looked at Mrs. Roh, and she appeared embarrassed. "It's bad word, Mr. Liff," she said.

"Roughly?"

She smiled a little, not as easily embarrassed as all that. Tien had told him that the Chinese, unlike the obsessively polite Japanese, had no difficulty at all being rude when they felt like it.

"It Vietnamese slang for bad white guy."

He caught Mr. Roh smiling privately. "I'm not sensitive, Mrs. Roh. Why do you think *thong miao* are Sabine's enemy?"

"They hate us all," she said matter-of-factly. "They say we take their town away. They say we buy everything, we buy all the good house. They think we all rich and we stuck up. You need to talk to somebody about the big fight here in 1970 and 1980 time. They still angry."

"I will." He turned. "*Mr.* Roh, you okay with that same-same? *Thong miaos* numbah ten?" Jack Liffey figured that the Saigon street slang might be a grievous insult to the man, a former college professor, and he wanted to see his reaction.

The man bit his lower lip and didn't budge.

"I'll find your daughter," he said finally to Mrs. Roh.

Mr. Roh snapped his head around and stared like a death's head at Jack Liffey.

"How many languages do you speak, sir?" the man demanded.

"I try hard, but it's very difficult for my weak brain."

"I speak eleven languages, including Ancient Greek and Latin, Mr. Liffey. I have five university degrees. I was dean of Russian and French Literature at the Faculty of Letters, Saigon University. I think I can still speak all those languages, though my best is still Vietnamese. And my second is Mandarin."

So, the G.I. slang had indeed insulted him. "Sir, you have me beat," Jack Liffey said. "I said that to get a reaction. I don't like being ignored."

Mr. Roh smiled a little. "I apologize."

"Sir, may I visit your daughter's bedroom? I'm not a linguist, but I know how to look for missing children. I realize it isn't comfortable to allow this, but it's helped me before."

The Rohs exchanged glances.

"You may do so, Mr. Liffey," the father said. "My wife will show you to our daughter's room. Please do not be disrespectful as you look it over. And please keep us informed."

"I'll keep your daughter in my heart."

*

"What was the very first song you ever bought, and on what media?" Maeve said, realizing immediately she should have said "medium." But who cared? The sensibility of the world now didn't care about rules; the sensibility of now was more about transgression.

Maeve was sitting on the edge of Bunny's bed, a little shaken by the talk with Gloria and feeling very needy, though Bunny was clearly glancing out of the corner of her eye at the laptop screen on her small desk. Maeve tried to ignore Bunny's hints of preoccupation.

Greenwood Avenue had been the last vestige of a stable home in her life. She needed it stay stable.

"'Losing my Religion,' by REM," Bunny said. "A CD."

"I had it on vinyl. God, we're getting old. I remember when Jennifer Lopez was married to Ojani Noa."

They both burst out laughing, and Maeve felt a wave of love for Bunny. "Tom Cruise and Nicole Kidman!"

Bunny's eyes went to the computer screen again, but Maeve tried not to notice.

"Time is so cruel," Maeve said. She was sinking into a kind of forever coziness with the so-comfortable Bunny, projecting it far into the future.

"Maeve, I don't know how to say this and stay mellow. I got work and you can be a real pest sometimes."

A jolt of electricity went up and down Maeve's whole body. Nobody had ever said anything like that to her before. "Oh, damn—I'm sorry."

"I just don't need you hanging out in my room all the time. I like you a lot, but I got other things in life."

"Sorry, sorry, sorry. I'm gone." Maeve jumped up.

Bunny looked regretful, but she didn't say anything to take it back.

"I won't bug you any more, I promise." Maeve hurried across the house, past a startled Axel drinking beer alone in the kitchen, and back to her outlying studio in the old garage. She bolted the door and threw herself facedown on her single mattress and wept.

*

Jack Liffey got home with two full grocery bags and plans to prepare something nice to eat, his major goal for the day. He had a whole notebook full of observations about the Chinese girl's bedroom, but the notes—Catholic missal, too-cute dolls, Girl Scout stuff, modest clothing, a few Chinese knick-knacks, a big stack of pamphlets from a group called the Orange Berets—had pretty much been blown away by the alarm bells at the end.

He'd been patting the underside of her desk drawers, a pointless exercise that never yielded anything useful except in old noir films. This time the devil blinked. A small aqua blue baggie had been taped there with Mylar, and beside it a hand-drawn map that appeared to be a walking trail across the border east of San Diego. There was a scrawl of Spanish on it: *esto es la chica Chuey*. This is the girl, Jesus. He'd tapped a smidgeon of the powder onto his gum, grimaced, and then tucked the baggie into an old copy of *Finnegan's Wake*. A book God himself would never pick up. He'd pocketed the map.

"Glor, I'm home! I've got the makings for drunkard's pasta."

There was no reply. He sighed, set the bags on the cracked yellow and green tile of the kitchen counter and headed up the staircase. It might help, he thought, to drive up to Bakersfield and shoot a few people in the head, especially her lover Sonny Theroux. Nah, it wouldn't help; but it would make him feel better.

She was face down on the bed, but he didn't think she was asleep. If only she would go see some pro to work on her psyche, but she insisted that would be the end of her career at the LAPD. Already she was on long leave and might never climb back onto the hamster wheel for promotion.

"Gloria, it's me. Your sunbeam."

Eventually she rolled over. "Very funny. You ain't no sunbeam, but you know what you are?"

"No." He felt a chill. No joking, Jack.

"Second sweetest man that ever liked me."

He could see that she was drunk, very drunk. At least it told him she could get up and down the stairs by herself now. He wanted to check in with her about the missing girl, get her advice, but it wasn't the time.

"You wanna fuck me near to death, cowboy?"

"The doctor said no exertions for another week."

"You think too much about doctors. Think about me. I'll just lie here and you do the exertions, wham-bam-thank-you-ma'am."

He missed Gloria's body a lot, but he wasn't stupid enough to meddle with her drunk.

"You want my asshole, Jackie? My mouth? It's all free, all one hundred percent Gloria. Okay, except this tit. That's about ninety percent Good Year. And this toenail…"She was staring at her toe, frowning, trying to recapture a train of thought.

"I could make the Thai pasta we like," Jack Liffey said. "Or I could thaw a couple of Nachita's big tamales."

Gloria looked up and stared at him distractedly for a few moments. "What became of my happiness, Jackie?"

Which happiness was *that*? he thought. "I'll make love to you gently, later, if you can stay awake."

"You mean, no more booze for poor Gloria?"

"Yes."

"I been wasting the best years of my life," Gloria said.

"On me?"

"I don't mean that. On the department. On pushing punks around. On going in doors where I'm not wanted and stopping family fights that ought to go on 'till some *pendejo* gets stabbed in his sleep. I try hard to stop cruelty every day, but there's an endless supply. You come into the Rancho with me—" The federal housing project in San Pedro. "—and tell me there's any end to drugs and beatings and blaming everybody else for it. I'm very far from God right now."

She seemed to be on the edge of sheer drunk fury. He sat beside her and rested his hand softly against her damp cheek. She closed her eyes and heaved a little.

"Nap," he said. "I'll cook something and surprise you."

"If I could make a whole new world, Jackie, I'd have *you* in it, but I sure wouldn't have no *me* in it."

*

Monica Flagg leaned in hard to the binocular eyepieces of her Celestron microscope in the county forensic lab. As with most evidence, you didn't learn much more with a scope than you did with the naked eye. The charred glob just became a bigger charred glob. She poked it gently with a sterile dental pick to bring another part to bear.

Her poking caused a section of grit to fall away suddenly. "Terry, c'mere! Check this out."

"On point, homes."

"I think it's some kind of bling." Down at the core of the melted mass, she could just see a single pair of interconnected wire loops, like an ornamental chain for beads.

She slid off her stool to give him room and he leaned in, resting fists on the counter as he got interested. "You'd better call the big Rosk. I bet you got a melted rosary."

*

Ed Zukovich and Marly Tom kept well away from the crowd that was rubbernecking on Garfield. On the far side of Monterey Park's main business artery a dozen cops were taping off the mini-mall with its vandalized signage and combing the ground nearby. A cherry picker was going up to the tall sign. There was even a TV truck for a local cable news outfit, Channel 18-Asian TV, swinging up a microwave antenna. Zook was running on dex to keep awake.

"Who'd'a thunk they'd take it so seriously?" Tom said.

"Probably calling it a hate crime." Zukovich shot him a glare to shut up.

"I got tons of hate."

At least two-thirds of the gawkers were Chinese, puffy moms with strollers, overdressed businessmen, lots of tidy young men in bright pant and polos looking like escapees from a golf magazine. Plus a few Americans and Mexicans. Zook recalled the days when he'd ridden his banana bike downtown to the hobby shop and seen nothing but Americans.

"Remember the big D-D?" Marly Tom said.

"'Course. Right there." Dixie's Diner, the best burgers in town.

"I met Tiffany there," Marly Tom said, and then sighed. "I miss her boobies."

"Dude, there's little kids here." You could count on Chink kids speaking good American.

"Who cares?"

There was a stir across the street. A uniformed cop trotted back toward what had to be the bigshot command center—a beige trailer where heavyset men in dark suits were standing around trying to look important. The trotting cop carried a baggie in one hand, and Zook could just make out what was in it. An unburst paintball.

Shit, he thought. Might still be fingerprints. It might even be Beef's. Their weakest link. Get him in a room with some tough cop clownin' on him, and in ten minutes they'd all be in county jail.

"Yeah, let's hope it's not his," Marly Tom said, reading his mind. "What about the weekend kegger?"

"I'm on top of it. It'll be at the power lines."

"Good," Marly Tom said. "You look all dexed, Z."

"Hush. I'll talk to Mr. Hoity-Toity Seth. His Tea Party's bringing somebody into town to talk to their dinner party. We'll see if he's too good to come talk to the beer brigade."

"We're as good as anybody. This is a democracy."

"This is a white Christian republic, man. Don't forget it. We're gonna get our constitution back."

"'Course."

"Gotta go home. I think I'm gonna come down hard."

"Better living through chemistry."

FOUR
Soy Amigo

"Morning, Jackie. In your pink I hope. You find out good stuff for me?"

It was Tien Joubert's unmistakable tonal lilt on the phone. Ingratiating on the surface, but pushy under it.

"Tien, I've been at this job one full day. I've talked to her parents. I've seen the girl's room. Give me a break." He was still a bit ratty from dealing with Gloria's meltdown the night before.

"You know me. I pay for it, I get report in person. Friday you come see me, like old time. Seven at night. My relax time." As usual, nothing fazed Tien. You could insult her to her face and she would find a way to comment on your shoes.

"It's not old time, dear. It's new time. We've all got telephones. I'll call you Friday."

"No, no. How I trust you, I don't see your handsome face? I don't trust no voice. I pay double gas. This definite part of deal."

Jack Liffey had been wondering why Tien Joubert had decided to pay for a search for such a distant relative, and pay very well, but he figured he was finding out. Her endless automatic and probably meaningless need to try to possess whatever she saw—including himself.

He'd found out that despite all Mr. Quan Roh's degrees and languages, the poor man was running a mini-mart in a seedy area of Rosemead, the next town over, running it by himself eighty hours a week, including the dangerous night shifts. And he had no ownership share in the place.

"Tien, what's your relationship to this family again? My mind is going soft."

She laughed. "Jackie, your mind soft as big slab German steel. My born name Roh Tien, before Mr. Frenchman *fils de salope* René Joubert come along, and very short time he stay. You come see me Friday seven. You stay short or long."

He needed the money badly, and he could always sidestep her wiles. And it would get him out of Gloria's sour orbit for a bit, he thought. Far in the back of his mind, he recalled how much he had once enjoyed romping in a huge satiny bed with Tien Joubert and her utterly guiltless Asian sexuality.

"You was always sweet for a *gweilo*," was her signoff.

He laughed. "You were okay, too, for a slope."

*

"G'day all," Maeve said as she strode confidently into the big house's kitchen, trying hard to radiate good cheer. Axel, the only "all" there, had been dating an Aussie geology major named Barry Mackenzie for weeks, and "G'day" had become the greeting of the house, along with "chunder" for vomit, and "chook" (how weird!) for chicken. Everybody loved new idioms.

Right now her psyche was in so much upheaval about Bunny's rebuff that all she had was superficial cheer. She was relieved Bunny wasn't there.

"What's your run-and-tell, Axel?"

Axel looked really downcast. "Oh, cuss. Barry's decided that we should see other people for a while. You know what that means."

Maeve poured out some granola and skim milk. She'd learned recently to call it skim, a word that nobody who'd grown up in Southern California ever used, but the stores had started to use it.

"He seemed a really nice guy. Are you sure it's over?"

"I don't know."

"I hope it works out." Deep inside, she didn't really mean it. *Schadenfreude* was at work, and after her encounter with Bunny, Maeve hoped everybody in the universe was miserable.

Axel was hoarding their *L.A. Times* under her elbow.

"Can I see the inside stuff?" Maeve asked.

"Oh, sorry. Here." She pushed some of it over as Maeve sat.

"Seen Bunny yet?" Maeve asked lightly.

"I think she's on a funny track."

"Funny haha or funny peculiar?"

"What the hell is that?"

"Something my dad says—I think it's from prehistoric TV."

"Well, she was funny peculiar. She barged in this morning like Cleopatra on speed and snapped 'Hold my calls' like some Rockefeller. She grabbed one of your Pop-Tarts and ran on out without even toasting it."

Maeve crunched the first bite of granola, and she could feel some of her humanity seeping back. She shouldn't fob off a friend, especially one languishing in her own dumps. "It might be my fault, Ax."

Axel looked up as Maeve fell silent. She waved a section of the paper around ineffectually, trying to fold it in half. "Like?"

Maeve sighed. "I sort of made a pass at her last night and she flipped out."

"I didn't know you were into oh-six."

"I like boys and girls. I thought I'd made it clear to Bunny before, but she went ham. Said she was tired of me being a pest." It felt good to get it off her chest.

"Aw, Maeve. Give yourself a break. Nobody could not like you, you've got the biggest heart in the city. Though I'm not into the other stuff."

"Thanks, Ax. Everybody hurts. I just found out my dad and his woman are in trouble. And then Bunny shook me up. But don't worry about me. You've got big things on your mind, too."

"Don't be hangdog. An Ozzie dumped me drongo, as he'd say. But here we are—we've got a view of the hills to die for, college a half hour away, and we can eat whatever food we want with no mom. Mac and cheese forever. Think of the starving kids in China."

"South Central."

"Sure, Miss Bigheart." Axel reached out to press on her hand on the table, and abruptly she and Maeve both wept.

*

Megan Saxton did her best with the lukewarm shower in the Bide-a-Wee Motel in a very forlorn Morena, California, near the Mexican border. She stepped out and all of a sudden she was sitting on the sink, holding her bare wet feet high up off the tiles. A tan spider the size of a ginger snap ran in big circles on the bathroom floor. It looped across the tiles, a little blob of energy wound up to demonstrate some obscure scientific principle. Horror suffused her: the meaty legs, the *idea* of hair on the body, a blur of speed.

Not unlike the hideous Afrikaner himself. In an hour they were scheduled for the second installment of the interview, on assignment from *The New Yorker*. When the floor seemed spider-free, she hopped out of the bathroom to stand on the bed and wrap her hair in a towel. Moods padded up and attacked without warning. She missed Manhattan and the twenty-four-hour buzz of life.

Things were so much more primitive out here. Vi-oh-lence. Just phonemes, she told herself. Outside, a car door slammed. She walked gingerly to the window and parted the curtain a few inches. The windshield of a Humvee reflected back the sun, and the overbearing man himself stepped out. She had meant to drive to his place in her rental, but he had unaccountably come for her. Abruptly she whirled around, panicky eyes darting for any signs of the spider. There was nothing.

She punished her hair quickly with the towel, discarded it with her hair half wet, then tugged on a t-shirt and a pair of sweat pants. She felt her nipples erecting against the cotton in the morning chill and went back for an overshirt, more modesty than warmth. Then she went outside to head him off before he could invade her private space.

"Morning, dollie! I'm back from teaching the fat cats in the east the meaning of life."

"I was coming over to continue our interview later."

"We got up early because of a mountain lion," he said with his feral grin. "The local people are full of him. He is responsible for the death of livestock from Jacumba to El Centro, and pet kittens and cows and the odd drunk Mexican. Yesterday he ate a Buick, tomorrow he eats

San Diego. He's probably a couple hungry coyotes, but as long as it ain't a Communist, I say, 'Eat your fucking fill, Simba.'"

He carried a strange-looking rifle with a fat extra barrel underneath, and he nodded toward a couple of Latino men in camo jackets, kneeling to look at the remains of what seemed to be a small dog in the motel parking lot.

"I'm telling you, it's a good thing we got those castor beans. Super Hardi, he couldn't track a bloody zebra on Commissioner Street."

He hadn't looked directly at her, as she'd noticed before, but there was no one else he could be talking to. Odd man.

"Castor beans?" she asked.

"You like scouts? Castor beans got spots, but who cares?" He laughed confidently. His Chicano trackers stood and looked around.

"Is that a dead dog?" she asked.

"It ain't a live one, ma'an." He flexed his arm for no discernible reason, repulsive with muscle. "If the coyote's a Communist, I'm going to fuck him up."

"That's not very funny," she said.

His eyes came close to seeing her but couldn't quite make it. What's his problem? She expected reflexive menace, but found amusement. "I am *very* funny, duckie. I am whatever I say I am. I am the Charlie Chaplin of this desert valley." He chuckled. "'Course, I am also the stain on my new country's honor. Write that down."

She tried to imagine what sort of woman would be attracted to this abomination. He offered her his canteen—was it a bad joke?—and she shook her head. The muscles in his neck rippled as he threw his head back to drink, and she tried to remember it all for later. *The New Yorker* had no idea quite what they would be getting in her piece on the Border Guardians.

He'd sauntered over to his castor beans. She registered the cockiness, the brutal angular voice, the sheer physical beef of him. He was the sort of tempest force that young girls imagined they'd fancy sweeping over them—until one actually showed up. Someone threw an old sack over the dead dog.

He sauntered back. "I think your anger says I interest you."

"My anger says nothing. I'm always angry. I'm assigned to write about you."

Why had she said that? She turned to walk back to her room, and froze in place when she heard Hardi Boaz speak in a soft lilt in Afrikaans.

"What did you say?"

"An old expression. 'It is not the loudest moo that makes the most milk.'"

"Go to hell." She took three steps and stopped, remembering the spider in her room. "Do you know a hairy brown spider around here about this big?" she asked, turning back and making a big O with her fingers.

"Does it like bathrooms?" he asked.

She nodded.

"The hermit spider. Almost all of them are Communists."

"Is it dangerous?"

"Very."

"How can I kill it?"

He was backlit by the bright sunlight and it was hard to make out his face.

"You need an experienced killer." He came toward her.

"I was asking for advice, not help."

"Don't insult me. If I need some good English words, I come to you. When you need a killing, you come to me." He walked past and finally she fell in behind him. "This is the bonus that life gives you out on the frontier: you have a killer on duty."

"Not everyone would consider it a bonus."

"Let us track down this hermit spider and teach him the meaning of fear."

He walked with a slight bandy-legged roll, the rifle in one hand like a long piece of fruit. Simian, she thought, still taking mental notes. That might be too obvious.

Hardi Boaz wrenched open the door. "Freeze, motherfucker!" he shouted.

Everyone knew American films, she thought. She waited behind, scanning the threadbare carpet.

"Ah, the room smells of you," he said happily. With the barrel of his rifle, he disturbed the bath towel on the floor, prodded and lifted it. She wished she had sent him away. Having him prowl her room made her feel exposed and helpless. Her notes were on the table beside the coffee jug, her suitcase open on the bed with a black brassiere and black panties beside it, which reminded her that she was not wearing either.

He opened the bathroom door. "You're in the deep shit, my little spider. *Kom, liefling.*"

While he was out of sight, she flipped a corner of the bedspread over her underwear.

"*Een twie drie.* Come out, little comrade. Your pals have betrayed you."

Eventually Hardi Boaz came back into the main room like a predator. Hair was his motif, she decided. Even his knees were hairy above the rolled socks, and more hair spilled out the neck of his safari shirt to give her the willies. He passed close to her, his presence pushing her back like the bow wave of a tugboat.

"I think the little *kak* has escaped."

The voice was terribly close behind her, a swelling immanence.

"But you have not, my lovely friend," he whispered.

She gasped and her vision went pink. His voice had been very soft and close and now two powerful fingers held her neck. Another sound escaped her throat when his roughened fingers flexed slightly on her neck, immensely strong. She was near fainting. Blood thundered in her ears.

"Someday you must watch the lion mount his mate." The voice was very near her ear. "He comes from behind with great purpose and takes the neck hard to convince her to stay still."

She couldn't make sense of what the voice was saying, so calm and insistent. Tears started in her eyes. Her right knee shook violently.

"Stop it!" she insisted.

"Why?"

"*Stop.*"

"All right."

The pressure vanished from her neck. She clamped her burning eyes shut.

"I am on duty now. I will come back later, sweetling, to make love not war."

She could hear the small rattles of his rifle as he walked away.

"By the way, missy, the hermit spider is harmless."

When he had gone, a shuddering took her uncontrollably. Megan remembered her first story assignment for *Mademoiselle*, and the way the editor had praised her writing, how promising her future had seemed back then. It wasn't that it hadn't panned out, it's just that it had never gone anywhere that made her happy. She sat on the bed and wept with abandon.

*

"Stop!" Gustav Reik barked as he entered the big room.

His executive assistant, Bernadette Crouch, was writing with a squeaky felt pen on the whiteboard. She knew he couldn't stand that sound.

The homely woman with short red hair went right on writing.

"Hope you were happy with that useful idiot with the safari suit."

"What an odd clown," Gustav Reik said. "What did you think of him?"

"You don't care what I think. He's so primal he's probably a great lay."

"So am I."

"No, you're not."

The header on the whiteboard was *Freedom at Risk*. And the day's lectures for the gathering, with times and speakers:

- *The Myth of Climate Change*
- *How Taxes Kill Jobs*
- *Defunding Regulations*
- *Speak Money to Power*

"That's enough for now, Bern. Have you got the monthly audit?"

"It's on the piano." She gestured.

"It's not a *piano*," he said grumpily. It was a priceless Sabathil clavichord that his mother Wilhelmina had played every day of their enforced stays at what their father had called "the farm."

"Saxophone, then. I'm not musical."

"No, but you're hot as a pistol, as usual."

"How's your wife, G?" she said with an edge.

He decided to take the question literally, not as a *bug off.* "She's very busy with the ballet board that I bought her."

"You can afford it, you big libertarian cracker. *Forbes* says you're number four now after Warren Buffet."

He smiled to himself, opening the monthly accounting. "*Forbes* doesn't have a clue about the Bank of the Cayman Islands and several other places."

"La-la-la-la-la."

She had her fingers in her ears.

"What's all that?"

"Please. What I don't know, Gus-boy, can't hurt you."

"What you *do* know can't hurt me either, my fine sex object. I can arrange an underground nap in the New Jersey pine barrens for anyone."

He saw her puzzled expression, indicating she was not quite sure how serious he was, and he liked that.

*

"Nurse, is this the way to room 441?"

The short, dark woman, encumbered with an armload of linens, pitched her neck forcefully toward a side hallway. "Don't give up hope."

"Thanks so much."

Walt Roski made his way along the corridor of San Pedro's Little Company of Mary Hospital. Tony Piscatelli's wife had insisted on moving him here, only a few blocks from her sister's home where she could stay. The San Pedro hospital had no burn unit, but they made do.

He knocked once on the wooden door and walked in. There were two beds in the pie-shaped room, which was against the recent American fashion for making all hospital rooms private. On the far bed, near the window, a figure was rising up under the covers and groaning, then falling flat, over and over.

"Piscatelli?"

"Over here." The near bed, a dim figure lying on his side facing the door. The bed burred noisily all at once and pumped itself up to lift the man's body.

Shit, Roski thought. So much for thinking the man was pretty much okay. "Can I turn on some light?"

"Use the local one. This doohickey. My roommate doesn't like light."

A spotlight came on overhead, pooling on Piscatelli's face and chest. He was propped up on his side with pillows.

A groan, then another, from across the room. This was going to be a lot of fun.

"How you doing?" Roski asked.

"As well as can be expected, sir—etc., etc." The mattress, pumping and hissing softly, seemed to tilt the man a bit further onto his back. "It's like living on a tilt-a-whirl. But without the cotton candy."

"That could be arranged," Roski offered.

Piscatelli seemed to drift for a moment. "You're Arson, right?"

"Captain Walter Roski, County Fire. I won't offer my hand. They told me to stay back three feet."

"Infections and all that. I just had my cocktail of antibiotics and morphine, so I'm ready to talk. I'm actually floating a bit."

Roski checked his notebook. "I'll go right to it. Was your partner religious, Mr. Piscatelli?"

"Routt was about as devout as a chair."

"Are you religious?"

"Yes, sir. Very much so. I'm a deacon of the Holy Trinity Lutheran Church in Vallejo. I was praying hard for both of us when the firestorm hit."

"Do you have any idea why your partner would have a Catholic rosary with him in the fire shelter?"

A long pause. "Jerry Routt may have believed something, deep down, but he certainly wasn't Catholic. I've known him for ten years."

Walt Roski basically disliked religion. He'd arrested more than one young matcher over the years who swore that his beliefs required him to scourge the world with fire.

"Can you think of any reason your partner would be carrying a rosary? Maybe a new girlfriend gave it to him? We think it was made of amber beads and the heat ignited it."

Piscatelli seemed to be trying hard to reclaim a memory from the abyss, but the sensation passed. "Honestly, sir, no. If something comes to me, you'll be the first to know."

Roski asked the rest of the questions from his notebook without eliciting anything useful, and then left his card on the far side of the bed table.

"My card is right there. Don't touch it, it's full of my germs, but you can have the nurse read my phone number if you think of anything. I'll be in touch."

"Thank you, Captain. God bless."

"I can always use a blessing." Particularly since he was about to be read the riot act by his chief, probably with a note in his file, for once again feuding with the Feds.

*

Megan watched the man from a county animal welfare truck scrape up the remains of the dog. What an alien place, she thought. The heart of my darkness.

She was having trouble resisting the tug of the vodka bottle across the room. She turned on the radio, but the only thing she could get was Mexican rancheras or American country music. She wondered if she had grown any less intolerant of cowboy culture.

She listened to a male voice keening about a manly trucker carrying steel to Texas, and she wondered if the driver would be any less manly driving Tampax to Delaware. It was exactly the kind of unexamined American lying that always left her cross.

It was growing accustomed to your unhappiness that made you so self-absorbed, she thought. After us, the savage god—she'd read the phrase somewhere and it resonated.

FIVE

Set Big Cap Free

Tony Piscatelli could tell that the morphine was wearing off, and he was starting to feel the gnaw of medium-well-done soft tissue along his shoulders, but he resisted pushing the button on the nurse call. He was in a lucid time, and he wanted to stay in it. It was difficult to think productively against the pain—especially with his roommate groaning and humping away—but if he opiated again, his consciousness would become a vapor. He repeated a short prayer in his head, starting with an entreaty for the unknown groaning roommate. The nurse had told him it had been a motorcycle crash, and his roommate was only about nineteen. The age when everyone knew they were invulnerable.

Piscatelli recalled a visit from some arson desk guy, but didn't remember his name. Something about Jerry Routt and a rosary. Probably a morphine dream. Routt was about as likely to carry a rosary as a lava lamp. The man had once laughed out loud when Piscatelli told him about Martin Luther's big moment of crisis, throwing his inkwell at the devil.

"Dude," Routt had said. "I *know* that's not true. Europeans can't throw. They can only kick."

Yet something about the dream visit from the arson guy held him. Lying on his stomach, he did a few slow pushups before the airbed could start whirring and fussing with him again. He saw the arson guy's business card on the nightstand, so it was real. Something inside you is trying to get out, Deacon Piscatelli.

"Tony, look at this!" Was that Routt? Frustrating maybe memories.

The fire had been about to flame over. He'd just started getting worried, but Routt had yelled at him to come back. That was so like Routt, fastening on second things first. But he'd stepped back and they'd both seen something there on the ground. What?

Pain swept through him, and he thumbed the red button, then again, harder. Nurse, come now! Oh, Sweet Jesus, *now*. Our Father, who art in Heaven...

*

Ellen Chen, short blue hair and all, walked with intense self-absorption off the L.A. State campus into the empty parkland across Paseo Rancho Castilla. Spanish Ranch Walk. Another example of Southern California naming nonsense. The future, when it finally came, would be without such nationalist nonsense. Reason would rule, she thought.

Sabine hadn't phoned or texted in ten days now. That was their agreed definition of a political emergency. She sat to look out over much of the San Gabriel Valley below. Home.

She and Sabine were the last of the Orange Berets—the two musketeers, she thought sadly—pledged to fight for immigrant solidarity, human rights, not to mention the Revolution. Rah, rah.

Her dad had been badgering her that very morning about her grades, so she could get out of a second-best college and go to a really good school like Caltech or Berkeley. Her whole future depended on her grades. Her car would stop running, the stars would crash to earth. As politics had crumbled away into hopelessness for her, his incessant hectoring was becoming intolerable.

Now she had to worry about Sabine. Back when the Berets had been a viable Chicano-Chinese alliance of over thirty idealistic kids, and their blood enemy, the Commandos, had still been a rampaging racist gang, each of the leading berets had taken one of the thugs to watch. But as far as she could tell, the Commandos were down to three now, and the Berets had shrunk to two. Mosquito vs. gnat. Dear Lenin. Did you ever cry when things became this pathetic?

*

Overcome with trepidation, Megan Saxton parked in front of the isolated ranch house near the border. She had come from her motel again to carry on the interview with this strange man for *The New Yorker*. He had turned out to be another force of nature, truly frightening, but she had to go with that.

The flagstone patio beside the pool was an artifact from the 1950s, ribboned with blown-in desert dust. Hardi Boaz sat there in a cast-iron ice cream chair, wearing some kind of Arab robe. He glanced up and grinned. "You save me the trouble of searching you out, *liefling*."

He waved an arm grandly toward a pitcher of margaritas on the table. The gesture billowed his loose sleeve like a giant seabird trying to get airborne.

She set the tiny recorder on the table and turned it on, but didn't know quite how to begin.

"You have violent, piercing eyes," he said.

She felt herself blush.

"Have a margarita, lovely. It's proof the Mexicans are good for something." A smile acknowledged her lack of response, though he still didn't look directly at her. "The loud Boer has offered you a drink. I believe for the moment you are choosing to punish my magnetism with silence. That is fine, too. By birth I am pure South African beef, but now I am as big as all America."

He laughed a peculiar stage laugh.

"Look there." He pointed out at sparse chaparral beyond the hurricane fence surrounding the pool. "I can sit here with a rifle and hunt wetbacks and drug-runners. From this yard I protect the American race from a flood of mud people."

She checked to make sure the recorder was going.

A hard, dark point of abhorrence was congealing at the center of her chest, a numbness spreading through her, and she was losing her peripheral vision. The man talked and talked. What is this, what's happening to me?

"Go ahead and drink, sweet. I promise there is no aphrodisiac in it. I'm all the aphrodisiac any woman needs. I am the force of life, but my sweetest fruit is my gentle nature." He threw back his head and laughed.

She noticed a giant Rottweiler waiting just inside the sliding door of the house, glaring straight at her.

"My charm consists in not caring a damn what people think about me, especially the weak-kneed city pooftahs. I am the full-blown runaway id of the white people. I am the goddamn poet of our race, where poetry is written in grunts and growls and gunshots.

"I am the only thing standing between the sissy white people and the barbarian hordes. It's true, I may lose here, too, and the brown monkeys may end up running us out. Who knows? Even if you can give me mathematical proof that I am going to be overrun, I am still going to do my best right now to prevent it. And along the way I'm going to enjoy every goddamn minute."

She knew she should consult her notes, ask more about the Border Guardians, but her forehead burned. The odd harangue went on and on. She had been planning to slap him hard, but she couldn't move. An ice cube cracked like a firecracker in her margarita, and she almost screamed.

"Listen, sweetling, you didn't get yourself home before the dark, and your fantasy life is becoming real. The hairy Boer stirs, and his life force is in ascendance."

He stood and walked over to her. His great ham hands lifted her as if she were weightless.

"Yes, please," she heard herself say weakly. She hadn't even switched off the recorder.

*

Somebody had added a generous picture window to the back wall of the garage, really just a huge sheet of glass with unpainted moldings tacked up to hold it in place. The window offered a breathtaking view out over the hills east of her studio bedroom, though all that glass chilled the room at night and blinded her with sun in the mornings. She'd set up the studio portion of the room to be near the window and grab non-directional skylight from about ten on.

This afternoon she was using the light to study a still life she'd set out on a small table. A tipped-up cast-iron frying pan. A pebbly black Scotch Tape dispenser. A shiny black coffee cup. A study in tones.

She'd discovered she was better at tones than colors, and wanted to see how far she could push it.

Her teacher seemed so helpful and so genuinely impressed by the works she brought in on Tuesdays and Thursdays that Maeve had decided to ignore the half-inch wood Tinkertoy spools he had in his slit earlobes. You're trying way too hard, man, she'd thought.

She dabbed some white into the bare image of the pan and saw she'd gone too far. With acrylics you had to work fast and you couldn't move the paints around and blend later. She'd probably switch to oils. She realized it had been more than an hour since she'd fussed about Bunny.

There was a tap at the door, like punctuation to her thought. But it could have been anybody. Annoyed, she stabbed the brush into a jar of water and unstrapped her apron.

"Come," she called, trying to sound odd and mysterious.

She froze. It was Bunny herself, peering in with a hangdog look and carrying a flask-shaped bottle of Bunny's favorite, Mateus rosé.

"Peace offering."

Maeve's spirits soared. She felt faint and had to grasp the back of the sofa for support. "Thank you, Bunny. So much."

"Did I hurt you bad?"

"I was hurt."

"I understand, sweet. I laid my good down and my own problems gushed all over the place. I been under pressure in ways you don't want to know." She made a gesture, waving it all away. "I want to make it up to you."

Maeve wasn't all that fond of sweet Mateus wine, but she would have drunk battery acid just then. All her affection flooded back in. She couldn't help thinking—trying hard not to stare—what a glorious, abundant body Bunny had. Maeve plucked two washed-out jam jars from her painting supplies, opened the wine and poured. They sat face to face on the hooked rug.

"Can you tell me about this pressure?" Maeve asked.

"I need a cigarette."

"So smoke."

"You said this was a smoke-free zone."

"Girl, smoke."

Bunny lit up with a wooden match and sighed with relief. Maeve fetched a jar lid for an ashtray.

"I'm supposed to color inside the lines for now," Bunny said.

"Who said that?"

"Swami Muni."

Maeve was startled. She'd had no hint of another side of Bunny at all. The name sounded like a local bus line.

"He assigned me a boyfriend two months ago, like some zoo, and I didn't like the guy at all, but he told me I had to give him a try. He picks his nose, Maeve, and he never went to college. But I try to like him."

"You're the one who's going to get hurt," Maeve said.

Bunny hung her head for a while, and Maeve resisted the urge to sidle over and hug her.

"I still feel I have things to learn from the swami. I can be pretty shrewd."

"No, you can't. Why are you doing this thing?"

"I offered my searching soul to Muni at a retreat a year ago. He knew startling things about me with just a little talking. I know you're not persuaded."

"I'm here for you right now."

There was a sudden hammering at the door, definitely none of their roommates.

"Are you holding?" Maeve asked.

Bunny shook her head. "It's probably the guy. He acts like he's Thor, the god of the big dick." She giggled once. "Actually, the appendage is just so-so."

"I think I could get him beaten up if you want."

"Just get him to leave me alone."

After more door-banging, Bunny crouched down behind a Japanese screen. A muscular redhead with freckles everywhere tried to barge in.

"Stop there, freckle-face." Maeve stood against him as firmly as she could, and after a lot of mindless shoving back and forth, he backed off.

"I want to see my Bunny."

"Cool it. This is *my* home. Look, guy, my father runs bets, and his pals will teach you manners in an alley if I ask them to."

"What the fuck's the matter with you, girl?" His voice almost went shrill.

"You push into my room and ask what's the matter with *me*? If you've got a message, tell me."

"Bunny Walker is my woman. We been assigned. She's fat and a smarty-pants and I let that go 'cause I'm a good guy. Tell her I ain't strung out no more and to come over. She better."

"I'll tell her. Don't get in my face again."

Maeve was amazed how easy it had been to buffalo him. She locked the door, including her new deadbolt, and found her hands trembling like a kitten.

Bunny peered out, obviously impressed.

"You got any feelgood?" Maeve asked.

"I got some in the bedroom."

"Forget it. Stay here."

They poured out more rosé.

"The guy's a *pendejo*, as we say. You're not fat. You're perfectly proportioned."

Bunny laughed and brushed away a tear. "Thanks, Maeve. I know I'm a biggish girl. You've seen me in the altogether."

"A lovely altogether it was."

Then Bunny did cry a bit and hit the wine hard. She explained that the swami had her money and credit cards and some horrible letters against her parents.

"Maybe we'll have to take this swami down," Maeve said.

"You sound like the Lone Ranger."

"I am the Lone Ranger."

Bunny lay on the floor and wept silently.

Other lives made her own seem so idyllic, Maeve thought. She slid closer and rested a hand on Bunny's shoulder, comfort fashion. She knew better than to seem to take advantage.

"Maeve, if you'll promise to be my best friend forever you can have my body whenever you want." The woman said it like an offer of self-immolation.

"I'm your BFF right now. Just cuddle. I'll protect you."

*

"I got this brainstorm," Marly Tom said. "We write us a new phone app. Call it Whack-a-Chink. Bucktooth faces pop up out of holes and you smack 'em into big blood splashes."

"Work it out. I got to plan the kegger right now." Zook cradled a beer he wasn't planning to share.

Across the room, Captain Beef danced heavily at the beat-up old foosball console in the clubhouse, whiz-bang-rattle. He had no opponent but it was still taking him two or three spins to score.

"Beef, that noise is driving me to drink," Zook called.

"Put your mind at rest, Zookie. Just drink up and say, *thank you, Jesus.*"

"I ain't trying to turn you around. I need you over here for a minute."

Beef came and plopped down on a folding chair. "Hup-hup-HUP."

He'd been center when they'd all played football at Mark Keppel High.

"Okay, Mr. Seth tells me he's bringing in an important border defender and the guy is ours for the afternoon. I want to do a keg for right-thinking people the way we used to. The border guy will give a little inspirational talk about saving the U.S. of A. And we can gather the clans. Godfather Seth will be watching over us so we're all on our P's and Q's."

"Does that mean I can't wave The Big Captain in front of the girls?" Beef asked.

"Yeah, that's exactly what it means."

Captain Beef had a pecker bigger than the legendary John C. Holmes and at parties drunk San Gabriel girls tended to chant: *Big Cap! Let him free! Big Cap! Let us see!*

"We're all altar boys Saturday."

"Sure, Z," Beef assented.

"Back to your game, Beef. Marly and I'll handle the details."

Zook watched Tony Buffano waddle away. Keppel High had once been the powerhouse team of the Almont League, but ever since the Chinks filled up the school, they'd had a hide-your-face record of 0–10 for twelve straight years.

"We going for the power lines?"

"Yeah. The rest of the world's too civilized."

The area was unfenced, weedly land under the high-tension power lines that crossed town, fine for al fresco parties. They only had to push Sgt. Manny Acevedo in the Monterey Park P.D. to get his pals to look the other way for an afternoon. Open container in public, etc.

Zook still had dreams of reanimating the Commandos. It would be good to keep their name out there. "Seth can get real bucks, so let's be good to him."

They did a soft high five and watched Beef jig around for a few moments.

Zook had a sudden sour feeling. Life was whizzing past—his mom drinking too much now, an endless run of dead-end jobs. He'd won a scholarship to UCLA but chosen to stay at East L.A. City with his pals. Zook had tremendous loyalty to the last of the old gang.

"Zook," Marly Tom said softly. "You saw that shadow watching us the other night, the one Beef took a shot at."

"Coulda been anyone."

"I don't know. I think it was dogging us the whole time." He sighed. "What about that Chinese chick you said was following you?"

Ed Zukovich shrugged. "Must've given up."

*

"Seth, be a man," Andor said without inflection. "Show us what a he-man from the Golden State can do."

"I'm no big game hunter. I trained on an M16 in Iraq, but I never touched it after basic. I was in Legal Services."

Out on the verandah in Indiana, Andor was insisting he take the bolt-action rifle. The barrel appeared unusually fat. Seth Brinkerhoff finally took the weapon and sat on one of the rattan chairs.

Andor nodded toward the two deer browsing peacefully at a big salt lick about a hundred yards away across the pond.

"Don't I need a license or something to shoot a deer?"

Andor gave him a big stink-eye.

Gustav belched on purpose. "It's said that Lenin once dismissed the British Communist Party by saying that when it came time to seize the railroad stations, they'd all line up to buy platform tickets."

Andor chuckled.

"You quote Lenin?"

"I quote Ayn Rand a lot, too, but it doesn't make me a cunt. Afraid of killing a deer, Mr. B?"

Seth Brinkerhoff weighed the rifle in his hands. "This is a big one, isn't it?"

"You might say," Andor said.

"In the nineties, I sent my first kid to survival school," Gustav told him. "Toughen up the whiny little prick."

"What sort of stuff do they do there?" Seth asked.

"They survive. You never went?"

"I'm not sure we had them."

"That's California. You got Mr. John Chinaman Democrat representing your own damn district. He's one hundred and ten percent liberal socialist. I want you to get him out. Find out if he likes boys, find something."

Brinkerhoff sighed a little and settled with his left elbow on the verandah's outer wall and the rifle stock tucked against his shoulder, anticipating a bad recoil. A stag with lots of antler had wandered up to guard the deer.

Reluctantly, Brinkerhoff settled into the firing discipline the Army had taught him. Left hand cupping the forestock halfway forward, cheek firmly against the stock, open sights aligned on the head of the deer, squeezing the trigger a millimeter at a time until you felt resistance, breathe and hold, start squeezing again so you surprise yourself with the moment of fire.

All went well until a horrendous explosion went off near his head and the rifle butt smashed into his shoulder like a baseball bat in full swing, the rifle cartwheeling out of his hands.

"What the F—!"

Seth's chair fell over, and Andor behind him caught the rifle as it flipped. Gustav and Andor chuckled as Seth lay on his side.

"I love you guys," Seth said grimly. "Great sense of humor."

Across the small lake, the male deer's head and neck had just about disintegrated.

*

Piscatelli woke as his wife entered the room. He was reluctant to come back from his dreamless escape from pain.

"Tony, darling, I'm sorry, are you still drowsing?"

"It's fine, Jenny. Come over here, I want to see you."

He could see she wore rubber gloves and had sneaked in a small brown bag, but he was far more interested in looking at her comforting face.

"Are you at peace with Jesus, Tony?"

He was determined that she not unravel his composure. "You sound like you're giving me the last rites."

He was starting to hurt, which meant the morphine was subsiding and he might be able to think clearly.

"What's in the bag?" He wondered if this might be the big blessing of the Sheepshead Fire, to bring him and Jennifer closer together again. He'd begun to worry about their relationship.

She set out a digital picture frame that offered a slideshow of the family and their pets. She touched a button, and their daughter Greta said, "Get well quick, Daddy."

He could feel tears.

She rested her hand briefly on his forehead, weird with the rubber glove. "You're burning up. Oh my, I'm sorry." Wrong thing to say. "Let me get the nurse."

"Wait, please." The bath of emotion had freed his memory a little. "Is there a business card on the table?"

"Yes." She bent closer to the table to read. "Captain Walter Roski, Los Angeles County Fire Investigation Unit."

"That's it," Piscatelli said. "Would you call that number? Tell him that he should look very carefully about a hundred meters… southwest from where they found Jerry. Southwest. There will be more remains—an Asian girl, I think, with a bullet wound. It's over a berm, so it might be missed."

"What's a berm?"

"He'll know." He closed his eyes, visibly tense. "I love you so very much, Jen, but I have to go back inside now. Jesus bless."

*

Friday, seven p.m. as ordered. Jack Liffey pushed the doorbell set into the sparkly pink stone facing beside the door. For some reason, you just couldn't outdo Orange County in ugly houses.

Tien Joubert came herself. Probably a bad sign, but everything to do with the woman could be a bad sign.

"Jackie, hon! Right on time! Come in."

She was dewed with sweat and wearing a barely cinched flop-open robe, ostensibly a cover-up for being disturbed during her exercise and sauna, but he knew she knew he was always on time. He'd hoped to skip all the sexual teasing, but he did need the money.

"Hello again, Tien. Sauna time?"

"You betcha. Wanna try?"

"Some other time." As he came into the too-blue house, he noticed a teacup-sized Chihuahua going insane against Tien's leg. No yipping, though.

"Replacement for John Bull?" he asked.

"Nobody ever replace nobody. John Bull go up to doggy heaven." She picked up the dog, put it into her coat closet and shut the door.

He watched, but she seemed to have no intention of letting the dog back out, despite the hysterical scratching.

"I got special deal with Heaven. They give me half off, of course."

"You sure the deal isn't from the other place?"

"The way you dress, Jackie, maybe." She pretended to shield her eyes. "You got to let me get you good silk Ferragamo jacket. Where you get that corduroy? Pic-n-Save?"

He grinned, impervious on that score. "Salvation Army. If I had a silk jacket, my clients would think I'm stealing from them. Am I here for a sartorial roast or a report?"

"You sit. Lupeta!" she yelled.

A heavyset woman hurried in. "Yes."

"Jackie, you still teetotal man?"

"I am. Some green tea would be fine." She knew well that he drank ginger ale, but she would never honor it.

"Green tea for two, and bring us biscuits."

"Yes, señora."

"You've done well the last few years?" he asked. "Your businesses?"

She appeared to resist an impulse to sit down on his lap and sat opposite, her robe just about coming open. "I saw tech in trouble and got out. Then I see real estate head down shit creek. I bet against. Me and China good friend now. I import medicine, dress, toy, and other stuff, chemicals they put in food for good taste. My company grow three time in profit every year. Ten more year, I'm king of America, I tell president what to do."

He chuckled. "I believe it."

"Of course," she said blandly. "He and his guys better believe right now."

"Tien, you can't be beat. Just outlive all the bastards. That's my plan."

She made a face, as if assaulted by a nasty smell. "No good, Jackie. No no. You got to get *even*, bury the bastards deep."

He saw the entirety of one of her breasts, remembered caressing the small nut-brown nipple, her yelps and moans, and he wondered if agreeing to this meeting was another falter in the long, slow, ethical sideslip of his life. When I get home, give me some affection, Gloria, please. Tien's body was older now, of course, age showing in a little sagging and some vertical stretch lines, but she was still perfectly formed for her size. And the impact of a body never existed by itself, he knew that—it had to do with your relation to the whole person, all of its quirks, and maybe your flight from something else.

"Time to report," he said.

SIX
The Jewel in the Lotus

"It was wonderful to have a front-row seat for that whole struggle. Talking to the principals, taking notes in the city council and all the local meetings. Then I could retreat here with my colleagues to talk it over and write it up."

John Hollister was a frail emeritus professor now, apparently begrudged a small shared office with two other retirees, but back in the 1970s he'd led a team of colleagues and students in producing a Pulitzer history about the race crucible of Monterey Park.

Hollister and Jack Liffey stood side by side on the walkway of the former's office building at L.A. State College, looking southeast across the I-10 and over the grid of Monterey Park.

"We've never been able to study a flashpoint of immigration like that. When we came on board it was a real case study—Taiwanese businessmen arriving and facing a startling nemesis in Harry Batcher, a bitter city councilman, and his friends. They ran weekly newsletters about the yellow peril. But the town had dozens of white progressives, too, feisty Jewish ladies from New York who organized their own meetings."

Jack Liffey's old pal Mike Lewis had set up the visit with a fellow social historian. "Sir, I'm really more interested in what's going on now."

The office door behind them slapped open and an old man in a rumpled sweater almost toppled out. Hollister wrapped his arms gently around the man.

"Eddy, it's John."

The man's eyes looked disturbingly vacant.

"Let's go back in and finish your work. Your wife will be here soon."

He gentled the man into the little office. Jack Liffey could guess the problem. It was his father's, too. He'd just worked out a reverse mortgage on Declan's bungalow in San Pedro in order to hire a daytime caretaker, a really sweet Filipina who didn't seem to mind the man's random racist outbursts. At least the dementia kept him from writing any more of his white supremacy articles. Where did all that racial hatred emanate from? Jack Liffey asked himself for the millionth time.

Hollister shut the door softly. "Sorry. It's Alzheimer's."

"My dad's just about on the same off-ramp," Jack Liffey said.

Hollister couldn't stop once he'd been wound up. He told Jack Liffey about the crosscurrents of the struggle in the 1970s: "English Only" campaigns, groups attacking and defending Asians.

Hollister sighed. "You could say it was democracy at work, all that goofy door-to-door fervor. The nutballs fastened on coded symbols—like 'English only' or building a statue of George Washington downtown in place of a Chinese mini-mall.

"Decency actually prevailed—or numbers, if you prefer." He shrugged contentedly. "The whole area you see there is seventy to eighty percent Asian."

"At least you didn't have any dead bodies along the way."

Hollister pointed out a slope under some power lines just across the freeway in Monterey Park. "That bare spot. They found a sleeping bag full of bones there in 1977. I always felt if I upset the wrong people, the next bag would be me."

"I never knew."

"Sorry, I'm a bore about it. For more recent history, I'll call a man you should meet. Father Soong in Monterey Park."

*

Megan Saxton realized that for twenty-four hours she'd been no farther than thirty feet from Hardi Boaz. Lying in bed or being scrubbed and coddled in the bathtub or helping as he cooked crudely and loudly. It was comforting and terrifying at the same time, completely off her map. She wondered if she was having a nervous breakdown.

"Oh, lord, look!" she cried as he drove.

"*Magtig!*" he swore and braked hard. The Humvee dropped one wheel off the shoulder as it came to a stop.

A small, wounded antelope was dragging itself along the desert, a few yards off the road. The antelope's rear legs weren't working and the sun picked out flashes of white on the backs of the rear legs. Megan recognized the flashes as compound fractures, bone jutting through flesh.

Hardi Boaz yanked his rifle out of its rack and strode toward the animal. She got out herself as if drawn by his magnetic field, but she stayed on the pavement.

She thought she heard a bleat. The man said something gently as he squatted.

What she could see of the animal seemed to thrash all of a sudden. She moved to a better angle and saw him digging in a wound with a knife.

"Stop it, for God's sake!"

He glanced impassively back, not directly at her, then flicked his eyebrows. In one quick motion he set the barrel of his rifle under the antelope's chin. With an extraordinary echoing blast, the top of the animal's head disappeared.

She screamed, a complaint that seemed to have transmitted itself straight to her from the animal, and then she covered her eyes. She could still hear the terrible gunshot. A gentle man is writing poetry in a bee-loud glade somewhere, she thought, and this primitive has just killed an animal.

When she looked, he was digging in the wounds again.

"What are you *doing*?"

"Look, *mevrou*. I am not the Little Prince. This could be motorcar. But *this* in the side might have been a bullet, and I must know if we have armed border-crossers."

She gasped as he flipped the small animal over, what was left of the head lolling in a ghastly way. This is too primal for me, she thought. She felt a tremor in her legs.

He dipped two fingers in the wound, then stood and walked to the road and brushed his gluey fingers against her forehead. "The English lords blood little girls on their first foxhunt."

The smell was feral and disgusting and she pawed at her forehead. She must flee whatever held her near this strange, powerful man who couldn't look you in the eyes.

He walked a few paces heavily and then stopped and looked back with an almost wistful stoicism. "All your life, *mevrou*, the rim of your civilization has been patrolled by men like me to keep out the barbarians. My ring of defense makes possible your fine fantasies of how pleasant the world is, and you've always been happy to sacrifice men like me to your self-image.

"I must leave you for a few days. I ask you to stay and wait for me, but it is your choice."

*

It was Monica Flagg from the arson team who found it in the gravel and called him. Walt Roski hurried toward her across the burned-out wash. He fancied Monica, but it was only an idle head game. He was divorced and lonely, severely depressed, thirty years her senior.

She pointed to a patch of ground standing beyond a shallow berm, just as Piscatelli's wife had described. An oval area of burned earth, and one odd grayish shape poking up out of the ground where Monica had swept the ash away with a paintbrush. A small hip bone, maybe.

"That's human remains," she said. "Or I'm a bad dog."

"I hope I don't have to punish you." Her strange remark deserved that at least. He outlined the oval in the air with his finger as he always did to remember it. His memory clung best to gesture and body soma. "It wasn't quite firestorm heat, so there'll probably be more left. Where do you make the head?"

"If I had to guess, there."

"Call Terry to bring a sifting screen. There'll be more bone. Maybe other evidence. Wait."

Walt Roski took a ballpoint pen out of his shirt, stepped off the berm, and dragged the pen through a tiny irregularity in the powdery ash. Out of the ash came a trophy hooked on the plastic pen: a melted, misshapen set of handcuffs. Barely recognizable, but close enough.

"Crimeny!" she said.

"I wonder if a cop was involved."

"Even street kids can buy handcuffs these days, Walt. S-and-M fans on Hollywood Boulevard."

"S and M?" he asked innocently. He wanted her to have to say it.

"Sadomasochism, dear. You may have heard of it."

*

"Never stop questioning. A faith unquestioned will break like a straw at the first bad wind."

Jack Liffey lurked in the shadows of the church building to watch a circle of high-school-aged kids, mostly Asian, sitting in a circle on a lawn and listening intently to a short Asian priest, almost a midget, who spoke tranquilly in perfect American English. Father Soong? The St. Thomas Aquinas parish church was utterly undistinguished, a low stucco box of the 1960s that could have been a church of any denomination, or a big shoe store.

"Faith is everywhere—often where you don't expect it."

The man reached into a fold of his loose white frock and took out a strange object. It was an embossed brass cylinder on a wood spindle with a single lanyard tied to a small weight. He spun it for a while, with a soft grating sound.

"*Om mani padme hum*," he intoned. "This is a Tibetan prayer wheel. What I quoted is the prayer written on it. It means the jewel in the lotus. Or maybe something more complicated, no one is agreed. But everyone agrees that a prayer flies up to heaven at every spin."

Nobody said a word.

"Is no one going to challenge me? Don't you feel that's nonsense?"

Finally an Asian boy with a shaved head said, "It's laughable, father. What kind of God would want somebody to sit there twirling a top?"

The priest smiled. "And what kind of God wants you to watch me drink wine and mumble every Sunday? Question and doubt, but cling hard to what lives in your heart."

The priest noticed Jack Liffey waiting and glanced at his watch. "We've run way over. Same time next week. We'll talk about the jewel in the lotus. I want each of you to bring one doubt that you've entertained."

They stood up raggedly and the priest gathered himself, all four foot eleven or so, and made toward Jack Liffey.

"You must be Mr. Liffey. Professor Hollister called. I'm sorry we ran late."

"Jack, please. My father gets to be Mr. Liffey, since he's still alive."

"You're lucky, sir. How old is he?"

"Ninety-some. Whether I'm lucky or not…well. He was a world-renowned scholar on the supremacy of the white race. His work was published by a lot of fairly unevolved life forms."

Father Soong smiled. "We know a little about racists here in Monterey Park. My name is Theo, if that's the order of the day."

They shook hands and the priest led him toward a side door of the stucco building, and then into a spacious office.

"I'd love to know what you were up to with those kids."

"Please don't think I'm cynical just because I need to disturb some cynical teens. Those were some of the brightest kids in this parish. Most of them are going to lose their faith in a few years at college. I'm hoping a few of them will cling to a scrap of Christian charity." The priest shook his head sadly. "You'd be surprised how perfunctory faith can become even for priests."

"Would you tell me about Sabine Roh?"

The little priest seemed to muse on the request for a while, even shuffled papers to delay answering. "Sometimes it's very difficult, Jack. To misquote Tolstoy, all good girls are alike, but Sabine is gooder than good. She's kind, considerate to everyone, deeply religious and deeply into what she calls 'community.' She really means Liberation Theology, which she's been reading with her friend Ellen. Gustavo Gutierrez, Paolo Freire, even our own Dorothy Day and her Catholic Worker group. Sabine keeps telling me that she wants to become a nun and I try to dissuade her."

"Why?"

He let out a long breath. "Very few orders are going to allow her to express the social side of her nature." He closed his eyes for a moment. "It's so sad, or maybe worse. The Church has abandoned all the really elderly nuns. Go to any retirement center and you'll find eighty-year-olds on walkers looking after bedridden ninety-year-olds.

"Maybe it was presumptuous of me. I told Sabine that becoming a nun would probably end up infantilizing her. Young nuns have a kind of moral earnestness and a caring for others without any real personal connections to strain the bond. And there's always somebody around to take their good intentions seriously."

Jack Liffey wondered when the church, in its wisdom, was going to send this man off to deepest Congo with no way back.

"Please tell me about the Orange Berets," Jack Liffey requested. "You were their advisor."

"They're gone now, but it was a stroke of brilliance—a Mexican-Asian coalition to fight racism. But mixed with street theater." The priest was silent a moment. "Sorry—I actually choke up if I let myself think of a few dozen immigrant kids standing arm in arm to protect peace meetings from the rowdies. I'm blessed to have seen it."

"What's left?"

The priest shook his head sadly. "A snapping turtle that doesn't know it's dead. If you can help me reestablish contact with Sabine, God's blessing on you."

There was a brisk knuckle-rap at the door.

"Yes!" the priest called.

An Asian girl wearing a tight black leotard and a buzz cut of startling blue hair looked in. "Sir, I need to get an urgent message to Sabine."

"Do you know where she is?" the priest asked casually.

The girl glanced at Jack Liffey, and he did his best to seem utterly uninterested.

"She's gone to the mountains," the girl said.

"Don't be silly, Ellen. This isn't Cuba."

"I don't think it's literal. She's hiding out."

"What's your message?"

"To call me."

"Do you have any idea how I'm supposed to give her this message?"

The girl looked surprised, and then distrust flooded up through her. "Sorry to bother you, sir." She ducked out at once and shut the door. They could hear light footsteps running away, and the priest sighed.

"I suppose you wouldn't like to pass me this Ellen's address or phone number."

"I'm afraid I don't have it. She was in the Orange Berets, but she was a militant atheist."

There couldn't be that many girls with blue crew cuts, he thought. "One last question, sir: why did you show those kids the Tibetan prayer wheel?"

The tiny priest reclaimed the device from the folds of his oversized garment. He twirled it a few times pensively. "Next week we'll talk about the jewel in the lotus. It can only mean the eternal contained within the fleeting. The lotus flower lasts only a few days, and then it withers to make room for a seedpod for the future."

*

Ed Zukovich borrowed his uncle's Cadillac Escalade for his mission to pick up the border dude at LAX and take him to the Washington Plaza Hotel, the only accommodation Monterey Park had that might seem respectable to a celebrity. Of course, if you went outside the city a bit—to the Huntington Hotel in Pasadena, for instance—you had a truly swank place, but that was a lot more expensive.

At the American Airlines exit gate near the baggage claim, he held up his cardboard sign saying *Boaz*, like some dorky chauffeur, expecting to greet a stuffed shirt. Seth Brinkerhoff had told him the man was dynamite as a speaker. Dynamite was always good, Zook thought.

People were dragging rolling carry-ons out the doors, but he was a bit early. He elbowed his way to the front of the drivers in their monkey suits, feeling like a mutt in a poodle show. Zukovich had never even flown in a plane. His mother had been terrified of airplanes, boats, even long-distance buses.

All at once there was a bellow of laughter that set a nearby airport cop on alert. An enormous grinning man wearing a khaki bush shirt, khaki shorts, and knee socks had come out and was staring straight at Zook and the sign. His hands were flung into the air exultantly. The man-mountain used both index fingers to point straight at the cardboard sign and brayed again.

Zukovich flipped the sign over to see if he was holding it upside down, but no. "Is it misspelled?" he asked when the man came up to him. Oddly, the man's glance was fixed a few inches to Zook's left.

"Don't mind me, sonny." The booming voice had a really odd accent to it, with all the vowels twisted out of shape. "God put me here so nobody could get theirself smug about being civilized."

They both noticed two more cops heading discreetly their way.

"Uh-oh. I think I am in the deepshit already for being too loud. Like a gutshot rhino, hey. Let's go get my crap before the coppers decide to shoot me and ask later."

Zukovich followed him toward the luggage track that was already receiving suitcases from above. He noticed from the burned and crosshatched skin on the back of the man's neck that he was probably older than he'd looked at first. Zook didn't do well with ages, but he guessed late fifties. The big man was bowlegged but nimble. What a strange being.

"Gerhardus Boaz." He thrust out a big strong hand as they walked. "Call me Hardi."

"I'm Zook. Where do you come from?"

"San Diego. Though I rule Imperial County, too." He did his best to mimic an American accent, but it didn't work. "Of course, you mean before. I left South Africa in 1995, son. You can't expect a real man to go on living under *kaffir* rule. You don't know what *kaffir* means, do you? It was our word for nigger. Course, over there, there were niggers everywhere like ants."

Zukovich winced. A well-dressed colored couple nearby halted and turned to glare at them, but Boaz seemed totally unselfconscious about creating a scene.

"I know what you think, ma'an, but I'm not prejudiced even a little bit. Back home we said the Dutch and the *kaffirs* came to South Africa at exactly the same time. *We* arrived at the Cape in ships just as the blacks were climbing down out of the trees!"

He burst into laughter, and Zukovich wondered how to get his charge out of the terminal alive.

*

"Woosah! I got to chill."

Diana Yao had ridden up breathless on her goofy pop-popping Solex bike with its 49cc gas engine. She lived about a mile away.

"The engine cut out at Hitchcock and I had to pedal for a while before it came back."

Diana had left the Orange Berets some time ago to go back to serious math studies at L.A. State, but she was still loyal to Ellen and Sabine, so she'd responded to Ellen's distress call. She'd insisted on meeting in neutral Cascades Park not too far from her home. The grass slope, with its descending pool-to-pool rapids, had been built in the late 1920s as the grand entry to a housing development that had gone bust in the Depression and never been built. Emblematic of something, Ellen had once thought.

"Let's be cool," Diana said. "I'm still out of it, but I'll always be there for Sabby."

"Word up," Ellen said. "I need to find her."

"What do you know?"

"I know Father Soong doesn't have a clue. She was tailing that fat guy in the Commandos, the dumb one they say has the big thingy."

"Everybody knows about Captain Beef."

"He figured to be the safest doofus to watch, he was so stupid. I drew the intellectual." Ellen laughed. "The Zook guy who's read all the biggest clownsuits of the Cold War, like W. Cleon Skousen. He's their big thinker. Compared to an oak tree."

"El, I'm here because…?"

"I'm scared and alone in this, Di. Sabby told me she had a way to get close to watch that big guy. I don't know what her game was. She's changed a lot. Ever since her trip to Mexico, she's been a lot harder and angrier. Not that sweet nun."

"I never heard about her trip."

"Nobody really knows. It was a craziness to help her parents, but I don't think it went down well. Help me any way you can. You know her math friends. Just ask around."

Diana reached over and rested her hand on Ellen's knee. "You don't look too good, girl."

"The revolution let me down. Maybe I just want a normal life."

"True that," Diana said.

*

Gustav watched his younger brother Andor unfold the metal stock of his newest plaything, the SPAS-12 shotgun. It wasn't the assault shotgun itself that interested Andor so much as the specially fabricated B-2 Bomber shells.

Long ago, Andor had gone to a movie made by some pretentious Spaniard named Buñuel called *The Discreet Charm of the Bourgeoisie.* The only thing he remembered was one scene in which a bunch of rich and drunk party guests, wearing tuxedos and gowns, utterly blasé, went out on a verandah and fired an ordinary-looking pistol that blew the crap out of whatever they aimed at. He remembered like yesterday watching an elm tree burst into flames. I want *that*, he'd thought.

"You do like your powerful firearms," Gustav said.

"They make my dick hard."

"Sometimes a gun is just a gun."

"Huh?"

"You never read Freud?"

"Why would I read a Jewboy, Gus? Here, have a Bloody Mary. I think I'm learning to make them right."

"What's the secret, little bro?"

"Extra garlic and Tabasco. It keeps away vampires, too."

Gustav smiled dutifully.

"Who'd you send to speak to that California Tea Party group?" Andor asked.

"The South African with the short pants. The only guy who's ever successfully fired your T-rex."

Andor roared with laughter, a rare moment. "That big asshole is definitely the cutting edge. Maybe he'll sprain their pathological daintiness. All Californians are secret liberals, I swear. Must be the climate."

"Or bad schools."

"Want the first shot?" Andor offered him the STAS-12.

"Sure." Gustav had seen the Buñuel movie, too. "Andor, you know the real joy of being so goddamn rich?"

"Buying an election?"

"I meant personally. We can own all the newest marvels, lock, stock, and barrel. We can have our fun whenever we want."

"I don't get it."

"Drink up. Geronimo."

Gustav aimed the SPAS-12 at a big tree across the pond, a well-spread chestnut.

A tail of fire issued from the shotgun, along with a startling *whoomp*, and then the gnarled tree trunk erupted in flame about halfway up, crackling like mad. Before long, the gigantic crown of the tree began to tilt.

Despite Gustav's expectations, there was something a bit unsatisfying about the blast—perhaps that the weapon wouldn't destroy a city, a whole world.

*

"Bang, bang, bang—you're all dead!" Hardi Boaz shouted to the bikers at the bar, making pistols of both hands. Heads turned, of course. The stool squatters were generally as big and buff as Boaz himself, with sleeveless jean jackets, shovel beards, ponytails, and wallets on looping chains.

"Agh, boys, take it easy. I been promised they isn't no wetbacks or nigger-lovers in this place. So I'll let you all live!"

Ed Zukovich wanted to go hide in the men's room. He hadn't actually said anything about wetbacks or nigger-lovers. Boaz had asked to be taken to a place where things were "real white" so he could relax, and Zook figured the man didn't mean a cocktail bar in Beverly Hills.

This place was a famous biker hangout in El Monte on the way up to Chantry Flats Road in the mountains, where lots of Harley folks loved to ride on weekends. It was a stone-built old building called Rock House No. 2, with two dozen Harleys parked in front.

"Cool your jets, mister." A confident growl from somewhere at the bar.

"I'm cool as Dr. Death." Boaz gave a midair pump with one arm, then the other. "I been through a dozen nigger lands like a dose of salts, ma'an. The fainthearts can kiss my arse. Agh, sis, even a lot of them places ain't places no more."

One of the bikers stood up slowly. He was paunchy and had two teardrop tattoos descending from the corner of his right eye. "You got a problem, foreigner?"

"Hell, everybody gets a beer!" Boaz yelled and threw a hundred-dollar bill on the bar. The skinny bartender stared at the bill as if it was infected with leprosy.

"That buys about twelve beers, mister, with no tip. This ain't Cow City in the movies."

Boaz tossed down two more hundreds. "Beers all around, gents. And no offense. I'll make up any short, barman."

"Thank you, foreigner," Teardrops said evenly. "Let's take it easy tonight, amigo. Some of us been at work all day and got to smooth out."

As the bartender folded up the money, Zook tried to steer his charge to a table far in the corner.

"Join us," Teardrops said. Somehow the crowd at the bar opened up to make some standing room. "A big man like you buys me a drink straight off, I'm obliged to hold off thinking he's a sack of dogshit."

Boaz brayed his laugh and dragged Zook up to the bar beside him. "This my buddy, Zook. I'm Hardi."

"I'm Shank. Where the fuck you from with the clown suit and clown voice?"

They shook hands as if trying to crush each other's fingers, and Hardi Boaz took a while explaining he was from South Africa, but many years back. Boaz was still not meeting any eyes, but they didn't seem to be bothered.

"These days all my Boer brothers, the fat-arsed sissy guys that owns the Jag agencies, they all of a sudden start talking like Martin

Fuckin' Luther King, about how they going to love the darkies. They say we got to like our bright tomorrow. Man, through history, any dumb sonofabitch talks like that, he gets his dick chopped off. I had to leave for greener pastures."

The opened beer bottles began sliding from the center of the bar outward.

"I hear you," Shank said. "But let's keep things up close and personal. Some of my friends got Mex ol' ladies. We're pretty damn white here, but I'm not so sure about you."

"My people were so white they were Dutch!" Boaz crowed. "I been an American for ten years. What a great country we all got. We just got to keep it that way."

Zook relaxed and sucked down a lot of beer as soon as he realized he wouldn't get stomped. Hardi Boaz and Shank spun off on a discussion of what it meant to keep America great, and Zook listened closely as Boaz talked about building an armed "troopie" that hired itself out to ranchers along the California border to guard their property, chase off drug mules and wetbacks trying to come over. Boaz loudly invited Shank and all his friends to Zook's keg the next day to hear him talk about keeping America pure.

Uh-oh, Zook thought. These guys were a lot heavier than he'd bargained on. The teardrops were a prison tat for the number of enemies killed.

Much later, as people were starting to reel out of Rock House No. 2, the ponytail sitting beside Teardrops gave a huge grin for the first time, revealing gold stars set into his front teeth. "I'll come to your kegger, boys, and let's us shiver Old Glory right up your flagpole."

SEVEN
Saturday Night Challenge

After a bit of sleuthing about Miss Blue-hair at L.A. State, Jack Liffey found his way to an old craftsman bungalow not far from downtown Monterey Park. He waited discreetly down the block in his pickup. He'd usually been able to pal up to teens without putting them off. One thing in his favor was that old guys generally didn't count at all. And he never tried to hold his own with them or top their comments. His ego had become expendable long ago.

"You know a girl with a blue butch cut?" he'd asked.

"Gotta be Rosa."

He remembered the name Ellen, but he went with it anyway and waited now at the address he'd finally located. He didn't really think there were whole glee clubs with bright blue hair.

Eventually a little Yaris showed up, the exact equivalent of his own daughter's old Echo. But where did Toyota get these names? It was Blue Hair clambering out—definitely the girl from the church. He intercepted her on her way to the door.

"Ellen. Remember me from the church? I'm working for Sabine's family." She had a skirt on over the leotard now.

"The name is Rosa," she said belligerently. "For Rosa Luxemburg, the greatest hero of all time."

Amazing, he thought, a teen who'd read a book. "I agree, but if you're a political organizer, isn't your hair a bit too conspicuous?"

"Not where I work."

Disaffected kids at college, okay. "Fair enough. I started Long Beach State with a greasy flattop, long sides, and a D.A. You know what that was?"

"Sure. A duck's ass. 'Ducktail' is what L7s say."

He had no idea what an L7 was, but didn't think it was the time to update his dope sheet on teen talk. "Could we meet somewhere to talk, Rosa? Sabine's parents are terribly worried. I'll treat and I'll go away the instant you tell me to."

She glanced around, as if FBI agents might be behind the trees. "Down on Garvey to the left, you'll see the French Victory Restaurant. It's not very French or victorious but it'll be quiet. Be there in half an hour. I'll make my own way, thank you, and I'll buy my own Coke. I'll check the street first for white vans with antennas on the roof."

"Just me, Rosa," Jack Liffey said.

*

Jack Liffey parked at a city park between Ellen/Rosa's house and the cafe she'd specified. A half hour—why the delay? So she could say hello to her parents first? So she could summon her pals to beat him up?

It was early afternoon in the late autumn and the clear-sky sunlight was promising its usual lazy magic. Elderly Chinese men squatted near a nondescript building at the edge of the park, playing something on a checkerboard lying on the grass, the game pieces all white. There was a perfectly serviceable picnic table nearby, but they obviously preferred heel-squatting. Not far away, Chinese teens were playing a pretty good game of two-on-two basketball.

Here was Professor Hollister's laboratory of immigration, he thought. He tried to imagine being stuck with a group of Americans displaced to some far corner of China. He decided he'd probably feel hopeless about learning enough to fit in. How could anyone expect grown people to give up a lifetime of their culture?

A young Chinese couple in jeans strolled into the park with a lively boy hand in hand between them. The boy was maybe eight, and they all skipped happily to a swing set in a sandbox. Immediately they took up their gender roles—the woman and child sitting in swings to be pushed alternately by the man. Nothing about their manner suggested Asia to Jack Liffey.

The grizzled game board players laughed abruptly, and an old man covered his eyes and ran off. Sore loser. Another old man took his place.

The gangly little boy shouted something as he ran out onto the grass. He glanced back and pointed at his mom. She jumped off her swing and ran after him with the kind of tiny mincing steps Asian women often favored, twisting and turning to pretend to elude her son's lunges. The boy finally poked his mother's thigh, and the woman reverted instantly to a full-stretch Western run as she chased after her husband.

Okay, Jack Liffey said to himself. The cultural gap can be very complicated.

*

Rosa twiddled the straw in her diet Sprite and ate an occasional sweet potato fry from a paper tub. A low wall separated them from the sidewalk—presumably to keep patrons from absconding with the salt shakers. The counter menu inside had offered various combinations of grease and carbohydrates, plus something called the French Victory Special. He felt like asking the clueless-looking Chinese teen, when did the French ever have one?

Two tables away, a tiny older man with a business suit and a bad scar down his cheek sat opposite an astonishingly beautiful Chinese girl with long, dyed blond hair. She wore a chest sash like a beauty queen over a ball gown, but he couldn't read it. The two touched hands across the table now and again like lovers, but it was the lack of parity between them that made one suspicious—looking for adjustments.

"Go on," Jack Liffey said.

She wasn't Catholic, Ellen said, but she knew that Sabine had been close to Father Soong. She and Sabine had been blood sisters from their teens when they'd read the Brontës and Jane Austen together. Later they'd tipped toward reading Marcuse and Habermas and liberation theologists like Paolo Freire. They'd both scorned the Asian boys who pecked away at their computers, doing math. They yearned for a wild-haired Che Guevara.

"Where's Sabine gone to?" Jack Liffey asked.

"I wish I knew."

"Tell me about the Commandos."

Ellen/Rosa made a face and bonked her forehead with the heel of her hand in self-reproach. Jack Liffey liked the emotionality.

"Back in the day, they were dangerous. Satan's Commandos, a nasty motorcycle club, and then they became a hate-the-Chinese group. They were on the fringe of the Tea Partiers for a while, but the gang is mostly gone. A few scary guys, that's all."

She was interrupted by a whinny from the table nearby.

"I guess I should split right now!" the woman bawled. He could hear outrage in her voice.

"No no no. Please. I'm on top of it," the man insisted.

Jack Liffey took only a brief glance, as the woman seemed to be subsiding.

"Can we talk more about Sabine?"

"Maybe."

"I take it that's her given name."

"She has a parental name, too. I don't speak enough Chinese to order noodles in a restaurant. I think her original name was Suong— it's actually Vietnamese."

"I wanted to make sure it wasn't a *nom de guerre* like Rosa. So her family are Hoa Chinese from Vietnam."

"You're about the right age, aren't you? You were one of the baby-killers."

The word was like a cattle prod, but he let it go, then didn't. "Rosa, I had a peace symbol on my radar scope and my buddy had a poster of Uncle Ho on the wall above his. It was the best we could do."

"Goody for you." She looked about to stand and leave.

"Wait, please. I'm just looking for Sabine, and I have no interest in anything that's uncomfortable for you. I swear I'll protect any confidences."

Rosa/Ellen pursed her lips, poised on her own knife edge of trust.

"Sabine and I founded the Berets. I said orange was a lousy color. Combining brown and yellow, of course. I asked Sabby if we were fighting for Halloween."

He smiled.

She nodded a kind of surrender to him. "Sabby and me have been watching the last few Commandos as a kind of duty. You've probably seen the racist posters they put up. Losers like that often resort to terrorism as they burn out."

There was more bleating from the couple nearby, plus some table-pounding, and Jack Liffey forced himself not to look.

"My own target was the so-called brains—Ed Zukovich," Rosa said, studying her clasped hands. "He's only the brains compared to a cactus. We both ignored their poster artist, Marly Tom. His name is Tom McMarlin, and he's nothing, a nebbish.

"Sabine drew the big dumbhead, Antonio Buffano. He's known as Captain Beef and he's reputed to have the largest penis in the Western World. I wouldn't know. They're all sad cases, really—like dogs that were kicked a lot when they were puppies.

"That's all I know, Mr. Liffey, except that they're holding a keg party tomorrow afternoon. I can find out where it is if you want to check it out. But if I tell you, I want a report. Obviously I'm not welcome."

He waited, but there was no more forthcoming. "That's not all you know about your friend, is it? I know she wasn't clean as Ivory Snow." He mentioned the baggie and map he'd found in her room, and she stared hard over his shoulder at a ghost from some dire past.

"Please. It may help find her."

Ellen/Rosa banged her forehead with her palm again as she fought some inner struggle. "Sabby's family needs money bad, and a lot of people know that. Some of them aren't nice people—a few angry Latinos on the edge of gangs that we knew from the Berets. I told her to stay away from them, but she said it didn't matter what happened to her.

"It's her holy helper complex. Maybe she agreed to be a drug mule for one of them. She'd figure nobody would ever search a Chinese girl on a day trip to Mexico. If she went, it was by herself." Ellen swirled her straw. "It was maybe ten days ago if it happened, and I don't know if she went or even if she made it back."

There was a squeal, followed by a bray of anger. Jack Liffey's eyes slipped reluctantly to the table nearby, just in time to watch the woman stand up. She wrenched open her blouse angrily toward her companion. He could see she was flashing the little man and the world at large with large, firm breasts. The man with the scar jerked back in his chair.

"Happy *now*?" the Chinese girl shouted. She clutched the blouse tight as she glanced at Jack Liffey with murder eyes, and then scrambled over the low wall to the outside world. He guessed he'd just seen something to do with the parity adjustment that he'd wondered about.

"What else do you know about Sabine's big Mexican trip?"

She shook her head. "I'm mum now."

"Would you give me the names of any of the Latinos who contacted her?"

"I'm no snitch."

He had a sense he'd reached the end for now. "Tell me where the keg is," he said.

*

Gloria sat at the kitchen table and offered cooking instructions in her most lackluster voice. She was guiding Maeve in working up a complicated *mole poblano* for the chicken that was browning in lard in a cast-iron pot.

"*¿Qué hubo, señor pito negro?*" Maeve said, addressing a foot-tall dried black chile that she held in front of her face and then licked to taunt Gloria.

The odd slang pun—*What's up, Mr. Black Penis?*—only really worked if you knew both languages.

"Use proper Spanish, girl. That thing's not no pecker I ever seen."

Maeve held up another chile. "*¿Qué es esto, mi reina?*"

"*Una pasilla, mi chica.* The pasilla's not terribly hot as chiles go."

There were also three fat green anchos, and a mulatto that looked like a big raisin. Real Mexican cooking could be damned complicated, Maeve knew. Her old boyfriend had been satisfied with ordinary burritos and tacos, which he'd splash all over with dollops of hot sauce.

"I thought you were decidedly not Mexican," Maeve said.

"If you stand up and burn in a church long enough, you're a

candle, hon. My *pendejo* fosters insisted I learn to cook *their* way. No frybread or roadkill stew. I must admit, American Indian cuisine leaves a lot to be desired."

"How about telling me about your growing up?"

"What do I get in return, chica?" Gloria was sipping her beer slowly.

"What do you want to hear?" Maeve said.

"I want to hear the whole truth about Mr. Gangster Alberto Montalvo next door, your irresistible impregnator. I knew him way back to a sullen nine-year-old and a twelve-year-old wannabe, throwing gang signs at me like an animated little monkey. I also want to hear the whole truth about who you're fucking now, or whatever you call it with girls."

"My two for your one."

"My one is *mucho grande*, sweetie. I haven't even told your dad about the fosters in Baldwin Park."

"Deal. You first, Gloria."

Gloria went on giving cooking instructions on the complex recipe, but interlaced the "stir in"s with a tale of being dumped by Child Services into an East L.A. she'd never seen before. After her mother's death in Inyo County, the disorderly little Indian girl had been found breaking dishes and throwing food against the walls in her trailer.

"More beer," Gloria demanded.

Maeve took no time deciding. She brought a Corona and had one herself.

Gloria karated the bottle caps off with the heel of her hand against the edge of the table, as she liked to do. "These two scumbags took in foster kids as their only source of income. If they wasn't both dead now, I swear I'd drive out there and kill them."

The household had averaged about six, and the Delgados regularly pitted the kids against each other, to teach them about "real life." Boxing, wrestling, even spelling bees—whatever they weren't good at. Those not directly in combat had to watch and root. The main bout was always boxing at the end.

"Bless me, curse me. I'm sorry, my chica, I couldn't rise above any of this."

What Gloria had learned was how much she could enjoy hurting—sometimes to escape her own pain, but sometimes for nothing more than riding a wave of cheers. Early in her tenure there, the stringy little girl had resolved to get herself out of the house on top or die at it. She still had visceral memories of punches that had drawn screams.

"That's so awful," Maeve said.

"Or is it just the way things are?"

"I totally deny that," Maeve said. "People can cooperate."

"Come along with me on a few night patrols—if the brass ever reinstates me. America is an ocean-to-ocean freak show."

"Some people are decent. Like Martin Luther King."

"Like your dad, hon. He's the second-best man I ever met. And years ago, your dad briefly met the love of my life."

That hurt, Maeve thought, but it must have welled up from somewhere deeply honest. Truth night stumbled on. Maeve noticed that Gloria had become withdrawn, maybe even crying a little inside with the memories of her big love. It was startling. Maeve had never seen anything but ferocious strength in the woman.

Suddenly Gloria leapt to her feet with wide eyes and staggered straight toward Maeve like a Frankenstein, some kind of urgency driving hard against her broken hip. Gloria gave a terrible bawl of pain but wouldn't quit the mad charge until the hip gave way and she began to crumple. "Freeze!" Gloria shouted. She rammed her hip against the old O'Keefe & Merritt for support and slapped at Maeve's back. Maeve winced and turtled her head down, expecting another blow. Then she noticed that her blouse was on fire and ripped it off.

Gloria hissed on an inhale and swallowed back her pain. "Chica. You were going to turn into a human torch."

"My bad. I thought you were going to teach me Challenge Night." She put her arm around Gloria's ample waist and helped her back to her chair. "I guess I'll do better when I've grown up."

"Hon, you've used up that line. They don't make bras any bigger."

"Oh, I'm sure they do."

Gloria settled with a sigh and smiled for the first time. "Your turn now, or I *will* teach you challenge. Tell me about Beto next door."

Maeve could feel herself blushing. "That's tough."

"So was my turn, hon. Flip the chicken over now and turn it down to simmer. You can start chopping up the onions."

"You know I was really—what?—insane with sex. I would have jumped off a cliff for him. And I had a really bad time when I submitted." Luckily, the banger was off the grid somewhere now, probably Mexico.

"Anybody would've had a bad time with that kid, hon."

"I had a real fight deciding on the abortion. It wasn't the best year of my life. Thank god Beto didn't learn he'd knocked me up. He'd probably have killed me for the abortion." She was trying hard to be suitably tough, but didn't feel she was doing very well at it.

"Is that what turned you against guys?"

She shrugged. "It's not that crude, *Tia*. But I guess it left a big sore spot that a gentle girl could caress."

"I'm missing something here. Can you tell me what it is with girls that makes you feel so good—is it just looking into each other's eyes? The lack of all the *pendejo* swagger? What's the really big thing for you: fingers or toys or tongues?"

"Gloria!"

"This is truth time. I want another beer. And I genuinely want to know what it is that turns you on with girls."

Maeve took her time getting the beer. "Something inside me just clicks. I'm not hiding any secret." As Gloria opened the bottle with her chop, Maeve abruptly put it together. Gloria was interested in turn-ons, not because she was considering the lesbian thing, but because she was caught up in a non-arousal funk of her own with her father. This is for professionals smarter than me, Maeve thought. She could barely cling to the edge of her own sexuality.

There was a scraping sound outside, and then the familiar muttering exhaust of her dad's pickup on the driveway.

"Saved by the bell," Maeve said.

"Not forever, chica. *Y no me vienes otra vez tus quentos de hadas pendejos.*" And don't bring me any more lousy fairytales.

"*¿A un tiempo, que si...todo en la vida eras mierda?*" Maeve said.

Gloria laughed conspiratorially as a key fussed at the door.

Once upon a time, what if everything in life was shit?

*

Seth Brinkerhoff found the big man lying on a chaise out by the pool
of the Washington Plaza. The amenities of the hotel were something
of an afterthought, since the pool was surrounded by asphalt and
squeezed between a parking lot and an alley. Not quite five stars.

Hardi Boaz was all by himself poolside. Maybe the Chinese didn't
swim. It was the top hotel in Monterey Park, and had been basically
a Chinese hotel since about 1980. In all his years representing rich
white clients in the San Gabriel Valley, Seth Brinkerhoff had never
been inside the Washington.

He paused a moment at the pool gate, held by the altogetherness
of the big hairy man on the chaise who wore only swim shorts. His
head was thoroughly tanned like a day laborer, but the rest was a
big white side of beef with the letters AWB tattooed across his chest.
There was also a flag, a whirl of three black sevens in a white circle
on a red background that looked dangerously like the Nazi flag.

What have the Reiks done to me? Brinkerhoff thought. He'd
asked for an inspirational speaker, wanting somebody like Ron
Paul or Michelle Bachman for his Tea Party dinner dance, and this
was what they'd sent. Apparently, "inspirational" was a flexible
concept.

This man was the founder of a border watchdog group along the
California line east of San Diego. "Don't worry, sir," the Reiks' gal
Friday had told him, "this guy looks like a rough edge but he's a
really rousing speaker." Like the damn overpowered rifle the Reiks
had made him shoot. The episode still smarted.

Brinkerhoff was perfectly content to lend this side of beef to the
lowlife bikers who were run by the son of his old realtor pal; Zook
was actually his godson. But Brinkerhoff was not quite so content
to have the man address his dinner-dance fundraiser in the Legion
Hall the next day. At least he'd get an advance look at the keg party.

"Mr. Boaz," Brinkerhoff announced as he entered the pool area.

"Me."

The big man stirred and the chaise under him groaned, but he
didn't meet Seth's eyes.

"I'm Seth Brinkerhoff, chairman of the Tea Party Express here."

"Hardi Boaz. I'm your Commie-stomping Christian patriot. Lock up the virgins."

The accent was bizarre. "I guess that's what I'm here to talk about," Brinkerhoff said grimly.

"You got me some virgins?" The big man pretended to come alert.

"We're in the process of becoming a respectable part of the Republican mainstream, Mr. Boaz. So we're all virgins in public. Can you tell me what that AWB on your chest stands for?"

"It's ancient history. *Afrikaner Weerstandsbeweging*. Afrikaner Resistance Movement, to you. We did our best to keep the *kaffirs* from taking over our lovely birthland, but our leaders sold us out. That's a long time ago, and I'm an American now. Hail Washington. I got real fraternal feelings for all the San Diego ranchers afraid of the Beaners coming across every night. If you got a nice car outside, they're probably stealing your hubcaps this minute."

"Mr. Boaz, the borderlands are apparently a little bit different from the rest of California. Up here we gave up that kind of talk a long time ago, even if we believe there's a grain of truth in it."

Boaz squinted. "That why you stuck me in this dink hotel? The beds even *smell* yellow."

"This place is ranked two stars. It's the best in town. If you want to move to a Big 6 Motel, let me know."

"I'm bighearted, ma'an." He slapped the left of his chest, quite hard, as if to demonstrate the location of his big heart.

"What's your border group called?" Brinkerhoff asked. Bernadette had been unwilling to tell him, and he was worried that they might have a really embarrassing name that would leak out, like the Bean Stompers.

"The name ain't important, man. They can call us anything they like, long as they quake in their bloody boots. I hate sissies who're afraid of words."

"Who is it supposed to quake? The wetbacks?"

"Sure, long as it's you saying it in this super-pure ecology, in the homo-commie part of California."

"Mr. Boaz, you can say anything you want at the keg party tomorrow, but at the dinner, please try to stick to a Christian and patriotic agenda without mention of race and without profanity."

"Fuckin'-A right!"

Brinkerhoff turned to go, but turned back after a few steps to stare at the neo-Nazi tattoo. "By the way, sir."

"Ya—here we go. Rub enough snake oil over the world of ideas, we got us a bright tomorrow."

"Please wear a very opaque shirt."

EIGHT
Over and Under

Rosa/Ellen summoned Jack Liffey with a phone call early the next morning. She opened quickly, the blue hair especially brash in the glare of the sun.

"Good morning, Mr. Liffey," she said.

"Ohio," he said brightly.

She smiled. "Don't even try."

He'd been told it meant hello in Chinese, but without the right intonation it probably meant *My penis is on fire*.

She thrust a flier into his hand, a Xeroxed invitation to a keg party that afternoon with a hand-drawn map.

Patriot Beer Bash!
Meet an American Hero!

"How did you get it?"

"It's like a rave by invitation. They stand on street corners and leaflet only the target audience. I'm not sure how they define their demographic, but it certainly isn't me. I got it from a neighbor kid who looks like Elvis Presley. I want my report."

"You'll get it. It might help more if you tell me more about the drug connection."

"No."

A baby began to squall inside. "Yours?"

She nodded. "My dad will never forgive me unless I become the head of Microsoft. I'll call you tonight."

"One quick question," he blurted before she could shut the door. Something she'd said nagged at him. "What on earth is L7?"

She smiled, then made an L with one hand in front of her face and a 7 with the other and slid her hands together to form a square. "It's from texting, Mr. Old School. A square, a nerd."

"Well, twenty-three skidoo."

*

Ambition had failed her and nothing had replaced it. Megan Saxton knew she wasn't very likable, but what could one do about that? Left alone in this nowhere for a day now, she couldn't stop ruminating on her life. Successful at this, successful at that, blah blah. But unbearably empty inside. In the bottom of her small suitcase, fetched to Hardi's house now, she found the Xeroxed Christmas letter from her sister in Texas that she had never opened.

> *Hi there, super friends,*
> *Jus' another greeting from lil ol' me here in Harlingen.*
> *Whew! What a busy life Dick and me and Bobby Joe and Beth and Jessica had this past year. I can't believe there were only 365 days to it...*
> *...Summer we all trekked up north to Dick's family in his favorite state of Iowa and we had a real wacky time with them, with Dick's dad still "beating the band" about Iowa State and the missus "cooking up a storm" for all the massed legions...*

Megan Saxton's eye skipped down the page, dreading even more moronic quotation marks.

> *...Down to the Galveston beaches with the "three little stooges" in tow...*
> *...Tornado touched down across town and sadly killed little Beth's "bosom pal" Grace from Crockett School...*

A photo fell out onto the floor, and she leaned out awkwardly in an attempt to reclaim it without changing position in her chair.

The husband and wife—her sister—stood on the lawn, grinning and making horn-signs behind each other's heads. A sixteen-year-old lout clutched a football and two girls glumly posed on their knees. Susan had aged noticeably even from last year, her hips spreading fast.

But why was she grousing? Susan looked happy. Every one of the single, self-reliant women Megan Saxton knew in Manhattan and Brooklyn went through periods of despondency and doubt, lonely terror and suicidal despair.

And why didn't she just jump into her rental car and drive away from this place of testosterone horrors? She had made the attempt twice and failed.

She tried to imagine her face in place of Susan's in the photograph. She doubted if she could ever summon the energy to conjure that suburban ranch house out of the maelstrom. In a way she admired Susan, though utterly without envy. You are what you want to be, she thought, if only you can figure out what that is.

Do I really want to go on playing with this big hairy gorilla, probably a borderline autistic of some sort, who's without a particle of reflection or self-doubt?

*

Sujjested Donation 10$

Jack Liffey couldn't remember seeing an actual beer keg since his college days, but they hadn't changed a bit. Two of the ribbed aluminum kegs sat side by side on a concrete patio. Below the patio was a wide strip of abandoned wildland under crackling high-tension power lines. At the base of the nearest power pylon, down a shallow hillside, someone had piled up sturdy milk crates and set a plywood sheet across them to make a rudimentary stage. Maybe seventy-five people swarmed the front edge of the stage, talking and drinking beer. A few big men wore torn-sheet armbands—security, of course. A boom box on the stage was thumping away. Angry black rap music, a nice irony. As far as he could see the crowd was entirely white.

Uphill the powerline easement was open to a paved road parked up with cars and motorcycles far into the adjacent neighborhoods. Jack Liffey made his way up through a hirsute sample of humanity to the crush at the kegs. The women were at least as rough-looking as the men.

A fortyish bald man in a sleeveless denim jacket pushed in line ahead of him, talking to a man with a ponytail. "They sat in that hooch all day watching the flies zapped by the bug light. Hillbilly TV."

"Dig it."

Jack Liffey had worn jeans and an old Pendleton shirt. They looked him over carefully. "Lookatcha, bud—your clothes scream undercover." Maybe his jeans were too crisp.

"I'm no cop. I came to hear the border guy."

They got their beer and dismissed his existence just as a noisy outbreak down the slope drew their attention. A lot of push-and-shove and eventually one of the shovers vomited over the other. It was not going to be a tranquil afternoon.

The music cut off and a boomy voice rolled across the hillside. "Hey, hey! Bros and gals! Listen up!"

Jack Liffey drafted himself a beer. He wouldn't drink it, but he had to have the prop.

"Back it down!" somebody shouted.

The hubbub died down a little as order was repeatedly demanded.

A skinny speaker on the stage waved a baseball cap over his head. He wore one of the white armbands. His other fist held a ludicrously small microphone corded to the boom box. "Listen up, boozers and boozettes! America's for Americans, right?!"

A half-hearted cheer greeted the declaration.

"Hey, lemme hear you! *America's for Americans*!"

The roar was louder, echoing off the nearby houses. Jack Liffey guessed the crowd was over a hundred now and folks were still strolling in from the street above. Why did the police tolerate it?

"We got some interesting company today, brahs and sisses! A soldier who's been busy stopping up our borders like a big can of Drano!"

Jack Liffey smiled at the mixed-up simile. He descended toward the stage, careful not to take a sip automatically. He'd been sober for fifteen years now on his own hook. A dry drunk, as he'd been told his teetery condition was called.

"This border hero was born overseas and, I warn you, he talks pretty funny, but he's a real *legal* American now and he's our brother in the fight for the white. Let's give it up for the border guardian, Hardi Boaz."

A stocky man leapt onto the stage to a smatter of applause. He was dressed bizarrely in a safari shirt, khaki shorts, and desert boots, straight out of a Tarzan movie.

"Mah fella 'Murcans, I wanna thank y'all for havin' me here at your party!"

Jack Liffey wondered if he could be hallucinating. The desert warrior was doing his best to produce a Texas drawl, but it was so overlaid with tortured vowels and glottal stops that he doubted many of the partiers could even pick out the words. Fortunately, the man quickly dropped his strange hybrid voice.

"Gather up close-like, friends and patriots. I want this to be a campfire talk, just between me an' you. I won't bite you like no tick on no mangy dog."

Reluctantly the crowd compressed a bit toward the stage.

"I was born in a land far away, and when I grew up it used to be a lot like America. But it's gone to hell, like a dollar knife tryin' to cut rocks. We was a proud white country with a real civilization, but we got overrun by our own mud people, thieves and no-accounts who are as dumb as dirt. Okay, you can't blame dirt for being dirt. The real problem was the white traitors, big city lib'rals, who opened the gates. The pansy college boys who don't even know enough to piss downwind! J'yee-ziss, ma'an, they no worse traitors than traitors to their race!"

That got a bit of a boo from somewhere. Jack Liffey could hear the South African accent reclaim the man's voice as he tried, without much success, to work up a rhythm of oratory. A burly guy was scurrying around in front of the stage taking photographs with his cell phone, also wearing an armband, but no one took much notice of him. Jack Liffey guessed most the crowd was busy trying to work out who this cartoon, fat-kneed wild man was.

"Ma'an, you got to hear the shit the city lib'rals talked when they felt they had to give account for what their fathers did to our mud people. They talk to some cowpat dirt-farmer, they say the niggers are the children of Ham and it's gonna take them centuries to learn to walk upright without scraping their knuckles. But when they talked to the fuckin' Brits in the cities who got all the currency, they got to make new names for things every ten minutes, like some sidesaddle sissy. They made up so many words for kissing black ass I can't remember them all. One man one vote. Colorblind. Multicultural."

The big man plucked at one of his buttocks, almost rammed the microphone up his ass and farted loudly into it. There was a strangled gasp from the crowd. This was an amazing moment that Jack Liffey knew he would always remember with a kind of fondness.

"There's your multicultural! Might as well try putting socks on a duck!"

A confused titter, maybe just puzzlement, rippled through the crowd.

"I hate sissies afraid of words. Fuck the *kaffirs* and niggers and brown people and wetbacks, over there and here, too. You tell 'em, Hardi."

People around Jack Liffey seemed ill at ease, whispering to one another, probably afraid they were being mocked in some way. He figured they might get most of the rant from the abusive epithets alone, but it would be weird beyond weird to them. And these were not folks to appreciate being made uncomfortable. They may have come for a hate-fest, but they wanted a familiar and comfy hatefest.

"Sorry, all of you, if ol' Hardi wanders away from the point you care about. When I get worked up I run off the rails. I'm a hundred and ten percent America now. I'm here to tell you my Border Rangers are the last chance right now for the fighting whites down there who live along the border. These good white folks are threatened every night on their own ranches by armed Mexican drug-runners and wetbacks, and we got to protect them.

"I got no wish to be no better than ol' George Washington in building a white country. Stronger and meaner and quicker, yah, but not tidied up for no limousine lib'rals in Beverly Hills. White people built a fine country here and we gonna take it back yet. Here's what I say to all the mud people: Touch us, you tar barrels, and we'll lop your fuckin' hand off! You tell it, Hardi!"

A few partiers still straggled in from the road, and the man railed on about his work along the border, the nightly armed patrols in Jeeps and on horseback to keep out the plague of mental defectives.

"We need a government that'll do what's necessary. What we oughta do, we just nuke that land across the border. It's all desert anyway, and we sure got plenty extra nukes stored up. Let the Mexes walk tiptoe over on the other side, that's what I say. We gotta break bad. We gotta send all the wetbacks home. Then we just keep nuking the borderland. In ten years nobody can cross and everything calms down and we become just like any other goddamn country, a big respectable nation with a bit of a lousy past. We got to say all that right out loud."

Jack Liffey almost felt sorry for the man. Nothing about the tirade was working very well with this crowd. From time to time there were buzzes and local cheers, but the rant was so outlandish and so far outside their experience that the crowd had little idea how to react.

"As far as I'm concerned, I'll do this dirty business for white America forever. I'll shoot every one of these muddies crossing the border. I'll personally expel Mexicans and then I'll drive up to L.A. and soak Che Guevara t-shirts in acid and hand them out to all the Jew hippie girls demonstrating against us—let them burn their tits off. I'll do whatever the white nation needs to do to beat off the impure. I lost one country to the mud people and I ain't losing my new one!"

Even random hurrahs had died away.

"Listen, I'll take the whole filthy rap on myself and my pals, and two hundred years from now we'll be known as the George Washingtons of the new white America, the guys who took back the country, and maybe some people will think of us as those regrettable bad boys who went a little over the top but it can't be helped. I sure as bloody hell won't be known as that poet, that sissy, that *woman* who wept over the tulips when the mud people took our country away. Are you with me in this?"

The crowd was stunned silent, though a few decided they had to display a little enthusiasm. A faint cheer began in a couple of pockets and seeped out slowly.

Jack Liffey was interested in the sheer megalomaniac power of the man. He carried something even odder, too, but Jack Liffey hadn't worked it out. Once in a great while he seemed to talk aloud to himself from an inner voice.

"Bang!" he shouted into the microphone, and the crowd recoiled at the reverberations and the squawk of feedback it set off.

"Listen, my fainthearted friends, do your country a favor. I know this town is full of Ching-chong yellow invaders." He pointed all around the shallow canyon. "This is wall-to-wall slopes. Dinks, Slants, John Chinaman. My white folks, shame on you, you ain't done your duty to scare 'em away. You got to begin the fight at home."

Hardi Boaz tucked the microphone into his shirt pocket with another bit of squalling feedback and reached downward. The skinny man who'd introduced him dug into an olive canvas bag and handed the speaker—oh, no—an assault rifle!

Jack Liffey could see it was an over-and-under M16 with the fat tube of an M203 grenade launcher under the barrel. His first sergeant had kept one in his billet, and he'd seen plenty of them in the Tet Offensive. The sight of the weapon was as electrifying to him as to everyone else. He hoped it was just a prop.

"Listen, fainthearted friends, here's my gift to you! Fight back! Go on, Hardi." His voice was just audible with the microphone in his pocket. There was a flash of teeth, a rictus of a smile, and Hardi Boaz shouldered the assault rifle. A cold hand took Jack Liffey's spine. The big man tilted it up into a high arc. An amplified *bloop* sent a grenade arcing out into the Monterey Park suburb.

"*What are you doing?!*" somebody shouted.

"Bloody firepower, ma'an, I can't get enough!"

The first grenade detonated somewhere out of sight and he slammed the launcher tube forward as the thin man tossed him another grenade. As if in the grip of some bloodlust, he closed the breech and fired again, off to the far left this time. He pumped the M203 open, caught another grenade in midair and loaded it. This time he swung and fired to the right.

"*Get* some!" he shouted. "Here I am, Ching-a-lings! Get some!" The invisible explosions echoed across the easement and punched Jack Liffey in the chest. There was no indication of damage out there. Yet.

The man stopped firing, and Jack Liffey could hear that something had changed in the crowd, and maybe in the surrounding suburb, too—a world stunned into a new tentative condition.

Hardi Boaz plucked the microphone from his pocket. "Fear not, my tenderhearted friends—these were only flash-bangs today. The rest is up to you. Save our white country. Send your own yellow people the big message to go home."

Then the Afrikaner was gone, leaping off the platform and swallowed by the crowd. The atmosphere hovering over the keg party had gone private and expectant, and Jack Liffey could hear the crackle of the power lines clearly and then an *oooh* from the crowd. Sirens began to wail in the far distance.

"Time to book, bro," he heard.

People began to move purposefully uphill toward the street. Before long the pace of the dispersion picked up, everyone picturing the arrival of masses of police in a very bad mood. Sirens were all around the compass now, approaching, and Jack Liffey saw several people up at the patio helping roll the aluminum kegs inside the house. For an instant he saw the thin young man who'd handed the speaker the rifle. Who are you, sport? he thought, watching the young man. We must meet.

Jack Liffey worked his way uphill as fast as his age and the crowd would allow, heading toward his pickup and home. Everything was a bit unreal. He'd felt strangely aloof from the keg party from the beginning, amused at its oddball nature.

What if he'd grown up among angry Boer kids in South Africa, he wondered, mired in some outdated view of what was possible? Or among lost and inarticulate teens in America—kids who could barely express their rage at a changing world and a faraway elite who seemed to run it.

Life was too damn difficult, he thought. Crazy violence was probably the only protest left for those trapped in a shrinking pocket of history.

He watched the partiers hurrying toward their cars. For most of the afternoon he'd been patronizing these people, treating the keg party like a Little League version of the Nuremburg Rally. But the sudden whirl to violence had turned his own detachment against him. He felt a little sick. *Are you really so superior?*

His pickup was caught in the tangle of escaping cars. Sirens approached fast, and he felt a surge of sudden gas pain in the middle of his chest. *Stress?*

*

"You're the only game in town, Gloria," Maeve said in the kitchen.

Gloria wore an odd pained expression. "I bless the day that wanting Jack brought his wonderful child into my home. I mean that, hon."

Maeve didn't know how to respond.

"I'm a mess." Gloria's voice was a whisper.

"Aw, woman." Maeve came and knelt beside the chair to hug her legs. She knew depression could strike deep, though she had no idea what to do about it.

"Thanks for staying the evening, Maeve. I'm going to need help pretty soon, I think. I'm about to—I don't know. Break into bits."

Maeve pressed her forehead against Gloria's knee, feeling helpless.

"My rages are scaring me, hon. I wish I'd been in Iraq. I could call it all PTSD."

"Your whole life has been an Iraq."

"Do me a favor, hon."

"Of course."

"My weapon's in a cardboard box in the second drawer upstairs. Take the box and hide it somewhere in the house."

Maeve felt a chill of real alarm.

"Oh, Glor." But there was nothing to argue about; she knew she didn't have the strength and wisdom to give Gloria the comfort she needed.

The large angular pistol was in a leather clip-on holster, her badge-wallet beside it, plus another black clip-on with two spare magazines.

And a pouch with pockets for handcuffs and another with a spray tube of Mace. It was like Batwoman's boudoir.

Maeve flipped the cardboard top back over the box to cover the terrible sight.

Back downstairs, box well hidden: "You've got to hold on, Glor. You're strong—a real role model for me. And for Dad. I know he loves you to death."

Gloria covered her eyes and began to weep as if she'd just lost a child.

*

It took very little time for Jack Liffey to find out where Hardi Boaz was staying. Ask for a big, loud South African.

As far as he knew, the missing girl had had to cross the border somewhere near where he patrolled. Who knew?

The Washington Plaza Hotel wasn't much, but it seemed to be the only hotel of substance in Monterey Park. The lobby was definitely for Chinese guests, with bilingual signs and black lacquered furniture as tokens.

He stood a moment near a chest-high vase and tried to consider Boaz's exotic notion of expelling all Chinese and Mexicans from America, so common to the Tea Party. Quite apart from the fact that Mexicans had preceded Anglos into the Southwest by two centuries, it was like trying to get the chocolate syrup out of a milkshake. Intermarriage, centuries of common citizenship, and a twisted skein of cultures and families had connected everyone. It was ridiculous.

"Mr. Boaz, please, and tell him that his fainthearted friend is here," Jack Liffey told the blank-looking Chinese woman at the desk. "Use that expression."

He waited in the lobby. Before long he had to wince at a shrill whistle, like a referee calling time, as the huge man emerged from an open elevator across the lobby, two fingers in his lips, glaring off somewhere to Jack Liffey's left. His fists went to his hips, the tactical commander watching over the battlefield he controlled. The man had changed into another set of freshly creased bush khakis, slightly darker. An obligatory costume.

He came straight toward Jack Liffey, still without meeting his eyes, and Jack Liffey began to wonder about something like high-functioning Asperger's. It would explain a lot.

"I'm telling you, ma'an, it's a good thing I found some like-minded friends here in L.A. I got plenty of enemies, and it's still a strange country. I myself couldn't recognize a bloody liberal zebra in a herd of patriotic horses. Hardi, you talk such rot."

The man hadn't acknowledged Jack Liffey directly in any way, but there was no one else he could be talking to. Now and again a corner of his mouth flicked, like a grazing animal involuntarily reacting to a fly.

"Fainthearted friend." He laughed louder than necessary. "You know what the *kaffirs* used to call me? They called me *Meneer Koppelkop*. It means Mr. Fuckhead. I called them Communists. Are you a Communist, too? Oh, don't be so rude to this man, Hardi."

The big man laughed confidently and stared at the far wall of the lobby, his laser glance whizzing right past Jack Liffey's face.

"I think the Communists left the building a couple decades ago. But I'd like to talk to you, sir."

"I leave in two hours, friend, hustled out of town by the cowardly lions of the Tea Party Crybabies, even though we got the same big pals with the same big moneybags. But come up to my suite and help me finish my gift whisky, Mr. Faint Heart. You seem straight up. I always like that. The guy may be a danger, Hardi. Nah, no way."

The large man waddled a bit as he walked toward the elevators, not looking back.

"The press says we are the neutron bomb of the Campo area. We are responsible for killing wetbacks from El Centro to San Diego, and also pet kittens and sick cows and the odd drunk farmhand. Yesterday we ate a Volvo, tomorrow we eat the Palomar Telescope. But as long as we stop mud people and terrorists, I say, let's eat." He stopped talking for a moment and flexed his left arm, hard with muscle. "Come see the wetback I captured in this stinky Chink hotel."

That gave Jack Liffey a real chill—the image of a Mexican bellboy in chains in the room—but he followed the man into the elevator. Hardi punched the top floor button repeatedly with evident satisfaction.

"What's your name, fainthearted friend?" He stared hard at the pinging digital floor indicator.

"Jack Liffey."

"And what do you do, as Americans say?"

"I hunt for missing children, sir. I hope your group doesn't eat children, too."

The man laughed heartily, but his laugh was devoid of any suggestion of humor. Jack Liffey had expected menace, but saw only a kind of theatrical evocation of various emotions, like a robot who'd learned how to be human from a book.

"Unless the children are Communists. Then I got to fuck them up bad."

"That's not very funny," Jack Liffey said.

Boaz's eyes browsed the elevator with his hard, indirect stare as if he couldn't quite find Jack Liffey. "I'm funny if I say I am, Mr. Jack Liffey." He flicked the corner of his mouth and then smiled grimly. "I am the guy who makes it safe for all the sissies in San Diego and L.A. to complain about me. I'm only doing what I'm good at. And fat cats pay me damn well to do it."

Fat cats, Jack Liffey thought. He didn't even want to know. What good would it do? Somebody he couldn't touch. Who had paid James Earl Ray to kill King? There was far too much of that in America.

The elevator doors came open on seven, and Jack Liffey followed the man to a large suite. Just inside the door, a military-style canvas B-4 bag was already packed and waiting.

The sheer, physical beef of the man in the delicate, Chinesey suite was hard to ignore. He went to a swing-open bar and poured himself a scotch from some expensive-looking single-malt bottle. Jack Liffey declined.

"Behold, I show you my captured wetback now, Jack Liffey." He strode to the mantel of the false fireplace and touched the top of an upended drinking glass with surprising gentleness. "A tiny wetback."

He slid a laminated information card under the glass before lifting it. Jack Liffey approached and saw a large cockroach, scrabbling this way and that as its horizons went berserk.

Thank heavens, Jack Liffey thought.

"All of these cockroaches are Communists. You need an experienced soldier like me to track them down. This is the bonus this Chink hotel has without even knowing it. I teach any invader the meaning of fear. You the man, Hardi."

"Flush the bug, please. I need to talk to you."

"*Ja*, you in the deep shit, my little roachie," he crooned. He seemed to be able to make eye contact with the insect. "*Kom, liefling. Een twie drie*. Come out, little comrade." He dumped the bug onto the mantel. "Your pals have betrayed you, *liefling*, and it is time to learn fear. Don't you love this part, Hardi?"

Boaz was backlit by the tall west window and it was hard to make out the expression on his face. His oddity no longer seemed quite so harmless.

"Mr. Boaz, I came here because you struck me as a man who's never afraid to tell the truth." Flattery almost always worked with those who thought they couldn't be flattered.

"So you say." Boaz grasped a roach leg in two fat fingers and held the insect up, wriggling. "Look at this little *kak*. Life is short, Commie."

The big man took a Bic lighter from his shorts and flicked it beneath the insect.

"Aw, man, crush it. Stop this."

"You are indeed a faint-heart."

Boaz brought the flame up to the roach and a crackle sounded clearly in the silence. Jack Liffey looked away reflexively.

"Oh, ah, *liefling*. The determined commie-killer now blows out the flame and lets you live one minute more. In pain, *ja*."

"Man, stop it. Just kill it."

"You're as bad as Emperor Nero, Mr. Liffey. Thumbs down in the arena. Who are we to question another precious minute of existence on earth, even if it means a little pain?"

"A missing girl's life may be at stake," Jack Liffey said. "I need to talk to you before your ride to the airport comes. I have a strong feeling you wouldn't hurt a defenseless young girl."

There was a sudden sizzling noise and he looked up to see Hardi Boaz toss the flaming insect into the fireplace. Jesus Christ.

"*Agh*, sis, the big loud Boer has done the deed, Mr. Liffey. I hope you can pardon it, but I consent to your disapproval, too, if necessary. I am as big as America, I am a beacon of white dominion, and naturalized American bison." He laughed his strange stagy laugh.

"A Chinese girl, crossing the border maybe ten days ago," Jack Liffey said. "I'm sure you'd never hurt a child." He wasn't sure in the least, but he needed to flatter whatever the man possessed of human decency.

"I get the idea, faint-heart. Life is tough all over. Where I live outside a tiny town called Campo, if I wanted to put in a nice bed-and-breakfast, I could offer hunting rights, and your Southern senators would fly in on government-paid junkets to sit on the patio, and together we could potshot any bloody thing that moves in the valley. Javelina, deer—and, of course, wetbacks. The big bad border is only a half mile from my house. You tell him, Hardi, you the man."

The tic at the corner of his lip had grown more pronounced and compulsive.

"Listen to me, ma'an. I'm put on the earth to enjoy myself and help a few others do the same. In a few years we're all buried in the dirt, you know it, so why not enjoy while we can? I want you to know that I personally have no desire to be any more saintly than your average San Diego congressman who beats his Mexican servants and *schtups* their daughters when his smelly wife is at the supermarket. It's the real world, eh?"

"Have you seen a Chinese girl?"

"You want to know if I seen some loose-goose Chinee?"

"That's about it."

"I like you for some reason, *Meneer* Jack Liffey. You got brass balls to front me. I could strangle you right now. There is pathology to every kind of politics, eh?"

A chill went up Jack Liffey's spine.

"But, no, I grant you your tomorrow. Maybe I see this Chinese girl, maybe not. You want to pry into my business, you can jump off a tree into snakes. This Liffey guy is a hell of a guy, Hardi."

The big man turned his head slowly and his glance smoked Jack Liffey's cheek with a fierce blow-by. All the bravado seemed to melt away.

"There's an empty place growing where my dreams was, Jack Liffey. Come out to my place near Campo someday and we'll talk and shoot some coyotes. Hardi, tell this guy directly that you like him fine."

"That's great," Jack Liffey said. "I get it—no comment." The invitation was about as tempting as a vacation in North Korea.

Jack Liffey went down the elevator and waited again in a corner of the lobby. In a half hour, he saw an angry-looking man in a business suit enter the hotel and the elevator dinged him all the way up to Boaz's floor.

He still didn't know what to make of Hardi Boaz. Could the man or one of his vigilantes have run into Sabine? He wondered if the girl's map led anywhere near Campo.

NINE
Fate Always Has Other Plans

Gloria awoke against her will with Jack Liffey shaking her shoulder gently.

"Let's not rush the day."

"Breakfast is served."

She rolled onto her back, pulled the covers up to her chin, and shook her head at the coffee and toast he'd brought on the sick-in-bed tray. Instantly she changed her mind and plucked the coffee mug off the tray.

"Thanks. Did I tell you Maeve and I had a talk yesterday?"

He picked up a slice of toast rather than let it go to waste. Eat it to save it, his mother had always said—a Depression baby to the core—but Gloria scoffed at that. *Throw it away to save it, for Chrissake. I eat what I want.*

"I didn't know Maeve came."

"We had another truth time, but your clever daughter got more out of me than she revealed about herself."

He'd have to talk to Maeve and find out what she'd learned.

"Maeve says she's still caught between cocks and cunts. And I told her she better make up her mind." She sighed. "I think her painting craze is wrecking her college work."

"I was afraid of that."

"You can't save everything on earth, Jackie."

"My daughter is first in line." He was resting his hand on Gloria's knee on top of the covers, as innocent a touch as he could manage.

She gently moved his hand away. "Sorry. I can't handle being touched yet."

"Anything else you want for breakfast?"

"A Walt fucking Disney true-life, all-happy world."

He couldn't help thinking of the Mike Fink keelboat at Disneyland. In 1997 it had capsized and dumped fifty terrified tourists into brackish water, leading to the whole ride being torn out. Disney true-life worlds had their problems, too.

*

Captain Walt Roski rang the doorbell with dread. He carried a briefcase containing an eight-by-ten photograph of the charred remains of a rosary, plus a similar photo off Google of what the amber rosary probably looked like before the firestorm. This was the part of the job everybody loathed.

A Chinese woman opened the door a few inches and peered at him.

"Mrs. Roh? I'm the man who called. Walter Roski, from the county fire department. Can I speak to you or your husband for a few moments?"

There were six girls from the San Gabriel Valley who'd gone missing at about the right time, and Sabine Roh was the fourth on his list. Reported missing three days after the Sheepshead Fire broke out.

The woman let him into the house with a worried expression. "You come about Sabine?"

"I need to ask you some questions," he said carefully. No show-and-tell until you pump them dry. It was the rule of thumb, hard as it sometimes was.

She led him apprehensively to a sofa in the living room. A middle-aged man sat across the room, his side turned stubbornly to the guest. He seemed angry.

"Mr. Roh can't talk now. Working in head. He not being impolite. Can I get you some tea?"

"No, please. Could you confirm for me the day you came to feel your daughter was missing?"

"Feel?"

"Please. Tell me how sure you were when you reported it. She never stayed over at other homes without telling you?"

The woman took a deep breath and confirmed the date—Sheepshead plus three—and no, Sabine was a very considerate daughter. She never stayed late, even an hour, without calling home. He ran down his notebook, asking all his prepared questions. There were no obvious hits until he asked one of the standards that almost never got a response—if anybody had contacted them on their daughter's behalf.

"My cousin in Orange County very rich woman, sir. She worry and she send a man to help look for Sabine." The woman rose and retrieved a business card from a sideboard.

Jack Liffey
I Find Missing Children

And then a fax and a regular telephone number. Lord, who used faxes? So twentieth-century. No e-mail address. Roski guessed he was a useless old duffer, one of those window-peepers who had trained up on divorce work. He probably still took photos with a film camera.

He copied down the information and ran through the rest of his questions with no more alerts. The man across the room hadn't stirred but was obviously listening to the conversation.

"I want to show you two photographs, Mrs. Roh. They don't show a person or anything like that. But I want to know if either of these photos means anything to you."

He laid out the before-and-after photos, and the tense woman immediately threw back her head like a wounded animal and let out a wail of pain.

I'll take that as a yes, Roski thought sadly.

She crumpled into her chair, hiding her face with her hands, and the inert husband finally levered himself erect with a cane. He hobbled toward the photos. Roski slid them around on the coffee table for him.

Mr. Roh froze in place, glaring at the photographs, and then he seemed to wilt. "This country is very punishing, sir," he said bitterly, in lovely American English, with a bit of a French accent. "In Vietnam, my wife and I were Roman Catholics. We were also ethnic Chinese. By those facts, we were enemies of the communist state twice over. We managed to leave in 1984, and our daughter was conceived in a refugee camp in Malaysia. Sabine idolized the women who taught her here, the Sisters of Charity of the Incarnate Word.

"Our daughter was determined to become a nun, with a political mind. I have no idea what romantic novel she got that idea from. Perhaps Graham Greene or Robert Stone. She never wavered from her mission." The man paused for reflection. "I think Sabine didn't understand that fate always has other plans."

*

Mint tea was a new departure, Jack Liffey thought. With Tien Joubert, it was usually either strong French coffee or Chinese green tea. Maybe she had a Moroccan boyfriend. They sat out on the dock in Huntington Harbour beside her ostentatious yacht. It looked like an ordinary yacht on steroids.

"Report Number Two, please. This gotta be about Sabine."

"The boss requires. The hireling complies."

"No snark, please."

His eyes were drawn to the next dock west, where somebody was mooring a long slim cigarette boat, one of those oceangoing rockets with several muscle-car engines that could churn out a thousand horsepower or more. He knew Southern California marine yards built several hundred of them every year and about twenty of them were used for legitimate offshore racing. The rest were busy running drugs up the coast at a hundred miles an hour on moonless nights.

"So, where she at?" Tien asked.

She was wearing a loose robe that, with every breeze, rustled open a little near the upper danger zone, and he was doing his best not to torment himself with his memories. He already knew exactly and intimately what was being offered, and it was a hell of a ride. It wasn't like he was getting his ashes hauled at home, as his pal Art Castro would have said.

"Patience was never your long suit, Tien. I talked to the girl's parents, her priest, her friends and political allies. Did you know she was in a radical group?"

Tien went absolutely still. "More, please."

"Maybe not as we knew radical groups. They were a mix of Chinese and Latino kids. Their focus was getting high school kids to stand up to racism. Their main enemy in town was a bunch of biker assholes who called themselves the Commandos. Both groups are pretty much extinct, but there's still bad blood."

"You say this word 'Latinos,' Jackie. You mean Mexicans?"

"There're a lot of countries to the south, Tien, and a hell of a lot of Spanish-speakers were born right here. Can you tell the difference between Taiwanese and Hong Kongese and mainlanders?"

"In one-half second. And *tong yan*, too. That mean overseas Han, like me. Singapore or Vietnam or Indonesia. Absolute, we all hear it."

Somehow the robe had crept up in her southern danger zone, too. "I believe you. Let's say Mexican Americans. But there's another problem I found out about." He told her about the fact that the girl might have tried to bring drugs across the border to earn some money for her family.

For some reason it didn't seem to worry her. "You go find out about all that. You real good at that. What car you drive now, Jackie?"

`It came flying in from left field, the way she liked, but the implication he knew well. Everything was A-list brand names. A car without a rich pedigree was just rust in waiting. "Why, for heaven's sake?"

"I forget how much I really like you, Jackie. I can take care of you good, get you nice Porsche Targa, Tullio shoe, Armani Black Label suit. I learn a fancy new trick in bed, too."

"Jesus, I don't think I'd live through that." He didn't want to tell her he drove a third-hand Toyota pickup that was twenty years old and full of dents.

"Peekie-boo," she said with a coy smile, opening her gown to show him one small upright breast, little more aged than ten years earlier, with its tiny brown nipple. He remembered the feel of it under his fingers.

He put up a hand to block the sight. "I'm living with someone I love, Tien."

"Pish." She shrugged but closed the gown. "I got good family, all got education, you know it. I dating big handsome triathlon man, thirty years old, all muscles. I like his American smell, too, like you, though Mummy always say it's like spoil butter. But he no good really. I know he want money. You always hate money. I never understand, but it make me feel safe. Make me trust you."

"I've seen too many people hurt by money. Not the lack of it, though that happens, too—but mostly from having a whole lot and wanting more. What I liked about you was that you were never crazy about grabbing money for its own sake. You liked the business of making deals, bargaining and doing favors, and money just seemed to flow to you."

"Deal is best thing, sure. All real business is complicated deal. I give you nice car, you give me name of important man to know. You give commission on one thousand bale of cotton and I give American green card. We're all cat in clover."

"Are you really happy in America, Tien?"

That knocked her back a little, as he'd hoped. It took her some thought. "I love everything America, Jackie. If I start over again, I go to a very good doctor right away and get round eyes, big falling tits, the whole American cookie. To me small means defeat and weakness, like 1975. I want to be big and powerful like you."

"Don't you know how powerful your money makes you? I've checked. You could buy one of the medium-sized states. You could eat anyone you want for lunch." An unfortunate phrase, he realized.

"I want to eat your big membership, Jackie. That the begin of my new trick. You gonna love it."

*

Zook was still fuming. He'd been bitch-slapped by Seth—the fucking lawyer—and told he'd made the grown-ups change plans for their own dinner. The kiddies should stay home and eat their peas. And, by the way, think about clearing out of the storefront clubhouse.

"What possessed you to hand that guy a grenade launcher?"

"He asked." Now that Zook thought about it, it didn't make a lot of sense, but it had seemed like a great idea at the time. Have a lark, impress some prospective members, and scare the Chinks in the bargain. Harmless flash-bangs. Glorified firecrackers. Where was the hurt?

But this pole-up-the-ass cocksucker had just warned him that the police were looking for him. Somebody had ratted him out, probably Seth himself.

"Get yourself lost for a while, loser."

Zook couldn't carry what he needed on his Harley, so he backed the half-restored 1953 Studebaker Commander out of the garage where his dad had left it decades ago. Zook had lost interest in further work on the car, it was so damned uncomfortable lying underneath and getting grease in his face. The 230-cubic-inch V-8 still ran okay—a pathetic hundred and twenty horsepower—but it *was* from sixty years ago. The brakes were for shit, but he could always stop with the handbrake or the transmission.

Get yourself lost for a while, loser.

The acid words still made bile rise. They always thought they were better than working people. Tea Party Seth was no better than those white-wine liberals in their Rockports.

He packed a week's worth of clothing, some beer, some finger food, and a handful of books into the Studebaker and headed north for the foothills. Way back in the day, his father had acquired an old cabin cheap from a college fraternity that had been caught hazing pledges and given the choice of leaving campus or giving up its party cabin. In his teens, he and his dad stayed at the place from time to time, but mostly it had rotted away until, in their heyday, the Commandos fixed it up and brought it back as a party house.

Zook stopped at the end of the asphalt and unlocked the yellow gate to the Serrano Fire Road. *Only three cars at a time*, the fire marshal had warned him, or they'd have their gatekey confiscated. Still, at party time you could get an awful lot of people into, and onto, three cars—clinging to the hood and roof, howling and yelling the last mile up the dirt road to the cabin.

He noticed fingers of seared chaparral above the firebreak and worried that the cabin might have burned out. Nobody'd been up

here since summer. It would break his heart. Not just the parties—
he'd first read Nietzsche here. It was his sacred place to mull life
over deep.

Coming around the last bend, he was relieved to see that the cabin
was whole, though immediately he went on alert. A steady issue of
smoke rolled off the stovepipe chimney. Two chopped Harleys and
a bad-boy tricycle squeezed into the parking pad next to the stream.
He got his back up. This was *his*, dammit.

Zook pulled just off the fire trail. He could tell that the metal
music coming from the house covered any noise he could make, so
he walked straight up to a window where the curtains were open.
One of his kerosene lamps was flickering on the table and somebody
had dragged an old party mattress into the main room.

A naked young girl, maybe thirteen, was kneeling on the
mattress giving a reluctant blowjob to a man wearing nothing but
a jean jacket, both his hands pressed to the back of her head. Tears
were rivering down her cheeks. A fat man in denim with droopy
eyes and a ponytail watched and encouraged. The fourth figure
in the room, a blowsy-looking woman wearing nothing but an
unzipped racedriver jacket, sat against the wall and seemed to be
masturbating.

What a zoo, Zook thought. He knew the Thinking Man had to
protect children whenever he could, but these animals could be the
Gypsy Jokers, meth heads who'd kill you rather than walk around
you. He manned up gradually and retrieved his Walther PPK from
the glove compartment.

Okay, Nietzsche, he thought. We'll see who I am. Pussy or man
of action. He pulled the plank front door open, and the woman in
the corner looked up and screeched. Zook lifted his Redwing boot
and stepped on the buttons on the boom box. The silence was a
relief.

"Who the fuck are you?" Ponytail said. The voice was both wired
and slurred.

"If I wasn't so classy, I'd shoot you all," Zook said. He let them
see his pistol but didn't aim it. "I own this cabin."

"Ah, shit. It's the Zook." That was the bare-assed man. He reached
down and hauled up a pair of used-up jeans. "So where you been?"

"Attending to patriotic business." He didn't recognize the man, but might have met him on a ride.

"Let's get a look at that piece you got."

"Never you mind. It works."

The little girl wrapped her arms tight around where her breasts were just developing. "I live in Santa Monica, on 1019 Ashland," she gasped.

"Don't be saying that!" the big woman snapped.

"Picked her up hitching?" Zook asked.

"Came to us and said she was real hot to trot," the woman said. "But she ain't."

"Would you folks take the party down the hill? I've got a group coming in." He wanted to find some way to help the girl, but there were limits to what even a stand-up guy could do. It was all a matter of odds. It would be a weird universe indeed if these folks weren't armed, too.

"Dig it," the man on the mattress said. "That PPK is just a little popper, Zook. If you want some heavy stuff, come see me. Tony Two in BP."

Baldwin Park, an even rattier working-class outlier ten miles to the east. "How do you friends know my name?" Zook asked.

"Every swingin' dick in the valley knows the Commandos."

That was gratifying. The partiers gathered their clothes and belongings.

"Why don't you leave the girl here, sort of like rent," Zook said without any emphasis. "I could see having some fun myself." The girl tugged on a t-shirt and shorts.

"We'll take good care of her," the big woman said.

That felt to be as far as the Thinking Man could push things. They pushed the girl out the door ahead of them.

"Watch your ass, man. I hear every cop in the valley are after you for that kegger." Zook stood beside the doorway, the pistol limp in his hand.

Ponytail yanked the girl onto the bench seat of the trike. "Sit the fuck down or I'll give you a flying lesson off yonder cliff."

Zook bit his lip, the pistol's unused force shaming him a little. Welcome to the big bad world, girl, he thought.

Before starting up, the trike man said, "Take it all quick, Zook. Ain't no second chances."

Zook's inertia burned inside him. He needed to do some deep thinking.

*

The mother's despairing wail had been unendurable, and Roski heard it even as he walked away from the Rohs' house. He'd had to tell them about the body that had been seen in the fire zone, and then ask them to agree to DNA cheek swabs as soon as he could send out a lab crew.

Bump up, Rosk. Firefighters said that to one another—bump up—after the death of a pal. Toughen up and try to move on. Nobody ever said it to a civilian.

He checked his notes and was about to dismiss contacting this ludicrous "private detective" when he reminded himself that you never knew where the break might come from.

The phone number gave him a throaty woman's voice.

"I'm trying to reach Jack Liffey," he said.

"What's he done now?"

"Can I just leave him a message? This is Captain Walter Roski, from the L.A. County Fire Department, Arson."

"Captain," she broke in before he could go on. "This is L.A.P.D. Sergeant Gloria Ramirez, Harbor Division. I live with Jack. I hope he hasn't torched a nuns' home."

Her voice was so self-possessed that Roski laughed. "No, Sergeant. That's pretty well excluded. But I need to talk to him."

"You know, I do, too. He can be very entertaining."

This was all inducing him to reassess the man he'd assumed was a plain screw-up. "Does that mean he's away?"

"For the day. Can I tell him what this is about?"

"I usually don't, but since you're L.E...." How did he know she was actually law enforcement? Her confident voice? "It's about the Sheepshead Fire, Sergeant, but I can't say any more right now." He gave her his cell number and got off before he could make a bigger ass of himself. Sometimes he could be a sucker for the ambience of things, and the woman sounded like somebody tough as nails whom he'd like a lot. He'd been way too long without a girlfriend. Or even a friend.

He looked over his list of missing girls and wondered if he should just double underline Sabine Roh and forget the others. All he really had was a mother's abrupt tears at the sight of an amber rosary. He'd talk to this priest who'd known the girl.

*

Jack Liffey wiped his sweaty forehead on the silken sheet, like rumpled cloth of woven silver. His face was next to one of Tien's tiny, perfectly formed bare feet.

"You in bad way, I can tell. How long you been needing big fancy boom-boom like this?"

He smiled to himself. Yeah, she'd learned some new tricks, all right. "I never need a five-dollah short time, Tien."

"You say. But life all about short times. Love the one you with."

Who'd sung that, he wondered. Those hopeful, horrible olden days. "Do you know about guilt, Tien?"

"No say that, Jack. You here right now with me. You know my pussy. My mouth know you." Yes, he thought, and then there was the tongue stud she'd had installed, not a common Asian practice as far as he knew.

"I feel what I feel."

"Don't you go on-off like radio," she said.

And what now for his intentions? Was this just a brief payback for Gloria's affair? Or should he disrupt everything in his life and move himself into the egregious yacht out there? What a thought. He hated boats, but he did get a kick out of this formidable woman, several kicks. Her utter unselfconsciousness. Her focus on the immediate moment. Infinitely forgiving, wanting to please; her mind bustling, full of plans and backups and backups for backups. Never at rest. The perfect personality in a go-for-broke, dog-eat-dog country.

He readjusted to lie face to face. "I always worry about tomorrow, Tien. It's who I am."

She shrugged solemnly. "Dig it. Tomorrow we both dead."

*

Somebody knocked lightly and didn't wait for a reply before opening. Between the fingers of one fist, Bunny was strangling two Corona bottles. "G'day, Maeve. *Mea culpa* or something. I think I owe you big time."

"Why?" As if nothing had happened. Maeve stood at a canvas, dabbing at the back view of a Francis Bacon-esque leg, working from a digital photo of a corpulent model from her life class. Bubbly thigh and cellulite butt—Maeve was doing her best not to find it repulsive. All life was sacred, all bodies.

"You been good about it, but it was my bad. That was really messed up. I'll make it up. I'll be happy to pose for you right now, if you promise no funny stuff."

Maeve's heart started to pitter-patter. Just glancing at Bunny's luxuriant body, even clothed, turned her on immensely. "Sure, no funny stuff. I'll do my best to separate desire from art, though I can't tell a lie—your body is a real glory of nature."

Bunny decapped the beers with the church key that hung on a string from the fridge handle. Maeve thought of showing off Gloria's ostentatious pop-off chop some time, but decided she'd better practice in private.

"Imagination is fine," Bunny said. "But be sure to knock on the door before you try to open it."

Jeez, was that a tentative invitation?

"For sure." Maeve brought out a fresh canvas already stretched and primed. Amazing, she thought. Two months ago she didn't even know what stretching a canvas was, or gesso, didn't know the difference between oils and acrylics. "You can undress behind the Japanese screen and come out with a towel."

"No, I'm fine."

Bunny seemed to toy with a private smile as she tugged off her bulky sweater with that lovely cross-arm maneuver, and Maeve wondered if undressing in her view was a way of Bunny teasing herself with forbidden thoughts.

"Please get comfortable and think about something neutral. I'd like to have you unconscious of your body. My teacher says too many women have internalized a male eye."

The faint grin returned. "Then I'll think of myself as a sight for a female eye."

Maeve just about fainted as the underwire bra came off.

"The cool air feels good."

"Knock knock," Maeve said weakly.

*

"Can I have a Bentley, hon? That horrid narrow entrance scraped the Jag's fender," Adrianna complained. "It just *barged* at me."

"How about I get you a driver," Gustav Reik said. He was home, briefly, in his Fifth Avenue penthouse overlooking Central Park in the Seventies. He owned the top two floors of the Hewitt Building, and kept the lower one as office, probably worth more than his entire hometown of Verdigris, Oklahoma.

Adrianna was his arm candy, of course, bleach and scalpel and silicone, with the intelligence of an armadillo, but she had an art history degree from one of those SUNYs out in the sticks and could almost hold up her end at a New York cocktail party. He'd bought their way onto the boards of a dozen cultural foundations.

"Aww, Gusty."

A lot of his Southern friends shook their heads in dismay that he'd chosen to live in Jew York, but you didn't have to be a Jew to love good ballet and opera and art. And good food, which was not to be had below latitude forty. Roughly Washington, D.C.

He waved his hand toward Adrianna's portion of the penthouse. "Addy, please turn left. I need to boil a hog for a few minutes." It was his way of telling her he had confidential business on the telephone.

She nodded obediently and hurried away.

He speed-dialed his administrative assistant, Bernadette Crouch. The woman was indispensable to him, as sharp as anyone he'd ever met, and her politics were bang-on libertarian as far as he knew. If only she weren't so buck ugly, he'd bend her over her desk more often. Why couldn't we swap brains and bodies, he wondered.

"Berny, has anybody backed out of the retreat?" He never wasted time on howdies. Manners were for also-rans.

"Hi there, Gustav. Yes, my cancer biopsy was negative. Thank you very much for asking. Only a few of our stalwart capitalist friends have declined—Mr. X from the aerospace company, Mr. Y from brokerage, and Mr. Z from hedge funds." They both knew about phone hacking, of course, including the government's big Echelon, Prism, and Omnivore spy projects. Not to mention the fact that *Mother Jones* magazine had somehow obtained an audio tape of their last retreat and promulgated it word for word to make a number of tipsy Republican governors sound like Herman Goering.

"The lawyer from Southern California?"

"Not a peep from him. Why does that small beer lawyer worry you, Gus? You sent him the biggest pain in the ass in our planetary belt as a guest speaker."

"I love all my children, each in his own way, Bern," he said, but smiled privately. He knew, like Andor, he had an uncontrollable practical joker gene. "Even you. This year is going to be important. We need a billion more to fight the socialist president."

"Good for us. I'm always invested in knowing that somebody who deserves it is going to end up crying."

"Never us, for sure, kiddo. See you in two weeks."

"But you should keep in mind that private wounds often reveal what is damaging on a much larger scale."

He frowned as he hung up. Bernadette was always tweaking him, and he had no idea what the hell she was getting at. And her cancer scare, for Chrissake. Had she actually told him about that? He leched for her on sudden urges, but he couldn't be expected to care about such a homely woman.

*

All roads met in Monterey Park these days. Jack Liffey was back on Garvey Avenue at a little sidewalk table in front of the wonderfully named Bon Mar Ché, and right across the street was The Sweet Blanket, whatever that was, tucked beside what must once have been a Dunkin' Donuts but was now Wei's Boba Teas.

Jack Liffey was still addled by his romp with Tien, but he did his best to calm down as he waited. He'd called home guiltily from her place, with some excuse that sounded lame even to him, and Gloria had completely ignored his fibbing and told him that a firefighter of some rank was urgently looking for him, and given him the number. It had to be about Sabine, of course. Too much at once. But that was the nature of life. The firefighter had picked the Bon Mar Ché.

A beige Ford Crown Vic pulled up in front, driven by a hefty middle-aged man with a tidy moustache. Nobody on earth drove those lumbering cars but cops and local officials with access to motor pools.

He'd liked most of the firefighters he'd ever met---truly decent people intent on doing good in the world—and he wondered if he'd like this one, too.

"Walt Roski?" He stood and held out his hand to the harried-looking man.

"Jack?"

"Yeah."

They shook hands in a perfunctory way. Roski seemed pre-occupied, but he did look Jack Liffey over in a snoopy way. "Let me be direct," Roski said.

"Oh, please. I live for it."

The man nearly smiled. "When I heard you were a private detective, I assumed you were a flake. Just another failed insurance adjuster. Your wife disabused me."

Jack Liffey was about to say they weren't married, but why? "Be even more direct. What's your business?"

The waiter appeared and they both ordered iced tea. Roski brusquely told the waiter not to show his face again after bringing the drinks. Jack Liffey had never heard that before, but he liked it a lot. Over-officious waitstaff were an American affliction.

Several noisy motorcycles took off on a green and upshifted together, loud as a bandsaw. As they passed Roski opened a briefcase.

"This is as direct as I can make it." He laid out two eight-by-tens, the before and after of an amber-beaded rosary that had clearly been incinerated. "Mrs. Roh went into wails of distress seeing this. This one was found in the Sheepshead fire zone with the remains of a firefighter. He was near the burned remains of a girl. I'd like to know what you know about Sabine Roh, so I don't have to pad around town tromping all over your moccasin prints."

TEN
The Eighteenth Brumaire

"Maeve, I want to thank you for introducing me to a whole new world…whatever you call it." Bunny was glowing.

Is that what I did? Maeve thought. I thought we were making love.

"That was my first time with a woman, you know."

"Frighten you?"

"A little, but it's like sinking into amazing comfort and protection. I've been so forlorn all my life. My big brother used to make me… we won't go into that."

"It was also lust for me." Maeve swallowed hard. "And I was loving you."

"Wow, Maeve. Let me adjust some."

"Of course."

*

Back home, Jack Liffey tiptoed upstairs to look in on Gloria, who seemed to be dead asleep. She was snoring like a trooper, so he descended to the kitchen and set out what he'd need to thaw to make lunch, wondering if that would do anything for the guilt he felt. Then he called his sociologist friend Mike Lewis for some practical insights about dealing with the lunatic fringes of the Tea Party, and about cocaine from Hermosillo, which was where the girl's out-of-scale map seemed to start.

Unfortunately Mike started out with a lecture about Karl Marx's book *The Eighteenth Brumaire* and how the rich had been hijacking populist movements for centuries.

"Thanks for the really big picture, Mike. Anything practical?"

"These guys are probably only dangerous on a local level. Of course, you're the local level."

"And drugs in Hermosillo?"

"That's the Beltran Leyva cartel, a small and declining one. Sinaloa's moving in on them. Poor Mexico. You been asking around a lot about this?"

"I'm on a job."

"Jack, do me a favor."

"Sure."

"However silly it seems to you, go look out your front window this minute."

With a chill, Jack Liffey carried the cordless with him and pulled a lacy front curtain aside so he could look out at Greenville Street. A weary ice cream vendor with a pushcart. Two kids under the hood of a Chevy.

"Nothing special, Mike."

"Good. Keep looking."

*

It had taken Zook a while to collect the discarded beer cans, drag the mattress outside to air it, and put the rest of the cabin back where it belonged.

He'd rehung his wonderful old canvas sling chair from a roof beam near the stove and slid back into what he thought of as his Nietzsche perch. A little side table with a beer and a few joints, where he could sway and drift to his heart's content, reading the masters and real Thinking Men.

He started with W. Cleon Skousen's lectures, digging into the world's secret power structure. Zook skipped forward to his first dog-ear.

FDR's adviser Harry Hopkins treasonously delivered to the Soviets fifty suitcases of secret plans and half of America's supply of enriched uranium, and later the Russians built the first Sputnik with plans stolen from the United States...

Skip.

But the U.S. Constitution was never based on the Enlightenment. It was drawn entirely from the Bible.

Skip.

The secret world order began to use the Communists, a regimented breed of Pavlovian men whose minds could be triggered into immediate action by signals from their masters.

He was getting bored, but he lit his first joint.

Rich Nazi-capitalist families of the New World Order like the Rockefellers and the Rothschilds have used the Council on Foreign Relations and loony left-wing forces for years—from Ho Chi Minh to the American Civil Rights Movement—to serve their own power.

It didn't quite gel for him. Not pointed and clear, like Nietzsche. He set the book down and drifted off into his favorite daydream. He was riding across the plains on a powerful horse, carrying a Remington lever-action rifle. Once in a while he'd make a dip into a suburb to shoot a snotty liberal traitor holding a wine glass on his patio, then gallop away.

*

The department's Serology/DNA lab had moved into the new Forensic Science Center at Cal State – LA. Still the blood lab had kept to its peculiar tradition: six days a week, if you sent in a sample, it would go into the boundless hopper. But on Tuesdays, if you had something genuinely urgent and were willing to wait in line, you'd get your results that day. A few days at most.

The PCR version of the DNA test—you'd have it in three days.

The odds of a mismatch were still one in many million, perfectly good to steer an investigation, even if it couldn't convict O.J. Simpson.

Roski waited forty-five minutes among disgruntled L.A. detectives. Amazing how many of them were overweight. He dropped off his bone fragment, then phoned Jack Liffey again.

"Jack, you were a real sport to fill me in. Investigators get used to a whole wall of jive, as I'm sure you know."

"Yeah, I fell in love with you, too, Walt."

"I'd like to reciprocate with a little show-and-tell to keep you on my side. Do you want to see the spot where I'm pretty sure your girl died? I have to go there anyway."

"Jesus, this is a strange life. Of course I do."

"Meet me in an hour at the top end of Serrano Place against the mountains. It's between Sierra Madre and Altadena. A big yellow fire gate. You won't miss it."

"Since we're best pals now, I'll bring lunch."

*

Before he could get out the door with his lunch package, the phone rang and rang. Jack Liffey hesitated but went back and grabbed it before it could disturb Gloria.

"Jackie, this no good for me. My heart go pit-pat too much. I forget I like everything about you, even you old man wrinkles. All you boy dogs so lucky. You wham-bam and run away and don't care about us girl dogs."

It wasn't strictly true. His own heart was pitter-pattering a bit, too. A cop in Orange County had once told him if he was crazy enough to sleep with the dragon lady, he'd better count his body parts going out the door.

"You're a wonderful kidder, Tien."

"You come back right now I do something that make you die and go to heaven. Heaven got me, naturally."

He smiled. "I'd probably prefer the jokes in the other place. I'm on my way now to talk to a man who knows something about Sabine."

"Sabine can wait. She wait forever now, in fact. I still warm for you, warm outside and wet inside. Jackie, I never feel this before. I mean it. I going crazy. Don't hurt me."

How much to believe? Tien Joubert was as hard as a stainless-steel nail, and she could curdle your blood with a moment's shift of tone, but maybe she was having her own version of a late-life crisis. He'd never worked out her age, but she had to be pushing sixty, maybe from the other side.

"Tien." He glanced guiltily at the staircase to where Gloria slept, and then nudged an inner door shut. "Don't push so hard. Everybody's afraid of so much need."

"You no like my big boat? It can be your boat, we get crew and sail to Hawaii, Acapulco, make love all the day. Get airplane, too. Buy whole island someplace. I got hundreds millions now, no kidding. You talk to my accountant. I need a good man to go the rest of life. Time drip away, Jackie. I been working too hard to enjoy."

He tried to imagine himself as Tien's kept man, dressed like an ad in *GQ*, worth many millions—some of which he could give to Maeve, of course—and he tried to imagine what various people would think of him fixed up like that. He enjoyed the presumed outrage of his ex-wife, for instance, but Maeve was something else. And his feelings toward Gloria were a mess. He'd loved her intensely for years, leaning steeply into the hurricane of her resistance.

"Tien, I know you're sincere whenever you start saying millions. I'll come down there early next week, I promise. We'll talk about cabbages and kings. Right now I'm on the job. A girl's missing." He recalled the way Tien's finger would play with his penis totally without embarrassment, soft as a flower petal.

"Cabbages?" she said.

*

As he drove, he could smell the tamales cooking and guessed his pal Art Castro's theory of engine-block cuisine was probably working. He wound uphill toward the vertical wall of the San Gabriel Mountains. Not many cities were caught like this between the ocean and truly alpine peaks. With periodic earthquakes, of course.

In the turnaround where the pavement ended was a yellow gate made of six-inch welded iron pipe. A four-wheel-drive Jeep Wrangler with official "Exempt" plates was already there, and he parked beside it. Roski must have swapped at the motor pool.

"Thanks for coming," Roski told him. "I don't meet that many guys I want to talk to."

They shook hands again.

"This investigation is probably outside both our comfort zones," Jack Liffey said. He saw Roski sniffing the Mexican smells emanating from his pickup. "I wasn't kidding about lunch."

He lifted the hood to show two big tamales double-wrapped in foil nestled on the four-banger. Foil-wrapped corn tortillas were draped over the radiator. A plastic tub of salsa sat on the battery, and he had some ginger ale in a cooler and a couple of beers for Roski.

"I've heard of this," Roski said. "But I thought it was a redneck joke."

"My first try." Jack Liffey put it all in a wicker picnic basket Maeve had given him years ago. "We can eat on the road."

"Might as well stop, Jack. I know a place." At the gate Roski reached up into a steel canister welded to the gate post. To make it impossible to use a bolt cutter on the padlock within. He unlocked the gate and swung it open.

"I'm in a funny place in my life, Jack. A bad marriage, kids that took sides and still don't like their old man much, and a belief system that hit the skids some time ago. There's been little real friendship."

Why did he keep running into people like this? He must have a homing beacon for the wounded and forlorn.

"The only emotion I get now is a kind of loss."

A volcanic ash seemed to have deposited itself over the land, Jack Liffey thought—the remains of a burnt civilization, poisoning everything.

"Relax, man. I brought you beer."

Roski drove them through the gate onto a rutted dirt trail and got back out to lock up.

*

Bunny had gone off to drama class and Maeve made herself coffee in the main house. She'd stopped going to anything but art, and felt guilty about it, but that's just the way it was. Her sense of guilt was basically just an internalizing of her father's wrinkly scowl. Fiercely principled eyes, a face the size of a mountain, his finger always pointing out the rocky upward path—the more difficult one.

She wondered if she was really in love with Bunny, or just letting her lust drive her. She'd always let passions blast her into orbit. Or was this hesitation just a kind of gradual dialing down of her inner fire, the first step toward "growing up"?

*

Roski's Jeep bounced hard up the fire road. Jack Liffey recognized the thousand-yard stare on Roski's face, driving with white-knuckled intensity. That stare had been how they described guys on the way home from 'Nam after a horrible tour. Later it became known as PTSD. He wondered if there had been a single big bottom-out for Roski.

At a crest a rock banged their teeth hard, and then the road smoothed again. The firefighter was driving too hard for the road.

"Walt! There's no hurry and you're fucking hurrying. It's folly."

"Sorry. I've got this maniac urge in me."

"I can see it."

"I should do another tour to burn it off. I did three. Desert Storm for Bush One and Enduring Freedom twice. Toward the end, the danger became a drug. Like your war?"

Ahead the chaparral had all been burned out by the fire, charred and ugly.

"Forget war, man. Peace is hard enough."

The four-wheeler slowed down, and Jack Liffey eased his hold on the door grip.

Ahead there was a short bridge across a streambed, just past a ramshackle cabin. An old Studebaker was backed into a parking pad. Jack Liffey recognized the lanky young man out front, who sat on a bright green folding chair reading a book.

"Don't slow down. I know that kid."

"Me, too. I talked to him once about fire regulations. The place got a bit rowdy from time to time."

"How far to where you're taking me?"

"Maybe half a mile. Who was he to you?"

He took the rickety bridge slowly with a creek boiling downhill beneath it. Beyond, maimed stubs of brush poked up through the burned land. The smell was unforgettable—wood smoke, car ashtray, cat pee, and a physical scratchiness in the back of the throat. Time had run out here.

"Jack? The guy?"

"You heard about the fuss at the keg party?"

"Film at eleven. Were you at that mess?"

"The kid back there was one of the organizers. I bet the cops know exactly who he is."

"Who knows?" Roski said. "Police intelligence. While I see many hoofprints going in, I see few coming out."

Jack Liffey knew it as an old military putdown, and it was nice to see it was still around.

"If you want to talk to him, I'll show you how to get into the fire road."

Roski yanked the wheel rightward to take the Wrangler up a side trail that was unbearably steep, and then hammered over a rise and surged out onto a broad graveled wash and finally stopped. A central meander in the wash carried runoff water, silver as molten metal. A work area in the wash looked like an amateur gold mine, with slanted sieve boxes and yellow tape tied to traffic cones, cordoning off an area the size of half a tennis court. The wash was lined with the scorched trunks of sycamores and alders.

"How many years to grow back?" Jack Liffey said.

"Too damn many."

They got out and walked solemnly toward the police tape.

"We're figuring that's her head end," Roski said, pointing at the upslope portion of the taped area. "We don't think she died in the fire. Our guy reported seeing a bullet wound. Her forehead."

He told Jack Liffey about the handcuffs, though he knew he shouldn't. It was a hold-back evidence point.

"You're pretty sure it's her?"

"I'm not sure the sun will rise tomorrow, Jack, but I'll call you when the DNA is in."

"Thanks."

Somewhere down in the city behind them an emergency siren spooled up, and the sound seemed to scoot up the dry wash past them.

"I'd like a beer."

They returned to the truck and Jack Liffey broke out the engine-block barbecue. Roski unwrapped his foil and munched away dully as if he'd lost his sense of taste. He talked half-heartedly about the way a chaparral plant community recovered after a fire.

"The plants are phoenixes, bless them. Ceanothus, sage, and fireweed can't even germinate without a flash of heat. And when we go overboard suppressing fires, other plants elbow in. Chamise and toyon, the things that mark overgrazed land. Ecologists always say they hate the interlopers that don't belong. But, you know, I always figure even sewer rats have to live."

Jack Liffey barely heard. His feelings were in an uproar, wondering what he was going to say to Gloria.

"I hate firebugs with a passion," Roski said abruptly, with real emotion for once. "They kill my colleagues. Even losing a structure is an unforgivable kind of failure."

Jack Liffey glanced at him.

"I took a degree in philosophy, you know, but there was no specialty in the study of failure."

*

The blue-haired girl was sitting on the old glide on Jack Liffey's front porch as he drove up. All he could see was the hair, but if it wasn't Ellen/Rosa the big oddsmaker upstairs had gone berserk.

Coming back down the hill with Roski, he'd seen a kerosene lamp glowing inside the cabin. True to his word, Roski had shown Jack Liffey another gate entry two blocks east, where a broken padlock under the metal shield was twisted around to seem locked but wasn't. I'll be back, he thought.

"Hi, Mr. Man," Ellen said. "I tracked down *your* house."

Jack Liffey sat gently at the far end of the glide. "Call me Jack, if you would. Do you prefer Rosa or Ellen?"

"That's a deeply epistemological question. Since we're not in a revolutionary situation now, everything should be normalized. According to Lenin. So I'm just Ellen at the moment and I can go ahead and vote for useless reformists."

"My daughter would adore you. What are you studying?"

"History." She snorted. "Around here it's all Tory history. Conventional thought, if you prefer. My dad wants me to study something practical like engineering, of course."

"May I ask why you're sitting on my porch?"

"You seem to be my only chance of finding out about Sabby." The girl still seemed to have a struggle over trust. "She's my better self. Please don't make fun of me."

"I wouldn't dream of it, Ellen. If she's better than you, she's a goddess."

"Yeah, sure. Have you found out anything?"

"Not yet. Do you really want the truth?"

"Wow, you go deep fast. I generally feel like a moral weakling."

"The arson people think a girl died in that fire, possibly an Asian girl. It may not mean a thing. But if it's true, I'll let you know right after I tell her parents. Right now I'll tell you about the keg party if you'll tell me what you know about the guy they call Zook."

"For sure, Mr. Jack."

"I'm sure you heard about the speaker who went nuts and fired stun grenades into the neighborhood."

"Oh, yeah."

"Zook was at the center of it, and there's too many coincidences. I want to talk to him."

She almost smiled. "You picked the right girl. Zook was half mine to watch for months when the Orange Berets were worthy opponents of the Commandos. He's almost comically intense about his beliefs. Ed Zukovich is his name. He went to junior college and thinks of himself as the big intellectual comer of Fascism for Dummies.

"He works off and on at dead-end jobs like fixing motorcycles, but he doesn't have to. His dad was a realtor and made a killing from all the Taiwanese and Hong Kongese moving into town. The old bastard hated his customers, but their money was green."

"You have a bright future in investigation."

"Just about the last job I want, old man. No offense."

"I have to make dinner, Ellen, but I promise I'll call you if I hear about Sabine. Cross my heart." He marked out a cross over his heart. "Does anybody still do that?"

She smiled but didn't answer.

ELEVEN

Beware of Straighteners

He'd used up the last of the frozen tamales on Roski, so he scrounged together a chicken penne he knew Gloria loved and hit it with extra chile and mint. When she glanced up woozily from bed and refused to hobble downstairs, he brought her a plate of dinner and a beer. Then he sat in the kitchen alone forking bits of the concoction out of the pot. Way too spicy for him. He knew he was dragging around his guilt like a giant wooden cross.

Gloria's cane suddenly rapped away, and he sighed and went up. She was sitting up in bed with the beer, the food still untouched on the floor.

"Can I get you something else?" he asked. "We have some of that ramen."

She shook her head absently and finished off the beer. Gloria was up to about ten bottles a day, but he'd decided not to nag. It wouldn't have done any good anyway. You couldn't tell her a damn thing she didn't want to hear.

"I want to talk a little."

"Of course." He put on his mental football helmet.

There was a bit of irrelevant hemming and hawing and talk of her discomfort lying on her side.

"You didn't call me up here to talk about your ribcage," he said.

She fell silent. An intermittent metallic banging started up outside, probably kids hammering on a dented fender, the ambiance of East L.A. "You should know Maeve and I had a frank talk, and I told her all about Sonny up in Bakersfield. She disapproved mightily, of course. I know you figured it out long ago. Your sixth sense was vibrating before I even left."

"Pretty much." His heart had already plummeted all the way to the floor and bounced, and he feared this was preface to saying she was leaving him for Sonny. Oh, no. Please, no.

"No, Jack, I ain't going up there to join no Sonny disaster. That's over."

She had read his mind, or his face, and the disavowal filled him with so much relief he didn't take in the next thing she said.

"Sorry, Glor. I had a senior moment there. What did you say?"

She glowered briefly. "I'll put it another way. I know you're sitting on a whole world of pissed off. I went and had my fun with another guy. I hurt you in the *cojones*. And now I'm less than half of myself and won't put out at all. You run around making food and caring for a crotchety bitch day and night. You're a good man, Jack, and I know I don't deserve you."

"Shakespeare said if we got what we deserved we'd all be whipped."

"Shut up, Jack. This is my turn. I know you deserve some payback." She stalled and seemed to be fuming, maybe at herself. "Hand me the food. I'm hungry."

He set the wood tray on her knees. She forked pasta in fast, like a hungry bear attacking a pile of steaks. She stopped long enough to enjoy a chew.

"You finally got it spicy enough."

The mound of pasta was half gone by the time she slowed down and finally looked up from the plate. He'd been so happy to see her enjoying something at last that he'd just sat back and watched. There might have been a tear in the corner of her eye. A glisten, anyway.

"Jack, there's nobody alive doesn't want payback sometimes for being hurt. You ain't Jesus H. Christ, whatever Maeve thinks. I want you to go find some filly out there who doesn't want to keep you and have some man-fun with her. My holdback ain't about you, honey. I don't know why it is, but I just can't get my pussy wet for nothing right now."

Jesus Christ, he thought. What kind of god of irony was running things?

"Please go look for a temporary slice, Jack. I know it'd take pressure off me."

Or not, he thought. It was the perfect opportunity to tell her about Tien, of course. But—absolutely not. Oh, no no. She was far more honest and earnest than he was, maybe too much for her own good. Wasn't cowardice sometimes a virtue?

"Gloria, I'll think about that, but right now we have to get you feeling better. How about I find you a therapist you can talk to in deepest, darkest secret? We'll pay for it off the books, and the department doesn't have to know."

She stopped eating again and looked up. Her eyes were pained and frighteningly sad. "Did I ever say I love you?"

Actually, no, she hadn't. "Sure." He felt his own eyes burning with tenderness and shame.

*

Maeve was in her nightie, staring contentedly out her picture window to take in the morning view across the canyon. The sun was well above the rugged hill line but just below the dark cloud that would snuff it out soon. The world seemed weirdly bright, though striped with ribbons of fog. More winter rain.

It was an awesome view: the mountain chaparral broken up by firebreaks, even a drift of smoke from a chimney. She wondered why she was so uninterested in landscapes. They could be lovely, even dramatic. Cezanne, Turner, Sisley, the Hudson River painters. But she liked focusing on a body, with all its blemishes. She wondered if her attraction to the body was too private and too obvious.

There was a rap at the door that she recognized—a hesitance along with an upbeat hello. Everything inside Maeve started to glow. "Come in."

Bunny peered in wearing a worn chenille bathrobe, which made Maeve's heart beat harder.

"Morning, Maevie. Can I come in?"

"You're a wonderful sight in the morning."

"Don't joke on me."

"Oh, wow, I'm not." Maeve was about to say more, but held her tongue because something was up.

"I had a bad night."

"Drop the dime. I can do coffee out here now." She discarded the dregs and put a new filter in the Melitta.

"Thanks. Nights can be scary."

"You mean your dreams, or something else?"

For some time now, from obvious self-interest, Maeve had been making a minor science of how women responded to jokes, hints, and overtures of lesbianism. Bunny was confounding her.

"All my life, flying in dreams has terrified me—falling, I guess. Last night, somebody gave me this big inner tube with a...like a membrane across it. A giant diaphragm." She laughed uncomfortably. "I just had to lay forward on it and it floated away. Then I surfed along, ten feet up. I couldn't wait to tell you and show you how to do it, too."

"And that bothers you why?"

"This new thing is scary, Maeve. I'll bet I've been a hidden L-word all the time."

"Maybe it just means you like me and I like you and together we can fly. Imagine no barriers, as John Lennon said."

Maeve poured the last of the steaming water and left it to drip as she walked back to Bunny.

"Show me how to fly."

*

As Roski had promised, the hidden padlock on the firegate was unlocked. It made Jack Liffey wonder how many of life's barriers were implied rather than actual. Maybe the lock on every tenth bank vault had been out of commission for years. All those unobtainable women had actually wanted you.

The yellow gate swung open with a screech and he drove through. There were so few landmarks in the burned chaparral that he was afraid he might be on the wrong fire road—but there it was finally, the cabin with the old Studebaker beside it. A '53? He still hadn't worked out a viable plan for approaching this kid, and now he'd have to wing it.

He parked beside the Studebaker, near a dropoff into the ravine that was running fast with rainwater. Water seemed to have come up a foot.

He wondered if he should pretend to be a member of the Tea Party. He had no rigid code about sticking to the truth, but truth sometimes helped in unexpected ways. Appeasing some fussy god.

"Hello, Mr. Zukovich," Jack Liffey said.

The young man at the plank door was dangling a book from his hand.

"My name is Jack Liffey. I was hired by the family of a young girl from Monterey Park who's missing. She may have disappeared up here. I have no reason at all to think you have anything to do with this, but it seems to relate to this area and I'd like to talk to you."

"Come again?" The young man's melancholy powder-blue eyes narrowed.

"There's a good chance the girl died a half-mile up the trail from here, about the time of the Sheepshead Fire."

"No shit. Wow. Come in, man."

He looked genuinely surprised, which was in his favor. The main room of the cabin was spartan but still untidy. A cluttered utility sink, a propane hot ring, empty food cans, an open bread loaf, and a big ice chest. On a table beside a hanging canvas chair a lovely old nickel-plated Aladdin mantle lamp was as bright as a hundred-watt bulb. He hadn't seen one in years.

"Everybody calls me Zook."

A single cot was against the wall with a sleeping bag. A small boom box on a windowsill. The room suggested an army billet out in the field in Vietnam.

"What are you reading?"

The young man showed the cover of his book. *The Heart of Liberty*. "It's lame," he said. "Philosophy for little people. No real mind challenge."

He went on talking about the real deep thinkers, like Glenn Beck, exposing a world of powerful Jewish banking elites—a zeitgeist that the young man had obviously lived in for years. Jack Liffey decided talking politics at all would only send him farther into loopy land.

"I saw a bus bench in town with an ad for Cookie Zukovich, realtor," Jack Liffey said. "Is that you?"

"That was a *really* old bench, man. Shoot it full of holes and then photograph it. The old man and me had issues. His real name was Casimir." He snorted, as if the name were shameful.

"Was?"

"He snuffed it a couple years ago eating oysters with a bunch of rich Chinks. Good riddance. Sorry to sound so doggy, but he beat the crap out of me and Mom when I was too little to stop him. I think it got him off. Hurting us, I mean. When I got old enough to threaten him with a baseball bat, he made me sleep in the garage."

"A lot of missing children I've looked for had stories like that," Jack Liffey said.

The young man stared intently at him for the first time. "Far out. You find missing kids. That's awesome, man. Want a beer?"

"Sure." He could pretend to drink.

"The old man was a bitchass of every kind. He helped sell the whole damn town to the Chinks, and when it was too late, he joined SAMP, Save American Monterey Park. Nobodies. Dark-suit assholes that didn't have no balls to really fight. Afraid of yanking on anybody's chain. Coors okay?"

"Sure."

"Me and some pals still prank the Chinks, but it's really just funnin' 'em. We paint out their signs or plant a stink bomb. I ain't stupid. I know the yellow man owns this valley now, lock, stock, and barbell."

Jack Liffey wondered if there was a crack anywhere in the young man's sealed worldview that might let some light in. He sensed a kind of struggling decency deep inside. Hunting for children had touched him.

The young man clambered into his suspended canvas chair. He pointed to a folding beach chair for Jack Liffey.

How to approach him? Jack Liffey asked if Zook had ever read Dickens. The young man barely knew the name. These recent American generations lacked all his cultural reference points. He tried desperately to think of a popular movie that dealt with child abuse. A video game, a hip-hop song—good luck.

"I have a weakness for children in trouble. You know, back in the 1800s in factories, little kids were forced to crawl around all day under cloth looms, unsnarling the threads. The owners insisted they needed the tiny fingers."

"Aw, shit. Where do you learn this stuff?"

Not in your books, you can bet the farm. They talked for a while longer, but the young man gradually got suspicious. "I was at your keg party, Zook. What do you think of that big South African?"

"Sketchy. He got me in deep doo-doo with the cops."

And it's all about you, of course, Jack Liffey thought. "Didn't you toss him the M16?"

"You wired?"

"Hell no. Check me out. I'm no cop." He opened his arms.

"It's time for you to bounce. I know the world, man, and the wolves eat the dogs. I'm hanging way out in this. That's why I'm in retreat here."

Jack Liffey took out the photo of Sabine.

"This is the girl I'm looking for, Zook. She's Chinese, but she's innocent of anything her parents or your parents did. Have you ever seen her?"

Zook stared for a few moments and handed it back. "Naw. I hardly never recognize Chinks. The round faces and slit eyes—they look so much alike they ought to tattoo their names on their foreheads."

"Could you tell me how many people use this cabin?"

Ed Zukovich touched his feet down to bring the swing chair to a stop. "Say what?"

"Not names. Just give me a round number. Five? Fifty? If she was up nearby, maybe she came here for some fun."

"Not many got a key." His suspicion was on red alert now. "Hey, how come *you* was at the keg?"

"I wanted to know why the USA is going down the tubes. But that South African guy wasn't any help."

"He was some weird noob. He couldn't even look you in the eye. My pal said if he'd gone and ordered a whole boatload of loudmouth sons-of-bitches, and they'd only sent that one, he'd still have accepted the shipment. Ha."

"He didn't make much sense."

Zook nodded. "It's hard to find people who want to straighten things out."

"Beware of straighteners," Jack Liffey said. "Life is a lot stranger than their theories."

The boy stared hard at him.

"I'll see you again, Zook," Jack Liffey said. Pointedly he left his business card on the table.

"I don't think so, man. Have a nice future."

*

Roski stuck his head in the door at the arson lab. "Do I need booties and a hairnet?"

"Not unless you've got the sniffles," Monica Flagg said. "Stay back five feet."

"It's hard to stay that far away from you, beautiful." The official DNA test would come from the blood lab out at L.A. State, but he'd asked a special favor of his local lab to do their own.

"Knock it off, Walt. I've got a steady now."

"All the sweetest dreams turn sour."

"Who said that?"

"I did, just now."

She scowled and discouraged him with a backhand wave. "You don't want to see all the bars and comparisons. I had to teach myself a lot about DNA science to do this favor. But you don't care about the science."

"Not so much."

"The race up the DNA graph paper has been run."

Monica Flagg held up a paper strip with a lot of fuzzy colored bars printed side by side. "In lane one we have the bone fragment. Running in lane two is the swab from Mommy Dearest. They sprinted side by side all the way to the finish line. You want a defensible courtroom number, I'd say it's one chance in fourteen million that these two aren't closely related. You want my opinion, subject one is absolutely the daughter of subject two. You said you didn't want to know the science, but see these two lines here? They're identical GYPA alleles. When those two are the same, I'm convinced. After all the degradation at the fire, your pals at the big lab will never be able to do an RFLP test anyway."

She used forceps to hold up the bone fragment.

"I'm morally certain that this is Sabine Roh. Sad."

"She's a lot smaller than her picture," Walt Roski said—the gallows humor of the lab. "And no boobs at all."

"Lay off the boobs, okay? I'm sensitive."

"Why, for heaven's sake? Your body is stunning."

"You ever had car batteries hung off tiny straps on your shoulders? You ever had a date whose eyes never met yours? You try to jog and your whole body wig-wags? You can't sleep at night for the backache? And everywhere you go even your own sex stares at you. Can you assimilate any of that?"

He held up a hand for a sympathy high-five. "Sorry, a lot of it never occurred to me."

She swept her gloved hand past his. "No touchie."

*

It was afternoon and almost time to report in to his paying employer. Jack Liffey was parked uneasily down the street in Huntington Harbour, half an eye on a big pleasure yacht sliding down the channel. What a strange place this was for her to settle, he thought. As far as he could tell, Tien didn't even like boats. But they were toys desired by the rich, so she lived with boats and owned boats and commanded boats.

He'd been stonewalling his thoughts about her for several days now, a brawl between the shame and lust running just about even. In the end—all else being equal—he was afraid lust would win.

"Good morning, Tien," he said as the door came open on her, not the help.

"Right on time. You got a crazy thing about on time, Jackie."

"You could pretend I'm not here yet if you like."

"How I do that? I take one look at you, then down at your bulge, and I want it. I want you bad."

"Think of me as a severe librarian, telling you to shush and sit still," Jack Liffey said.

"Ooh, yes. The naughty librarian."

I can't win, he thought. "Get me a soda, Tien. I'm very tense."

"Soda make you more loose?" she asked hopefully.

"No, but it gives us time to talk." And gives me time to try to figure out what the hell I'm doing.

"I get it. You pretend you only good friend, old style. I can play. Lupeta!"

They sat down in the maddeningly blue living room, and he noticed once again the giant art object of glass mirror squares set at various angles. He would run through fire to escape something as disturbing as that.

The Latina maid came in.

"Lupeta, *háganos algún refrescos* softies, *por favor. Y la cosa para me.*"

"*Si, mi reina.*" She withdrew immediately.

"Very embarrassing, no, Jack? She say my queen. No good in democracy. Dinosaur world stuff."

"Ask her: *reina de que?*"

"I know what I queen of. *Reina de su pinga, amor.*" She pointed at his crotch.

Something about her wacky sexuality always grabbed his fancy. "Calm down. Let's go out on the patio."

Reluctantly she took them out to the patio-dock, though the sky was overcast and the afternoon chilly. Jack Liffey gave her a concise report on his investigation. As he'd supposed, she wasn't terribly interested.

The maid found them with a ginger ale and an aperitif for Tien, an iced pale amber-colored liquid with a sliver of orange. It came with a bottle identified as Lillet. Jack Liffey poured his soft drink.

She made a face. "You still do little boy drink."

"Tien, I'm weak. If I had both you and booze in the same room, I'd melt into a puddle of protoplasm."

"I not know proto-plastic, but I get the idea. You in dog heat, too."

"I couldn't have put it any more vividly. Perfectly balanced by guilt."

She made a face. "In Vietnam they tell me the goal in life for girl is to stay quiet and oh-so-delicate and let family obligation make you little doormat that guys walk-walk-walk over. You know what I say to that? I say passion is what life all about. You find that, don't throw it away.

"You know I study in Sorbonne. Maybe I learn it there. Not Buddhist or Roman Cath. All I know for sure—all this submit and shut up stuff for women is big damn suck. It never make no great ideas or great life. Rage, rage, against end of light—somebody say."

"Dylan Thomas."

"Okay, this Thomas, he really know his P. Q. You my number-one passion guy, Jackie. You feel it, too—I think nobody ever tell you you got it. Remember our first time? We was fucking like two crazy kids in my old Porsche in garage, and you scream blood-murder. To wake my dead Grandma. Not fair you got to be with cold woman that don't know the hot in you."

"I never said that, Tien."

For some reason everything in his life seemed to be up for grabs. It was disturbing. Growing up in the changeless fifties, he'd acquired a comforting conviction that the world was a mapped place, known and predictable. But like most of the Baby Boomers, he'd had that outlook rasped away.

She tapped her forehead. "I know you in there, Jackie. You in deep *kim chee* at home with this cold woman."

Where did she get these revelations? "Forget that, Tien. You won't get to me by attacking Gloria."

"This no woman-woman contest." Tien was unbuttoning her silky blouse. "This you me. You want. You need. You take. I want, too. You make me crazy, my love. Please please, no make me cry now."

He experienced an overwhelming arousal.

"Jackie, you know you want. One time, think of you-self, what you need."

She stood up. Her gown fell and her small breasts were in the open air, the nipples puckering in the chill, her dark delta glistening, and he felt the pleasant drumming of big raindrops.

A couple in a boat passing along the channel stood and applauded. Rain began to patter comfortingly on the whole world.

"Stay tuned for big screaming hello, Jack."

TWELVE

Human Evolution

Jack Liffey settled wearily on the splintery glide on the porch, trying to keep at least the front door between himself and Gloria— out of hearing range if she started banging away, or at least keep himself within plausible deniability. The winter rains had come for real, spilling erratically off the house gutters that were choked with leaves. Another of the home chores he'd overlooked. On the way back he'd noticed that his car badly needed fresh wipers. A general and constant decay of things, including his recent sidestep into portable ethics. Oh, Jack. Oh, sad Tien.

Loco hurried out of the drizzle, shook himself once, and clambered onto the glide with difficulty. He snuggled against Jack Liffey, panting from the four front stairs and the two-foot vault. His age showed in a grizzled snout. He'd never fully recovered from bone cancer surgery and a long regimen of chemo. The half-coyote mutt had always had his own belligerent problems, but he'd become a lot more affectionate of late, as if the rational dog half had finally decided to acknowledge that his owner's negligible monetary nest egg had been sacrificed to treat his osteosarcoma. Never underestimate my sentimentality, Jack Liffey thought, fondling the dog's bristly snout. Or my sense of guilt. What the hell was he doing with Tien?

He wondered what it would be like to have so much money that none of your emotional relationships had to depend on it. All his life, he'd had to adjust to the available and existing.

The sky darkened perceptibly and the rain stepped up a couple of notches. He was happy to be under shelter, watching the slanting offpour from the roof. "What do you think of that, Loco? Water from the sky. Never happens in L.A., right?"

The flat yellow eyes searched upward at him, probably straining to make sense of the inexplicably affable tone of voice.

"It's okay. You and me, huh? I can sure make a mess of things. But you've seen plenty of that."

A flash of light lit the block briefly. Uh-oh. Four...five...six...seven. Then the peal of thunder. A little more than a mile, if he remembered right.

There was no question of Loco waiting around to calculate the distance in dog miles. He was gone with the sound, vanished from the glide like a disturbing thought to head for whatever hidey-hole he had in reserve.

The rap of the cane started up again inside, strident enough to cut through the wall of the house and the guilt. Coming, my conscience, he thought.

*

The nurse had told him that 347 was doing quite well for a crispy. He'd said nothing since he'd invited that comment with a dark humor inquiry of his own. Roski peered inside the room.

"You alive, Piscatelli?"

"What if I said no?"

"I'll just send Housekeeping in to water you."

The fire jumper seemed to smile, lying on his side on a bariatric air mattress that was noisily tilting him at an angle. He didn't smile with his eyes. Pain obviously lurked in the tension inside. "You're the arson desk jockey, aren't you?"

"Walt Roski."

"Thanks for coming, sir."

"In pain?"

"I pray, that's my way."

"Well, they say that what doesn't kill you. Jjust about kills you."

The fire jumper looked puzzled. "They bury Jerry Routt yet, sir?"

"Yesterday, partner. Fire trucks from all over five counties were flying the flag. A couple of antique pumpers. A slow code three to the cemetery. TV cameras. Mayor and chief at attention. Bagpipes and 'Last Call.' The whole nine yards."

"Routt woulda laughed at that, but not me."

Roski figured this was one earnest human being. "Nothing's too good for a man who gives his life fighting fires. I *so* hate firebugs." Roski set down his briefcase. "Can I get you anything?"

"That's what the nurses are for."

Roski smiled. "They're usually not so good about cheeseburgers or Little Debbies or Scotch, but you seem to be a rule-abiding man."

"Rules are made for a reason, sir."

"For sure. How's your memory of the incident? Still skating around it?"

"Yes, sir. I remember the roar getting loud and me yelling, 'Safe zone.' I must've shook out my shelter on instinct."

"You told me last week about Routt calling your attention to a dead girl."

Piscatelli nodded. "To be honest, I think I remember telling you a lot more than I actually remember."

Roski took out the photo of Sabine that Jack Liffey had given him. "I want to show you a photograph. It may have nothing at all to do with the fire. Just tell me if it brings up any thoughts at all."

Roski held the photo up and the smoke jumper's eyes bored into it. "Pretty girl. Chinese? Japanese? I told you she looked Asian, didn't I?"

"Never mind what you said. It doesn't matter much one way or another." And it probably didn't, since the provisional DNA test, but he had to check off all the boxes.

"The old brain ain't much good right now."

"That's fine, Tony. We don't need your ID so much."

"Is that girl okay?" All at once, the man began to weep silently.

"Let it out, my brave friend." Roski was about to rest a hand on a part of the shoulder that looked burn free, but he'd been told of the danger of infection. "A big box of rocks like you usually has powerful emotions."

*

Diana Yao had called Ellen. Her parents were away for the evening so they had the living room up in the hills to themselves. She had engineering books nearby as signs of homework in case her folks came back early.

"Thanks, Diana," Ellen said at the grown-up Scotch-rocks her old comrade had thrust into her hand. "Nothing is *ding hau* right now."

"I found out nothing about Sabine, but maybe she's off working it out with a boyfriend. Have you talked to her parents?"

"Yoohoo, I told you the Rohs hired a private detective to find her. Don't give me some Nature Channel story."

"Sorry. I've been asking around at warp ten because I like Sabby. I heard, maybe, about a trip she made to Mexico. And I heard she had a run-in with that dumb pudge with the famous big peter. If it helps you, the dummy likes the ponies."

"And you know this how…?" Ellen asked.

"I followed him to Santa Anita yesterday, just in case he was meeting Sabby. He spent all day searching the stands, I mean *all day*. Hunting for discarded win tickets, right? Think how hard that is. You've got to keep checking every race in your head, and they allow off-track betting now, so there's a bunch of tracks running all the time. It's harder than actually betting for real. What a doofus."

"Did he find any winners?"

"Would a ten-buck win matter? No, he didn't—not one. What a jackass. He'll be flippin' hamburgers at sixty."

"You going to keep watching him?"

"No. I'm out for good."

"Okay, thanks" Ellen said, resigned.

*

Gloria was sitting up in bed looking pretty grim, either angry or hurt, he couldn't tell.Making it hard to read was the cop way. "I get panics when I'm alone, Jack. Maybe not really panics. I feel nervous and tummy-upset, and I start thinking about Bakersfield. I try to watch TV but I can't concentrate." She sighed deeply and rolled her neck. "Did I tell you I killed two cops? Bad cops, but cops. And I was so helpless. You know, I got so wild I wasn't me anymore."

"How about I get you some regular visitors? Paula Green, Señora Gomez, Maeve—anybody else?"

She shook her head. "I got to deal with this."

The rain surged and rattled away on the roof like angry gods wanting in. A half-dozen leaks would need pots and pans soon, he thought. Just par for a hundred-year-old frame house. "Did something set this off today?" he asked delicately.

She scowled. "I got my butt bit off."

"Mood adjustment," he said, handing her the beer. "Tell me."

"Thanks, Jackie."

He sat down on the edge of the bed with a can of ginger ale and rested a hand on her leg gently on top of the covers. "I'd be happy to bite your butt, too."

She smiled without much humor, then her face went slack.

"Tell," he said.

"My captain at Harbor called. We talked a while, yadda yadda, of cabbages and whatever it is you're always saying. How was I doing as an invalid? Eventually he got around to using the word 'malingering.' Does that mean what I think it does?"

"Probably."

She grunted. "He told me he's reassigned all the jobs in Harbor Division. As if I don't exist no more. And he had his way of suggesting that I'm too emotional to be a good cop. Jesus Christ, Jack, I know for a fact that I'm the best detective sergeant they've had since Ken Steelyard. My clearance record beats everybody's."

She summoned a nasty smile. "I'd like to see Collingwood raped a few times and twenty bones broken and see how 'professional' the asshole is. Mostly I wanna know are they building up a 'terminate' book on me."

"Wasn't Collingwood the guy who read you the riot act for having a messy desk?"

She rested her forehead against his shoulder. "I used to just suck it up, all their man-woman crap. Forgive me if it spills over."

"Nothing to forgive, my love."

"You still love me?" She sounded almost startled.

"I've got ways of knowing that I do." Guilt, for one, he thought. "I think you and me are stuck in this lifeboat."

"You got a way of putting things abstract that loses me, Jackie."

"I'm just reflecting out loud. How can I help you keep your spirits up?"

"I wish I knew." She pulled back from his arm to take a swig of beer. It was a good sign that she'd touched him for a moment.

"You're my moral compass, Glor." And he meant it.

Was it just his own infidelity making him so affectionate and disoriented? So much pain and confusion surrounding him. The forlorn Chinese parents, the depressive Roski, the bewildered Zook, a daughter about to flunk out of her future, and Tien grabbing for him like a last-chance brass ring.

*

A half-hour later Jack Liffey was cooking up a clean-out-the-cupboard dinner when the phone burred at him. He was in a half-mesmerized drowse.

Burr-burr.

The telemarketers always called at dinnertime, but he decided to answer anyway.

"Is this Jack Liffey?"

"No, it's the stain on his honor." He couldn't get Hardi Boaz out of his mind.

"*Christ*, man. This is Walt Roski. What the hell's wrong with you?"

He came totally alert. "I was expecting somebody selling me a lower mortgage. I'm okay, Walt."

"You sounded like a man three sheets to the wind with his home problems."

"I don't touch the stuff."

"Okay. I've got news about your clients' little girl, Sabine Roh, if you want it. Or I can call back at a more convenient time."

"Right. One of your loved ones is on fire. I'll call later to tell you which one."

"Sorry, Jack. It's bad news. We've got the DNA back, and it says it *was* Sabine Roh burned up in Coyote Wash during the Sheepshead Fire. I'm sure you don't want to know the court testimony odds for this DNA test. Given the crucifix we found, I'm convinced."

"You mean rosary," Jack Liffey said. "A similar item."

"I'm not up on religious stuff. Do you want me to inform the parents or do you want to?"

"Whoa. How do you feel about that?"

"Let's say I'm ambivalent, but I can do it."

"I've done this before, too."

"One of us has to tell them."

Something was crackling too loud in the pan across the kitchen.

"I'll do it, Walt. I'm on a ski jump of emotion anyway."

"Jack, are you okay?"

"I'm fine. The sun will burn out before I'm in any real trouble. I'll take the Rohs."

*

The next morning Jack Liffey drove to the Rohs' house at nine o'clock, his wipers smearing in the rain. He didn't call first. There was absolutely no way to break news like this in stages. The U.S. Army knew that perfectly well and always sent its two Casualty Notification Officers to your door without warning.

Such an ordinary American house. With one Chinese decorative vase beside the door.

"Yes?"

"Good morning, Mrs. Roh." He tried the most neutral smile he could, but she started to have the tremors immediately.

"You got bad news."

"Can I come in? Is your husband here?"

She opened the door, but she shoved both hands out to stop him entering, as if she could push the bad news away. She'd figured it out, of course.

"Please."

Mrs. Roh collected herself and stood aside. "I'll get you tea."

"Thank you." In the dining area, Mr. Roh was glaring at him over a bowl of what looked like soggy rice that had been boiled into glop, with a hard-cooked egg sinking into it. Across from him Mrs. Roh's plate had a slice of dry toast with one bite out of it.

He sat at the end of the table without invitation. "Good morning to you, sir. I'm sorry to disturb you so early."

"'Stateside,'" Mr. Roh blurted out. "You know that word?"

"Yes, sir. G.I. slang for the United States. And 'back in the world,' and 'on the block,' and 'Jody's place,' several others."

"Thank you. Why the Jody expression?"

"I think Jody was the girlfriend you lost to a guy with a draft deferment."

"Ah, hard cheese. While you were busy lighting up villages."

"Exactly."

"Forgive me. I love American idioms."

"Sir, right now you want to hush and listen to me."

"I see."

Their eyes met and the man understood instantly, though his wife was still noisily getting tea.

"It's bad?"

"Let me tell you and your wife together. But please be prepared to offer comfort." This annoying man was going to have to take it in like a huge swallow of poison.

The man snapped out something in Chinese or maybe Vietnamese to his wife, and the woman came in without the tea, and after another barked order, she sat. Their eyes all met and disengaged and met again. Mr. Roh took his wife's hand hard.

Maybe in Asia this was all different. No more delay, he thought.

"Mr. and Mrs. Roh, the fire department has told me that your daughter died in the Sheepshead Fire. They ran a DNA test on some remains they found and it matched your cheek swabs. She probably didn't suffer. They believe she was already dead, shot to death. I promise you, if you wish, I'll find out who did this and have him punished. I'm so very sorry for your loss."

There was a stunned silence for a few seconds, then the mother threw her head back and began to wail. It went on and on. Jack Liffey sat quietly. Eventually she seemed to freeze up and sat in silence with her mouth wide open.

"There will be no five blossoms," the husband said dully.

Even now, he needed to explain, to be a professor. He told Jack Liffey that the five blossoms were marrying, having a son, being respected in a moral life, having a loving grandson, and dying peacefully in your sleep after a long, honorable life. In this reckoning, Sabine would not acquire a single blossom.

Nor will I, Jack Liffey thought. But I value daughters.

Mr. Roh met his eyes. "Beliefs are deep, sir, even if you feel you have no religious impulses. There will be no eternity now in my family."

The wail came again, and then the woman leapt to her feet and ran out of the room. "I'll go away now so you can comfort her," Jack Liffey said.

The man shook his head. "It's best to let her grieve. Mr. Liffey, can my wife, can we, touch—I mean *physically* touch—any part of Sabine? Please don't dismiss this request. It's important that we touch her remains."

"I'll arrange it, sir," Jack Liffey said. "And I'll find out who killed her."

"How old are you, sir?" the man asked.

"Sixty-four," Jack Liffey said.

"Do you fear becoming so much older, like me?"

"I fear not becoming older more."

*

Maeve was sitting on a stool, studying a still life that just wouldn't come together, when her contemplation was interrupted by a small knock on her door. Her spirits rose. Bunny.

"Come! I want—" She choked it off the instant she saw it wasn't Bunny. A short brown man stood in the door like a djinn appearing out of a smoke cloud. He had a face like old leather and an ambiguous smile, but instead of the flowing robes she'd have expected, he wore chinos and a polo shirt. He carried a tiny green umbrella over his bald head against the pouring rain. Maeve knew immediately it was Swami Muni.

"May I come in out of the rain, dear?"

This was going to be a tussle of wills. "Of course, Mr. Muni. Or is it Mr. Swami?"

Fussily, he rattled the umbrella to shake off water and left it upright outside the door as he backed in. "You are Maeve Liffey?"

So they were still even. "Please sit down, sir. What does one offer a devout Hindu to drink? Or are you Hindu?"

"The East has very broad tents. I am Buddhist, too. And the fourth way. The West is always hair-splitting. Green tea would be fine. Or tea without caffeine, thank you. My cardiologist insists."

He sat in a lotus position on the floor, his gaze fixed on her failing still life.

"That one's not working," she said. She went to the burner and started a kettle.

"But you have a good eye and a talent."

"I hope so."

She set out cups and teabags.

"Mickey won't bother you again."

"Mickey?"

"That large freckled boy who demanded to see Bunny Walker."

Maeve wouldn't give an inch. "Bunny said you *assigned* him to her, as if you were breeding animals."

"I thought it might help them both. I make mistakes. In the end I do nothing against anyone's wishes. I promise you."

"In the end, we're all dead," Maeve said.

"Possibly."

She watched him with her arms crossed, realizing it was an obvious defensive posture. A sign of weakness. This was going to be a duel for Bunny.

His face gradually readjusted into a comforting smile. "What we do in our group we call *work*. Enlightenment comes only with effort. This means bypassing your filters and defenses. Only the ears offer a direct pathway to deeper consciousness. The eyes always judge and filter. We're trying to evolve."

"I get it. A few special people get to become advanced beings." Unless the money for the lessons runs out, she thought.

"Could I see one of the paintings that did work out?"

Maeve went to her stack of canvases, reversed to the wall. She chose a large one, of Bunny, who was in the altogether, of course, but with her face turned away.

She brought it over and turned it toward Swami Muni. Rain had darkened the world outside so it was hard to see.

She sat quietly and drank tea for the next ten minutes as, every minute or so, he broke his study and silence and told her something about herself and her passions and her mother and father that he could not possibly have known.

It was called a cold reading, she knew, practiced by healers and grifters all over the world, but it was still very impressive. In the end she took up a lotus facing him, full of trepidation.

"What is *work*?" Maeve Liffey said.

THIRTEEN
My Dead Fly

Zook had been listening to the car crunching up the fire road for some time.

You take yourself off into a serious intellectual retreat, he thought, and suddenly every goof in the city shows up. He'd already had to put up with the Liffey guy. What now? He heard the car stop outside and, sure enough, footsteps approached. The fist on the door indicated it was no casual visitor.

The cop wore a dark blue raid jacket over his copsuit. His acne-scarred face looked especially unpleasant dripping with rain. Sgt. Manny Acevedo—once the Commandos' best bet for a friend inside the MonPark Police. Manny hated the Chinks, too. He wore a curl-down Pancho Villa moustache that did its best to distract from his tragic complexion.

"Zook, your *klika* got a big problem."

"Got no gang no more. Just a couple pals. We got our rights." Zook couldn't prevent it, he farted loudly.

"Sure, *hombrito*. And that's what your rights are worth." Manny pushed in out of the rain and pulled the door behind him. "Gimme a toke, a line. Anything you got."

"A beer okay?" Zook didn't trust the Mex cop, certainly not while he was wearing a raid jacket, even if it was just for the rain.

Manny gave him the stink-eye. "Yeah, right. You sure you ain't got no rails?"

"I'm in philosophical study here," Zook insisted. He gestured to the books scattered near his hanging chair, and Manny picked up a tented-open copy of a book about the fight to vindicate Joseph McCarthy.

"What the fuck is this?"

"Forget it. You want the beer or not?"

"Sure, *ese*. If you change your mind about offering a bump, I swear I ain't on no bitch patrol." He flopped on the lawn chair, and barked once, startling Zook. "I like you guys. I do. It'd be great if we could take all the *Chinos* down, but it's turning into an Obama world now. Especial since the department started hiring yellow. Give me a break; I kept L.E. away from your beer bash. We can still trade favors.

"You got to know there's a push on about a missing girl—Sabine Roh's the name," Acevedo said. "What kind of knucklehead name is that? A arson fireman thinks she's dead as a doorbob. They even dug up a bullet. So if any a you guys got a dirty piece, ditch it."

Ed Zukovich brought him a lukewarm Coors. All the ice in the cooler had melted a day ago. "Tell me, Sergeant Manny. What you want for any 4-1-1 from me?"

"Money ain't dick to me. I'm just stepping up to help *la raza*. Your fishbelly-colored *raza*, too. Maybe next week I ask a favor. Right now, a little weed or blow, please."

Zukovich knew he would have to give the dead girl some thought. First the Liffey guy and now the cop. Who knew how a perpetual straggler like Captain Beef would hold up with questions like this.

*

Rain ran in sheets down the awningless window of the church office. Just as he remembered, the room in St. Thomas Aquinas was painted an institutional vomit green. Father Soong was still strange-looking in his big white robe, like a man poking his head out of a tent.

There was a photo of Soong on the sideboard behind him, with a cop clutching either arm. Jack Liffey pointed at it.

"Antiwar demonstration?"

The priest smiled mildly. "Something like that. How I wished I'd been in Baltimore when the Berrigans poured their own blood into the draft files. I was stuck in a tiny mission church on the Rosebud

Reservation in South Dakota. A complex moral problem. The Lakota, like most Native Americans, are extremely patriotic. Their sons were almost all on active duty. I was their pastor. So I kept my mouth shut about Vietnam."

Something thrummed in the walls of the office, maybe just an excess of reverence. It was time. "I'm sorry to tell you this, sir. I've learned that Sabine Roh is almost certainly dead. She was shot and then left in the path of the Sheepshead Fire."

The man's features sagged, as if aging a year or two before Jack Liffey's eyes. His fingers pressed into both of his eyes.

"I just told the parents. If they're your parish, you might want to go over."

"I don't know how much comfort I have to offer. Sorry, that's my own vanity speaking. I liked Sabby a lot. I don't like her father very much. He has several advanced degrees in feeling sorry for himself. His daughter needed him badly, and he was lost in himself. Did he sit sideways, not looking at you?"

Jack Liffey nodded.

"What a prick—to use the ecclesiastical term. Thank you for coming to tell me, Mr. Liffey. I'd better go over there."

As Jack Liffey left, he looked back to see the small man staring down dejectedly at the Tibetan prayer wheel on his desk. Confusion everywhere.

*

Maeve stared guardedly at the CD that had been left on her coffee table. She was a little shell-shocked by her conversation with Swami Muni. The man had been humorous, self-effacing, soft-spoken and surprisingly unmystical.

Every time she'd expected him to veer off into mysticism, he'd talked about particle physics or neuroscience.

She felt a bit floaty, as if the guy had left a powerful intoxicant on the air. He'd also left the CD—Lesson One of *Work*, of course. *The ears are the direct path to the yearnings of the unconscious.* She wondered what her dad would say about it all. No, she knew.

Another light rap on her door—certainly Bunny this time.

"Hi, Bunny."

"Were you just entertaining who I think I think?"

Maeve made a face. "I can see why he interested you." In a different tone: "He told me the Mickey guy won't bother us anymore."

"Great." Bunny's eye went directly to the CD imprinted with a distinctive hypnotic spiral. "You're going to try *work*?"

"Shouldn't I?"

"Wow on wheels, Maevie. You seem so grounded. But then, you are ready to jump at anything you feel sometimes."

"My dad once said you only regret the things you don't do."

"Oh, I can think of some things I *did* do…"

Maeve took Bunny's hand. It was deliciously plump, warm and damp. "Bunny, we're both really young. Let's not have regrets yet. *Mi mosca muerta.*"

"I worry when you hide in Spanish."

"It's 'my dead fly' literally, but it means my sweet innocent."

"Innocent, huh? Be careful of that man, M. But I won't prejudice you."

*

On the car seat beside him Jack Liffey had a bag of sandwiches, and a couple of readable books that were carefully chosen to fly in sideways at a self-taught libertarian, sandbag his thinking a little.

Rain hammered on his windshield. He paused below the cabin because a cop car was parked next to the Studebaker. Jack Liffey waited discreetly for half an hour, but nobody budged, so he drove on past to take another look at the death site Roski had showed him.

He opened an umbrella and stepped out to investigate. The gravel wash was running half width with rainwater now. It would soon be full, and probably obliterate the crime scene entirely, but the ground told him very little except there'd been more digging. He'd watched Gloria work a crime scene once and been astonished by what she'd noticed. A square inch of tennis shoe imprint had got a killer caught.

Jack Liffey stooped at something shiny, but it was just a pebble. Life never tossed you a super clue unless you were a super sleuth.

In his experience, the only way to make a case was to stir the pot so hard that whoever you were looking for jumped out at you in a fury.

He wondered why he was putting so much effort into Ed Zukovich. Maybe it was because the young man was trying poignantly hard to find his way in a world that was beyond his resources. Jack Liffey was always a sucker for that.

When he drove back down the hill, the cop car was still at the cabin, so he drove home.

*

"Gus, it's the admiral's gofer on the line." Andor Reik meant the admiral's adjutant, a good friend of their family from back in the John Birch days.

"No names," Gustav said into the phone, and pressed a switch under his desk that automatically locked the double-glazed office doors on the business level of his building. The button also turned on a very expensive Chinese-made electronic jammer that killed every wireless signal within a hundred meters.

"Boy, howdy, this is for you," the gravelly voice said. "No hair and no horns left behind. The Navy is going to board your Sierra Leone ship before it gets to Iran. Some spook told them it was full of nuclear centrifuges."

"And when they find out it's only fracking and oil drilling gear?"

"It's still in violation of the trade ban, pard. I know your company is very, very patriotic about that."

What the hell was more patriotic than making giant profits off the towel-heads, for God's sake?

"We can't control what Nigerians and Syrians do with the tools we sell them. You hear me, spooks? And while you're at it, kiss your own fucking asses goodbye, because I can make sure you're stuck testing the temperature of the ice in Antarctica for the rest of your lives."

"Don't worry, my end is secure," the adjutant said. "Goodbye for now."

"Gus, it's me." Andor came back on startlingly from Omaha. How secure was it now?

"Yeah?"

"Don't be jumpy, bro."

Gustav hung up and switched to a new call.

"Ad, you shouldn't have been on that line. Forget it. You've got some work. First, get rid of the California chucklehead, that lawyer. Into the wastebasket of history."

"Can't our supposed friends stop the Navy searching our boat?"

"Hush now. The devil's runnin' up." He cut Andor off and leaned back in his Recaro desk chair, which had been rescued from a crashed Ferrari.

He considered his options. If the Navy was already steaming toward the *Kroo Sky* entering the Persian Gulf, it would be almost impossible to prevent a search. And the name Reik was plastered all over the oil equipment. But a lot of really big boys owed him.

Okay, let's see who feels froggy about this, he thought, as he punched a key that dialed straight into the Pentagon.

*

Late the next morning, Jack Liffey drove through the fire gate again carrying his picnic hamper with cold beer, ginger ale, two fresh meatball sandwiches, and the same books. He parked on the pad alongside the seasonal wash that was hard at work now. A big stream boiled angrily down its ravine, maybe two feet below the rim.

He wondered if the stream had ever flooded its banks—but the cabin was an antique and had obviously survived a century of winter storms.

Zukovich opened up after a knock, displaying a scowl. He was bare-chested in the cabin heat of the potbelly stove.

"Sorry to disturb your study, Zook. I brought beer and sandwiches and more books." He displayed the hamper.

"Are you fucking serious? You're way too spooky, dude. I don't want you here."

"Not as spooky as the cops. A big pal of yours?"

"He'd like to be. You didn't tell me the slope girl had been shot."

"Can I come in out of the rain, Zook?"

He still blocked the door. "You're suddenly an expert on what I want to read?"

"I did a lot of self-education myself. We're more alike than you know."

Disgusted, Zukovich threw open the door. "Bring the beer anyway. If it's cold."

"It's no big deal, Zook. I was just a guy like yourself, trying hard to figure things out."

"Yeah, yeah. Beer on the table. And why are you here again?"

Jack Liffey opened the hamper and took out the drinks, but not the books. "First, tell me why you're messing around with the cops."

"Fuck you, fuckwad."

Jack Liffey smiled. "Yeah, I knew your twin in 'Nam."

That silenced him for a moment, until he grabbed one of the beer cans. "Who's this twin?"

"He was an asshole that every officer and MP could play like a pinball. When I met him, I thought I saw a guy brave enough to speak truth to power, but he liked being their pal instead."

"Who said that about truth?"

"It's from the Quakers. But maybe you like being a cop's buddy too much."

The young man stared at him and seemed to make some inner decision. "Don't be so mean, Mr. Jack. Sit a while. You're a lot more interesting than the crater-face cop, cha cha cha." He found one of the foil-wrapped sandwiches and unwrapped it. "Ah, Mr. Torpedo." He opened the bun. "Mr. *Meatball* Torpedo, the best thing. This is from Ugo's on Ynez, isn't it?"

"Sure."

Zook was obviously very hungry, and began to eat at once. Jack Liffey sat down on a creaking lawn chair, relishing the warmth of the old Franklin stove. The rain pattered on the roof, roared for a while, then pit-pattered again.

"What is it I should tell power?" Zukovich said as he sat on his canvas swing chair. "And how do I get in touch?"

Jack Liffey smiled. Extra credit for a sense of humor. "That's your problem. I have no agenda here."

The young man still looked suspicious. "You're a funny old fucker, you know that."

There was a book on the floor beside him, and Jack Liffey glanced at it idly, recognizing the author's name right off: M. Stanton Evans. All those indelible names from his father's kitchen table rants—Philbrick, Skousen, Bouscaren, Bishop Fulton Sheen.

"I like stuff that's off the map," Jack Liffey said. "Sometimes it's really loopy, but sometimes you learn something."

"I like books that tell me what's going on underneath the media bullshit," Zook said. "I hate superior bastards lying to me and then going to eat sushi."

"Did you grow up in Monterey Park?"

He nodded. "It was already becoming chop suey town. Man, think of your own hometown and think of it turning into a foreign country before your eyes."

"I grew up in San Pedro, Zook. It was Yugoslav, Italian, Latino, Black, Norwegian, and Greek. *I* was the minority. A name like yours still feels like an ordinary American name to me. Roll call was Dragich, Mardesich, Zorotovich."

"It *is* American," he bristled.

"Say that in Kansas and see what happens."

The boy glared for a moment. "I bet you hang out with all the tame spades."

Jack Liffey laughed. "I hang out with a Paiute woman, son. What's more American than that?"

"Bet she plays your tom-tom in bed."

"Don't do that, Zook. That's my woman."

"Sorry, man, really. That was uncalled for. I know better than insulting a guy's old lady."

Jack Liffey looked into the boy's eyes, fresh and earnest. Was there any real hope? "Apology accepted."

"You want a doobie, man?"

He did, but it had been over a decade since he'd smoked anything. Rain rattled on a window like fingernails. "Maybe some other time. I've got to go soon." It was important to get out of there before the young man felt he was being crowded.

Wind wailed eerily in the eaves of the cabin.

"Whoa, you believe in Satan?" Zook asked, looking around.

"No."

"Me neither, I guess." He grinned. "But what if it's end-times right this minute?"

"Trust me. There's a lot to take care of before that happens. I'm going to leave you something—you can read it or not." He brought out an old paperback of John Berger's *Ways of Seeing*. A guy had handed it to him right after Vietnam and it had hit him like a mortar round. The book had made him rethink a lot. It was mainly about art, and the way art influenced the ways you looked at the world, and he bet it would come at Zook sideways.

"Zook, this book cuts into the lies people tell us all the time. Try the chapter about women. My card marks the place. Call me if you want to talk or if you just need a friend."

Zook finished off his beer. He didn't look happy. "Man, look. That book has an evil glow." And in the bright red pulse from the mica window of the stove, the white of the Penguin cover sure did.

Ideas always glow, he thought.

*

"Dad-o-mine, you've *got* to get a cell. I'll give you an iPhone for Christmas. I mean it. You're being an old fogey. Some fire department guy called *me* to leave *you* a message. I don't know how on earth he got my number.

"The guy said his name was Walt Roski and he needed to talk to you pretty soon." His answering machine read him the number, the same number Jack Liffey already possessed on Roski's card in his pocket.

"Wait," he said automatically, then realized he was only talking to a tape. He *was* an old fogey.

"Yes, I'm okay, Dad," her voice went on, anticipating him. "College is great. My friends are great. My painting is great. Well, it's getting better. Have you ever heard of a guy named *Swami* Muni? Don't get worked up. Just asking for a friend. Get a real phone, please. Bye." The machine stopped and whirred.

He wondered if there was any message she could have left that would have troubled him more? *Swami* Muni? He might not have worried about it at all if she hadn't immediately and transparently resorted to her emotional blackmail. He called her back, but there was no answer, not even a message bucket. Late afternoon. In class with the phone turned off—hopefully. Or maybe on a hilltop with this swami, waiting for the chariot of the gods to come pick them up.

How had Maeve become so impulsive? Was it his genes? He'd chased her down through a lot of open-hearted leaps, but he knew he finally needed to let go a little. And he had his own problems. Like Tien.

The next recorded call was Tien's voice. "Jackie, my great lover, I need you so bad. Why you always got a woman no good for you? I be too good." His hackles rose and he missed a few sentences as he raged inwardly at Tien for leaving a message like this on his home phone, which Gloria might easily have monitored. His skin crawled. Of course, Tien had done it on purpose. Poking a big stick into the passing spokes of his life.

"I hear maybe my niece-girl dead. You come see me, Mr. Big and Tough. Got to be. I expect you today. No telephone. In the person. We got to talk serious."

He was overwhelmed by a wave of tenderness for Gloria, and it felt so much like loss that he switched off the machine before retrieving the third call. He had to sit down to get himself together. Gloria had virtually ordered him to have an affair, but this wasn't what she'd had in mind.

After a while, he picked up the phone and punched in Walt Roski's number. He got the leave-a-message message.

"Walt, this is Jack. I guess we're playing phone tag. Please call my home number." He repeated the number. "It's got a nice old-fashioned recording machine with a tape in it. I'm here or—"

A *clack* meant Roski had picked up. "Hold on, Jack, give me a moment to clear some business."

"Sure."

Jack Liffey listened to the steady rasp in the ether, the abrasive indifference of technology, then Roski's voice came back. "Jack, I'm at the County Fire offices in City Terrace, a long stone's throw from your house. I need to see you."

"I know where it is. I'll be there—"

"No, not at the office. After 9/11, everybody's paranoid. You need clearance from God to get in. Let's split the difference and meet at the Mercado on First, the restaurants upstairs. *La Perla*. You know the place?"

"I could walk there if you give me fifteen minutes."

"Come on a skateboard if you want."

*

Thank whatever Mariachi god was in charge, the competing bands had ended their lunchtime sets and hadn't started up again. He was on the third-floor mezzanine overlooking hundreds of shops in the Mercado two floors down.

Jack Liffey glanced into the maelstrom down below—mobbed stalls of clothing, toys, shoes, CDs, and the magic potions of *botanicos*. The big-hipped waitress came and took his order for a Diet Coke and wandered off.

Before long Roski seemed to appear like magic, and sat down opposite. Jack Liffey realized for the umpteenth time that he wasn't really much of a detective. He hadn't even spotted Roski approaching.

"Hello, Walt. How about you tell me how the head of County Arson can't make a call to the gate to get somebody in."

He waved the thought away. "Let it go. I don't trust anyone these days. We've got a leak. Coroner data goes out to every sheriff's station commander and forty-six police jurisdictions. There couldn't be any leaks in all that, right?"

"I'm a helluva lot more interested in *what* got leaked than who."

The waitress came back with a Diet Coke and then suffered through an exacting order from Roski for any beer from Mexico that was in a glass bottle, as long as it wasn't Dos Equis or the surfers' favorite, Corona. He settled for an Indio.

"Your urgent news," Jack Liffey said when she'd gone.

"Wall Street is messing with our economy."

Jack Liffey made an unpleasant sound. "I think I've heard that."

Roski took two eight-by-ten photos out of a briefcase. "We heard there might have been a gunshot wound, so once the DNA test was positive, we went back to the scene and sifted some more. And we were watched over by a shiny-shoes from D.C. who called himself Smith. Hah. He's not my friend, I'll tell you that."

Roski laid out the eight-by-tens that had no need to be that large. The first was of a bullet that had mushroomed badly on impact. "A .45 caliber, a crappy garage reload that you can buy by the hundred at a swap meet in big plastic bags. Basically you use unjacketed reloads because you're an asshole and you don't care about degrading your weapon. And, oh yeah, you don't want to write your name down in a gun store."

He tapped the second photo. "This one is a piece of the frontal bone of a human skull. See the crack? They tell me it had to be a powerful blow, probably a bullet. Here's the rub: the bullet wasn't found under the skull. Probably in a shirt pocket, for Chrissake. When the science folks tell me the sun revolves around the earth, I believe them." He sat back and closed his eyes.

"Stay with me."

"You know what it means, Jack? Or *probably* means?"

"Please."

"We got handcuffs. A smashed skull. And maybe a bullet stuffed into her clothing, who knows why. This poor kid was killed somewhere else and dragged there."

They fell silent as Roski's beer came. A guitarist far across the interior space began tuning up and practicing, but the sound didn't invade their privacy. Roski seemed to want to relax, but couldn't get very close to it. He glanced at his watch, then at Jack Liffey's Coke. "You in AA?" he asked.

He'd told Roski most of it already, but the guy was lost in the null zone of his own troubles. "I got heavy into substances maybe fifteen years ago. I used to think I could mix it up with anything and come out on top, but it wasn't true. I lost a lot for it."

Roski stared into his beer. "Yeah. Iraq cost me a wife and two kids. I was in the Marine Reserves. We volunteered to be the guys they call up to protect the homeland if Canada invades."

"Walt, I was drafted to *invade* another country. Full of small yellow people like Sabine Roh." And Tien. "The only deal I had was being born in a country that never ever did things like that."

Roski nodded. "Somebody better be crying in Hell."

"You believe in Hell?"

"Of course not. What a stupid idea. Jack, I don't think I asked you here this afternoon to talk about a bullet. I asked you because I need a friend."

"Say what?"

"I know it's creepy. I'm supposed to be Mr. Tough and Competent. Most firemen are really good guys. But the guys who climb to the top…" He shook his head. "I go to lunch with my counterparts and they spend half the lunchtime talking about which is the best shopping mall, or arguing whether the Burger King Whopper is better than In-n-Out. After that, the inner life of my life seems to have crashed and burned."

A trumpet bleated across the mezzanine. Roski flinched and glanced around. "Ah, shit, that spooks me. Without calm-down drugs, I'd've been in orbit now. I'm a classic PTSD."

Jack Liffey thought of Gloria hiding her inner struggles from her captain. He stuck his fist out and Roski popped it from above with his.

"Homes." But Jack Liffey was thinking, why me? And a burning indigestion started up high in his chest.

"I could see you were a *mensch*, man."

"Don't go overboard."

Roski handed across a notecard with a hand-drawn map.

"What's this?"

"A favor. I had my staff find out where your loud South African lives. I think you told me you'd like another talk with him."

He hadn't told Roski any such thing, but he took the map, which looked a lot like the one he'd found in Sabine's room. Apparently the man wanted to use him for a little free investigation. They chatted a while longer, but Roski became increasingly self-absorbed, like a high-strung ballet dancer.

"I've got a wife to feed," Jack Liffey said. He didn't really want to add, but he did: "Let's get together soon."

Roski thanked him with a nod. "I've got a parrot at home to feed."

"Really?" Parrots seemed to Jack Liffey to have passed out of the real world into the world of Saturday morning cartoons.

"Fuck, no. I do all the squawking in my house."

FOURTEEN
The Social Presence of a Woman

The sensation of being lost was really only a game she was playing with herself in the desert stroll. Megan Saxton knew that if she glanced back across the weeds, she'd see Hardi's isolated house. She did turn for a moment and blinked, startled by the world's will to confute her. No house at all. Ahead somewhere was the dangerous border, so behind her had to be the house. But where exactly was behind?

She gave a single bird cry, as she once had at camp. Was she cracking up? She could do anything she liked here. She could strip her clothes off and laugh in the face of God. She did laugh, remembering the delicacy of Hardi Boaz's testicles in her hand. That a man so big would cry uncle if she squeezed.

Something moved in the dry grass, and she held her breath. Some ruthless drug-runner? A part of her knew it wasn't, knew it was just a breeze or a lizard or a nesting bird. She was playing with her fear, but she took the idea willfully and centered it in her head with the playacting impulse that seemed to have overtaken her.

"It's quiet," she said aloud. "*Too* quiet," and then she laughed. "Come get me." She brushed her foot noisily through the dry grass and there was no reply.

All the melodrama fed the mistrust she'd always harbored toward her mental faculties. She could never stay focused for long or think things all the way to the end, and it made her furious at herself and her parents' deficient gene pool.

Words were what she had and what she always came back to. Her diaries, poems, letters, essays to herself, and the A-list journalism. By unspoken pact with herself she did not look too closely at her words later, afraid they might not be good enough to make up for all the other failures. A haze in the air recalled summer days of hide and seek, and a burning smell evoked the taste of trash smoke, blue and damp and ashy. No, the sour smell was human shit along the cross-border trail.

"*Chuey. Tremenda cagada. El norte no es esta manera.*"

"*Lo sé.*"

Every hair on her body stood on end at the voices. It had to be drug bandits, armed and dangerous. She backed up a step, her eyes scouring the rolling expanse of shrubs. The faintest of breezes disturbed the weeds, the crazed womankillers behind every bush. She nearly passed out, and then she hurled herself out of her faint into a run northward. Her legs wouldn't work properly, and she veered left and right in the awkward gait of panic.

*

Ellen's cell phone chimed the Internationale, which about ten people in America would recognize. She was staying home, taking care of her little girl to give her mom a day off.

"It's me, Diana."

"Ellen?"

"So?"

"I know I said I was out of this, but Sabby's my best girl. I got some info on Zook. You want it?"

"Go on."

"This is from a nice old Chicana in the County Assessor's Office where they're digitizing all the property records. Luckily he's Zukovich, not Smith or Wang. She found me his family house on the north flats of MP, nothing special, but then she found something else. His family owns a cabin off a fire road in the mountains. It's just into the Angeles National Forest."

Ellen was thinking about the body Jack Liffey had told her was found up there.

"Those motorcycle asshats have been partying up there for years."

"Have you got an address?" Ellen asked.

"I can give you the GPS."

*

"I want you stay tonight, Jackie. You know it. I got business in morning but I can work it out."

He looked around her home with amazement. What was it that the French intellectuals called an event like this? An overdetermined conjuncture. Too many things shoving you toward the same thought.

Candles flickered everywhere in the room, come-hither lounge jazz was playing on an invisible sound system, and the table had a bottle of Cristal Brut Champagne with the cellophane still on it—plus, just in case, a bottle of ginger ale. To top it off, Tien was wearing a robe just translucent enough to taunt his imagination.

"Everybody's got business in the morning, Tien," he said. "If I stayed here tonight, my life would disintegrate. And don't phone my home again and leave a message like that. I mean it. If you do, you'll never see me again."

"Your life no good at all, Jackie. Too much pain, no joy. You one torment guy. You need me to make you whole new life. Now you just part of the *quan sat*."

That Vietnamese expression—a direct translation from the innocent American newsmen—had become a dark joke among the troops. Body count.

He wondered if he was just part of life's body count. Sometimes it felt like it. Wasn't that what Greek tragedy was? We're all guilty and we're all innocent because we don't have a clue what we're doing. *Quan sat*.

He noticed across the room that the giant viewstopper yacht was gone. "Where's your battleship?"

She shrugged. "Tax problem. I get some sea guys take her to Ensenada for a while. We say that her home. No tax."

He was sure she didn't know how deeply that offended him. He'd always paid his share without resentment—except for the part that went to wars and corporate subsidies. He'd been happy to build roads and give a little to the weak and unfortunate. I am the ninety-nine percent.

She pointed at a place setting across the dining table blazing with candles. "You sit."

He slid out the chair and noticed a small box wrapped with gold ribbon on his plate. Uh-oh. He'd been through this with her before, but it was clear she still felt she could buy him. He sat, wondering if he did have a price. A hundred thousand dollars? A million? Ten million? He picked up the box and reached across the table to set it on her plate. "No, Tien. We've been down this road."

"It nothing to me, sweet love. No pressures, no-no. That number ten."

He shook his head, but of course he wondered what was inside. A diamond as big as the Ritz? He might be able to pay for all of Maeve's college. "Tien, can't you see how this makes me feel?"

"You in bad way, I think. No big deal, Jackie. Small beer." She slid the ribbon off and handed across the open box.

How could he not look? He bent close to see a wristwatch in a velvet crèche. It was a gold Patek Philippe, with a diamond where the 12 should have been and only two roman numerals on the all-black dial. He could buy a Casio that performed a hundred other functions for fifty bucks, but he knew this absurd object was probably worth as much as Gloria's house, maybe more. What *is* my price? he thought.

"No, Tien. It doesn't work this way." He set the small box in the middle of the table. She didn't seem upset at all, and in the end her nonchalance was more attractive to him than the watch, though she would never have understood why.

"Forget watch," she said. "We eat." She headed for the kitchen, and he realized that for the first time ever she had no attendants hovering. Uh-oh again.

"You cooked this yourself?" he asked. She'd come back with plates holding two lettuce leaves with tiny squiggles of beige sauce on them.

"Not exact. But you lick your lips. Coming soon is slice of wagyu ribeye, wasabi spinach and har-lee-quin peppers." She'd said it all, as if she'd memorized the words, an immigrant waiter in training, but there was a catch in her voice. She left again.

What the hell, he thought. He could eat some caterer's best without obligation.

When she strode back into the dining room carrying the two dinner plates, her gown was open all the way down to the dark delta of desire. He could see that tears were running down her cheeks.

"You here right now, my big sweet love," she said desolately. "Can you keep me busy?"

It broke his heart.

*

Megan Saxton was about to crumple to the earth from the effort involved in running with her muscles so tensed up. Then she saw Hardi trotting toward her with an intimidating rifle in one hand, heard the steady clomping of his boots.

"*Mevrou*, get down!" he ordered.

She collapsed flat on the ground, gasping, and he sent horrible rifle shots in a steady banging out in every direction. Once, peeking up, she saw a little flame come out of the barrel. Then he waited, studying the terrain.

"¡*Venga matanza mí, pendejos*!" he shouted. "¡*Si tiene cualquier huevos*!" Come kill me, assholes. If you have any balls.

There was nothing but the rustling of breeze across the shrubs.

"You heard men speaking Spanish?" he asked softly, and she nodded.

He remained alert, but when nothing happened, he held his rifle with one hand and picked her up like a ragdoll with the other.

"I'm sorry. I'm *so* sorry," she said. She had little bluff left, she thought, feeling a primitive, numb shame that she was sure every girl would feel in the face of such power.

Her confusion seemed to summon the supernatural. They were abruptly surrounded by a whirring nimbus that shimmered in the air, creating a pocket of reddish—what? The atmosphere was molten, alive. Something grazed her cheek. The nimbus was giving off a hissing sound, some phenomenon that had to struggle to live.

She was absolutely alert in Hardi's arms, straining to understand, yet she did not want to understand too quickly. And then a ladybug landed on his shirt and she saw that it was a cloud of them, a swarm, many of them tumbling to earth as if victims of engine failure. She breathed through a slitted mouth, excitable, near some emotional blooey.

"Fear not, my woman," he said softly. "They just search for a new home, like wetbacks."

He carried her through the gate and into the house and then through the big living room with its horrible trophy collection of antlers and animal heads plus the one small orange beret on a hook. What was *that* about, she wondered.

*

Zook tossed a quartered log into the Franklin and bumped the fire door shut with his knee. He'd had canned chili for supper, and a hot dog grilled on top of the stove wrapped in a slice of soft bread. Jack Liffey's ice was down to meltwater and the beer was none too cold. He should put some cans out in the rain, which was roaring again like a good pushrod V-8 with a blown gasket, but he worried about two-legged predators coming up the fire trail.

He settled into the swing chair with the beer and the book the old man had left him. Jack Liffey had suggested he start with the thing on women. Within minutes he realized he'd never read writing like this—it surprised, jumping across gaps, forcing you to build your own bridges.

The presence of a woman is different in kind from that of a man. A man's presence is dependent upon the promise of power that he embodies. ... A man's presence suggests what he is capable of doing to you or for you.

By contrast, a woman's presence expresses her own attitude to herself, and defines what can and cannot be done to her.

Hay-sooze! He usually knew where shit was coming from or going, but not here. He pushed on into a way of looking at men and women he'd never thought of. It made him think of Sylvia, his spunky little sister who'd always said that he dissed her every time he opened his mouth. She'd fled the family for parts unknown.

From earliest childhood she has always been taught to survey herself continually. And so she comes to consider the surveyor and the surveyed within her as the two constituent yet always distinct elements of her identity as a woman.

*

Maeve wriggled comfortably on a floor pillow in the glass house on Canna Road that looked out to the whole Westside of L.A. She swiveled back to face the swami himself, who sat down comfortably in a lotus directly on the floor. He was in more characteristic swami attire: an orange robe with bare feet.

"CD number one was rudimentary. I don't want to drive anybody away. Evolving has to start slow."

"Explain evolving."

"Humans reached an end of physical evolution a hundred thousand years ago. We aren't going to develop another opposable thumb, or a blunt finger for pushbuttons. Any further evolution is going to be in here." He touched his temple. "And here." He poked his chest. "Both the head and heart are ninety percent unused."

I know where they are, she thought, but decided not to be hostile.

"There are generally three paths to enlightenment or evolution, but a few people in the Middle East discovered a fourth way. Madame Blavatsky, G.I. Gurdjieff, P.D. Ouspensky. I call this path *work* because it's not a weekend jaunt. Please shut your eyes and focus on the processes going on inside your body."

In for a dime, she thought, in for eleven cents.

His voice became a purr. "Maeve Liffey, relax and open your inner ears."

He told her that the first conventional path was the way of bodily struggle—the way of the fakir. He pronounced it fah-*KIR*. Those who took this path could develop amazing powers over their body: slowing their heartbeat, living without food for months.

The second path was the purification and stilling of the emotions— the way of the monk. The Albigensians, St. Teresa, the Buddha. He said he respected them all, but it had limits.

The third path was the purification of the mind—the way of the yogi or the way of Zen. Or in the West, the intensive study of philosophy.

She was tempted to peek at him but was afraid he was watching her like a furious animal.

"Our architects found the fourth path. You may have noticed that the other three paths require seclusion from the world, in monasteries or ashrams or libraries."

The fourth path had to be practiced in the midst of life, and it worked on all aspects of the human potential at once. But it could not be made explicit to the intellect. "You must discover it through work. That's enough tonight, Maeve."

"Oh, please."

"All right, let me offer you one more insight. You have a very tenacious and complex relationship with your father."

What girl doesn't, she thought.

"And you've had powerful transgressive relationships with both men and women."

A young man came in and disturbed them. "I'm sorry, Mahanta. It's time for the broadcast."

Outside the fancy house, Maeve was a bit unsteady on her feet. The rain was coming down hard.

*

They met for breakfast at Tia Chucha's in City Terrace, probably the roughest Latino area in L.A., maybe the roughest outside of Mexican cities under dispute by the drug cartels. Luckily very few bangers were up at seven. Jack Liffey was lucky he was up himself after a physically challenging night with Tien—and only because Roski had left him a beseeching call.

The night had been an emotional sinkhole. Jack Liffey had been out of control, and he knew he'd soon have to pay his dues for it.

Roski forked at a massive breakfast burrito of scrambled eggs, black beans, soft white cheese, chorizo sausage, onion, rice, fried potato, and green chile, all wrapped in an oversized flour tortilla.

Jack Liffey couldn't even look at that gut torpedo. He had coffee and a teacup portion of *machaca* spooned out of a big pot.

"I eat hard when I'm depressed, and I drink."

All around them, short brown manual laborers, born in rural villages, were grabbing a little food on the way to the tens of thousands of workshops that filled fifty square miles of flatland southeast of downtown L.A., the largest light industrial complex on Earth. Most had refried beans with a beer. He hoped to hell they had bathroom access at work.

"Sorry, Walt. I'm not a father confessor at seven a.m."

"Not required. I heard last night that my man Piscatelli is off the critical list. He's what they call guarded."

"That's a lot better than critical," Jack Liffey offered. "In my experience, critical means you're just about dead."

"I smell extinction all the time."

"I smell chili and beans," Jack Liffey said.

"I can tell you're not happy, too."

"Man, I was shot point-blank right over my heart in the L.A. riots and two little girls pushed me in a wheelbarrow to the hospital. I'm charmed."

"It's that kind of luck that makes me think you're somebody I need to know."

"I understand PTSD, man, but I don't know what I can give you."

"Want a bite?" He pointed with his fork at the outspilling burrito.

"Okay, to show trust in your cooties." He took a forkful of the mess and masticated it thoughtfully. "I think I'll let irony pass over."

Roski smiled briefly. "I need your help, Jack. Calling you was a distress flare."

"Do you want me to find somebody discreet to talk to? My wife has made me quite aware that somebody on the job has to be careful."

Roski sighed and seemed to untense a little. "Yes, Jack, thank you. I can afford a shrink. But don't *you* go away. I need an ordinary pal, too."

"Of course. But pros are better. Friendship makes things hard to deal with."

"At our age, lots is hard to deal with. I was fifty when the bastards sent me to Iraq for my third tour."

"No shit." They sat in silence for a while as several workers went out. "Can I ask one thing?" Jack Liffey said. "Is anybody on your side of the ledger looking seriously at those local bikers for the girl?"

"Those dumbbells? Really?"

"Dumb isn't always harmless."

"Thanks, Jack. I will now. The Feds are already looking at that strange South African guy down in San Diego."

"Why him?"

Roski seemed reluctant to speak. "Please be careful, Jack. I could lose my job big-time over this. The Feds say the girl was probably muling drugs across the border near this guy's house."

"Aw, shit."

*

Zook woke up, found a beer bottle near him with a swig in it and downed it, then made a face. Warm as spit. It seemed like the rain had stopped. He went outside to a bright icy morning, with a line of dark cloud on the western horizon that would be back soon. He washed his face out of a bucket dipped from the stream. The word bracing occurred to him. What the hell did it mean? The damn ice water was just plain horrible.

He used his propane ring to heat coffee instead of shavewater, the cowboy coffee his dad used to make. He'd tossed the grounds straight into a speckled blue enamel pot. While he waited, he started the Studebaker with a *grind-grind-BANG* and ran it for a while as he charged his dead cell phone.

Back in the cabin he had his bitter coffee, then Chocolate Trix moistened with water, very unsatisfying, and another hot dog wrapped in bread. He recharged the iron stove with pine and settled back into the swing chair with the odd book. He'd read the chapter about women three times and was pretty sure he was getting the hang of it. At the end of the chapter, he read it very carefully:

Women are depicted in a quite different way from men—not because the feminine is different from the masculine—but because the "ideal" spectator is always assumed to be male and the image of the woman is designed to flatter him. If you have any doubt that this is so, make the following experiment. Choose from this book an image of a traditional nude. Transform the woman into a man. Then notice the violence which that transformation does. Not to the image, but to the assumptions of a likely viewer.

He paged back to the photographs, picked a hey-come-fuck-me-big-boy nude and tried the experiment. It was too creepy. He tried to imagine a dude lying naked on a sofa, staring out at whoever like that. Straight guys didn't *do* that.

*

Gloria woke up with a jolt, her heart racing. She'd felt a big squirt of adrenaline spew into the organs in her back. She thought she'd even heard the *splut*. Whatever—she was instantly jittery and enraged.

Last night, very late, Jack had come in and showered, which was always a morning thing for him, not before bed.

She was pretty sure he was tapping ass. Of course she'd told him to do it, but that was a long way from him actually doing it. Jack! Against her will, she pictured his dick pumping in and out of an anonymous girl (young, thin, beautiful) and it tormented her.

Okay, woman, you're not a basket case yet. Think about getting out of bed, dressing, walking around a bit, maybe even forcing the stairs and preparing yourself to get back on the job. But the pain won out for the moment. Why *did* Jack stay with her? That was the mystery. She cursed him and ordered him around and still expected him to be a perfect partner. Nobody deserves the shit I serve up, she thought.

She tried to stand without the cane, felt an electric shock in her hip and sat back into the bed. It's only pain, woman. Weakness is not allowed in your household. She wanted so bad to get outside herself—this terrible hard shell she kept around her.

Jack was right. I need to talk to Paula if she's available. Maybe even Maeve. I do love that girl. Jack's indomitable issue. A very tenacious young woman with a strange aura of misdirected holiness all around her. Sort of like Jack.

*

After leaving breakfast with Roski, Jack Liffey realized City Terrace was almost halfway to Zook's cabin, so he turned north to the mountains. Zook and his dummies were connected to Sabine in some way. Or was it the noisy South African?

The rain started up again, but much of the night had been dry so the fire road might not be too sloppy. Driving up San Gabriel Boulevard, he noticed a full-sized animated gorilla outside a mattress store waving his arm at the traffic. Nothing special for L.A., except this gorilla's arm was on fire. The fur on the left arm had almost burned away to a wire armature, and a Chinese shopkeeper was on the sidewalk tossing a cup of water ineffectually at the fire. A faded sign in the shop window said, *I'm the Gorilla Your Dreams*.

And then he was past. He knew life never really seemed to settle into the rational.

The yellow gate was still unlocked, and he navigated the ruts and mud pools carefully. The fact that his pickup had high clearance helped, and he tried to keep one tire on the grassy shoulder.

The damn cop car was there again, this time blocking most of the road with the cop inside, so Jack Liffey noted the license number as he squeezed past and went on to the crime scene. He snoozed for a while in the pickup, trying to make up for a short and bad night.

He woke to a coyote yipping greetings from nearby. A blue heron glided in and settled into a big puddle to watch him warily. They stared at each other for what seemed an eon.

"Nothing to see here, dude, move along," Jack Liffey said.

When he figured enough time had passed, he turned the truck around and headed downhill. The cop was gone.

Zook opened the plank door right away. "Jeez, man. A guy comes up here for some thinking time and the place turns into a bus station."

"I'll take coffee. Tell me about your cop friend."

The young man seemed uneasy at the question but nodded him in.

"He's a jerk that thinks he's got a beef on me so he can wind me up anytime he wants. Like I give a fuck. I been in the graybar hotel. It's all fine." He handed Jack Liffey a speckled tin cup of coffee, probably the worst coffee Jack Liffey had ever tried to sip in his life.

"Why does he want to be in with you?"

Zook shrugged. "Because I'm cool. He probably thinks I'll be his fucking CI."

CI meant confidential informant. Jack Liffey saw the *Ways of Seeing* book propped open by the kid's reading chair.

"Did you like the book?"

Zook seemed to consider. "It blew me tight. I thought I had stuff all figured out, but…crap. Up to now it's just a party mix of all the jail philosophers."

"Who's that?"

"You know them. We're all just selfish cockroaches, looking out for number one. Kill the goody-two-shoes. *Oooh*, here's an idea. *Ooh*, here's another idea. It's the Tweety Bird philosophy of life. Jail shit is degrading to a thinking man."

"Nice description."

"I never thought of women like this guy does. It's weird. Who is this damn guy?"

"An art critic from England. But a special one. Try the last essay, too—it's about how advertising turns your head around."

"Oh, shit."

"Every once in a while it's good to rub against something different."

Zukovich walked a strange circuit in the room.

"We did this awful thing in the can," he said. "This was the real deal—California Men's Colony up at Obispo. We'd sit around and talk about our old ladies and what they was doing right that minute. It was all imagination and hate. Guys would get off saying, 'She's got five guys dicking every hole right now, including her ears.' We'd talk about how our old ladies always went for richer guys, or bigger guys, or stronger guys. Why do dudes diss their women like that?"

"You tell me."

He thought about it. "I guess they were all losers and didn't have no choice for a good woman. It's all a matter of the right personnel."

"Maybe it's a matter of what you value."

FIFTEEN

I'm a Mess

The map led Jack Liffey to an isolated ranch house in the scrubland east of San Diego, probably a half mile from the border. No cars were around, so he guessed Hardi Boaz was out on patrol or whatever he called it. There was a large desert tortoise at one side of the building in a pen that contained a waterhole and a little sun shelter, all enclosed by an ankle-high chain-link fence.

Jack Liffey wanted a glimpse into the house. He parked up the road and walked back. As he approached, the big tortoise headed toward him, swimming hard along the packed dirt, its legs making small scritching sounds in the quiet. He'd assumed these animals were stolid and even-tempered, but Jack Liffey was certain this tortoise was laboring toward him with murder in its heart.

The only uncurtained window was near the tortoise pen, and he peeked in just as the shell clanged into the wire fencing a yard away. Jack Liffey glanced down. The collision repeated itself over and over as if some gene had gone murderous in the tortoise. The hatred, or whatever it was, was awesome.

Inside, a man's living room, with mounted animal heads filling one wall. African animals mostly, so he knew he had the right house. Curly horns, straight horns. But his eye went to a trophy that sent a chill right through him. An orange beret hung on one of the trophies, and on another a straw farmworker hat. Trophies of human kills? What else could you think?

He heard a car in the distance and realized how exposed he was. Shit! Jack Liffey leapt the chain-link and hurried behind the tortoise's low shelter. The beast wheeled about and came toward him relentlessly, a very slow homing torpedo. Behind the shelter, Jack Liffey felt incredibly foolish.

A big Humvee parked in front and Hardi Boaz got out in full bush regalia, accompanied by a handsome, late-thirtyish woman wearing a button-down shirt. Something about her suggested New York and academia.

"I don't care," she snapped in a croak.

Jack Liffey watched them through his tortoise shelter without quite deciphering what was going on, as Hardi Boaz came around and slipped his arm up inside her loose shirt.

"Yeah, I want," she said.

"Can I hurt you?"

"Just a little."

Jack Liffey felt the tickle of a cough. Just then the sharp forward edge of the tortoise shell drove hard into the meat of his shoulder. He had to stifle a gasp of pain.

The animal butted into him over and over, its legs scratching away on the dirt like a mechanical toy. He could imagine the homicidal little eyes, and he wanted to pick the animal up and hurl it with all his might. Pain pulsed in his shoulder.

"Do it all," the woman bleated.

"*Dankie, liefling.*"

They went into the house and Jack Liffey rolled away from his tormentor, grabbing his wounded shoulder. The tortoise was already lumbering around to come at him again when he lifted one side of the beast with both hands. It must have weighed fifty pounds. Up in the air, two legs, neck, and tail worked at a steady cadence, fat metronomes. He flopped the tortoise onto its back, where it went on rocking as its legs worked against nothing.

Softly Jack Liffey said, "Fuck you, too."

*

Maeve sat scissoring her legs nervously off the cliff edge outside her studio. She was replaying the talk with the swami in her head. Human evolution or Looney Tune? He'd been all flattery...but, of course, flattery worked.

Weekend motorcyclists snarled along the roads below, Harleys and their Japanese copies. Heavyset bearded guys who fixed plumbing and installed kitchen cabinets during the week but on Sunday played Huns terrorizing the villagers.

Bunny peeked around the building at her. "You went to see the guy, didn't you?" She sidled out carefully and sat down beside Maeve, nudging up against her butt. "I'm not as worded-up as you, honey. I'm an actress. Mostly I say other people's words."

"Don't be so self-deprecating. You've got words."

Bunny hugged Maeve with one heavy arm. "Here's some words. A. Lincoln is on the five-dollar bill. And *a* Lincoln is a sweet ride. Tada." She kissed Maeve's cheek. "Please be careful of the swami, girl. I went a long way up his road, and there were surprises I didn't like."

"I'm just a student of the passing parade," Maeve said, intoxicated by Bunny's body against hers.

Bunny kissed her again. "Parade this. Swami told you that you have a really big soul, didn't he?"

Maeve cranked around to eye her but didn't reply.

"Yeah, he did," Bunny said. "You know what he means? He means you have really big tits. The swami may be holy as hell, but he's also a boob man. Start to worry when he goes, 'It's getting too warm in here.'"

"What are you telling me?"

"I didn't mind a little lookie-loo and even some nipple-sucking. I've never been hysterical about the sex thing, but it started getting to me, like—wait a minute. What's that little bitty dick got to do with my evolution?"

The mental picture was cheapening the swami and Bunny both.

"I don't know, I respect some of it. The sex was mostly charity. You've never given it up to a guy for the wrong reason?"

"Not that kind of wrong. I went head-over-heels for a gangbanger for a while, but it sure wasn't charity."

"We're different. I feel sorry for guys. They've got this thing about being in charge. That's why they drink so much at parties, you know—it's not to loosen *us* up. It's Dutch courage. It's such a relief being with you and escaping all that."

"I hoped it was more."

"Oh, honey." Bunny hugged her. "You're so smart and so dumb at the same time. Come inside and find out."

*

Jack Liffey had slipped away from the house to reclaim his car so he could arrive in a normal fashion. The beret he'd seen worried him, and he wondered how hard he could push this loud soldier-of-fortune.

Hollers and screeches came from inside. A real sexual ruckus, but he knocked anyway. After a while things quieted, and the man came to the door wearing a floppy Arab *jalaba*. The man still couldn't look him square on.

"Jack Liffey."

"*Magtig*. My fainthearted friend. You come to shoot some wetbacks?"

Hardi Boaz glanced at a door behind him. Jack Liffey saw a woman's bare leg kick the door shut. What gave him a real chill was the handcuff dangling from her ankle.

"Come out back. I get you any kind of booze."

"Coke?" Jack Liffey made a careful circuit around a softly gnarring Rottweiler and went out onto the fieldstone patio. Due south, well into Mexico, stark mountains all in lizard colors, gray and green, marked the horizon, wavery in desert heat.

The man brought his drink and handed Jack Liffey a little Coke bottle and a church key. An old six-and-a-half-ouncer from his youth. "These are from Mexico. The Mexes still use sugar instead of that shit corn syrup."

"You mean the Mexicans do something right?"

Hardi waved that away. "I'm getting tired to death of this fook-ing outpost."

Hardi's drink had a gin smell. He made some complicated pronouncement about holding off banditos and cartels. Wyatt Earp and Pancho Clanton. It had been simpler in South Africa.

Jack Liffey heard the patio door slide open and the woman whose leg he'd seen slipped just outside to wait in deference with her own drink. She wore drawstring pants and a t-shirt that said Iron Man Contest. The illustration was a man working at an ironing board.

"May I join the gentlemen?"

"Afternoon, my gorgeous. This good lady is Megan Saxton, a journo sent by the great *New Yorker* to write what a freak of nature looks like. This is Jack Liffey, whose life is devoted to finding missing children, a saint in our midst."

"Hardly."

"Do you know the Reik brothers?" Hardi asked him.

"Not personally."

"They been paying for the Border Guardians, but no money came this month. I wonder if they dumping me. Those *kaks*."

"You want help exposing them? You can signify by nodding."

"No."

They talked small talk for a while, but Megan said nothing. She watched Jack Liffey like a hawk that was about to pounce on something to eat. He remembered screeches and handcuffs.

Hardi said something about inferior races.

"Beating up your own blacks didn't work out so well, did it?" Jack Liffey said.

That touched a nerve, though the man's eyes still wandered. "*Ja*, sure, it breaks my heart. You bleeding hearts never understand that the dirty work of white people is not over yet. Ask this woman, she's felt the cock of a real white man."

The woman winced.

"Calm down," Jack Liffey said. "My strong-hearted friend, I need to know about the orange beret you have on the wall. You can tell me, or you can talk to the sheriff."

"The sheriff here is my pal." His voice was quite aggressive.

"No, man. The Feds can still deport you. A simple answer will do."

He stared into space for a long time, then shrugged. "I caught a pretty little Chink girl right out there packing cocaine north. About twenty kilos. She'd missed her pickup car, lost her water bottle, and had all her cash stolen by some coyote guide. She was amateur city. She wept like a baby and told me she was trying to save her parents. She thought I was *la migra*."

"What did you do with her?" the woman said, suddenly very interested.

He glared in her general direction. "Hardi, what did you do with the little bitch?" he asked himself, then shrugged. "I told her I'd let her go for a blowjob and her hat. She gave me both."

"Then what?" Jack Liffey insisted.

"The big Boer has a very generous soul. I drove her to the Greyhound in El Centro and bought her a ticket to L.A. And what thanks do I get? She spits on me. The ticket lady will remember me and her, you can check. The bus is in the poor part of that shit town that got no other part. Of course, I kept all her snort."

"Can I use the facilities?" Jack Liffey asked.

The big man thumbed to indicate where, but the woman spoke quickly. "My need is more urgent." She went inside.

"Why don't you get out of this crazy business?" Jack Liffey suggested. "You're not happy here. There's plenty of respectable security outfits. I could call a guy for you."

"I think I'll run with it for now. I like being an outlaw."

"The Reiks will dump you sooner or later."

"Maybe."

When the woman came back out, he went to the bathroom and found a scrawled note on the mirror.

Get me out of here! Please, I'm a mess. The big Joshua tree 20 min.

He snatched the note down. Every day seemed to take him right past something else that needed to be put right.

*

The house staircase was still an impassible cliff to her, so Gloria stood at the top landing hollering toward the front door, her cries muffled by the bandaging around her ribcage. Nothing. Eventually there was a phone call.

"Is that you, Paula?"

"I'm out front."

"Come right in and come on up. You're the best. Jack's out on his own job."

"I'm there, homes."

Gloria retreated to the bed in exhaustion as she heard the door downstairs come open and the heavy tread of shoes on the stairs. Paula was her best friend all the way back to the police academy, both early members of the brown-and-black club in the department. They'd both have flipped out long ago from harassment without each other.

Paula's short nappy hair appeared around the door. "You stuck up here, Gloria?"

"Can't help it. I'm old and raggedy."

"Girl, some decent guy comes around these days, I can barely get wet."

Gloria laughed and almost tore her chest bandages. "How's life in the Devonshire?"

"Mostly minor beefs. The murders all gang stuff. Yesterday I went out on an old man demanding that his priest marry him to his goat. I told the priest, why the fuck not if he can get the goat to say 'I do.' My captain promises I can finally have my promotion for a regular Tuesday date on my knees."

Gloria reached out and they held hands as Paula sat and offered a joint.

"Oh, thanks. Jack is so damn puritan."

"What's *that* about?"

"He had bad trouble back in the day. I swear the man's got discipline just short of God."

"Well, this is from God's own stash, girl, from a banger hanging outside Mary Immaculate."

"Open the window," Gloria said.

On the third try, she got the balky sash up. "Tell it, Sergeant Gloria."

As they smoked, Gloria got around to what she needed to say. "I was a big stupid, hon. Jack figured out about my date up in Bakersfield, and I got a really bad case of the guilties about what I'd been doing."

"Nuh-oh. Time for a bump." Paula brought out a second joint, waving the air to thin the smoke.

Gloria relaxed some after a hit. "When they make bud legal, I'm gonna buy a truckload."

"Go on, girl. Your guilties."

She felt her bliss evaporating. "I felt so damn bad about Sonny up there that I told Jack to go and have himself a slice on the side to get back at me."

"Word!"

"Shit, I didn't think he'd *do* it. He's so fresh and tight."

"What makes you think he took the contract?"

"We know, don't we? He come home late, smelling way too clean or hitting the shower right away. And he had some kind of bads inside."

"What he tell you?"

"I didn't ask. I didn't feel I had the right."

"Oh, girl. You got to make him suffer."

They both laughed and hugged for a moment.

"You know what worries me?" Gloria said finally. "Remember Joel Rothstein from the academy?"

"'Course. Who was it said every class always got one Jew to count the money on drug busts?"

Gloria waved that away. "Joey called me out of the blue yesterday. I think he was sweet on me in the academy. He's in the political unit now, and he warned me that Jack is messing with some crazy people. Mental cases training to shoot down black helicopters full of UN troopers."

"Lots of that hate around since Obama," Paula said.

"I wish I could make them all cry, girl. But right now I got to beg you to watch Jack's back. He's always trying to save their necks, these dickheads."

"I hear you. I'm way overdue for some time off."

Gloria wouldn't tell her directly to try to dig at Jack's sex life.

*

The Triumph of the Cowboy was supposed to be an exclusive watering hole uptown on the east side, specializing in comfort food like steaks and ribs but secure for the topmost skin of the Manhattan social fabric. The first person Gustav Reik encountered past the door was a man in a scarlet tuxedo grinning and holding out an oversized pair of scissors like a demented tailor.

"Hold still, sir, while I cut your tie off," he announced.

Gustav saw immediately that one large wall was hung with severed neckties. And everyone else in the room was sans necktie. Another joke of Andor's, not to warn him.

"Touch my tie if you want to die very slowly," Gustav hissed. He'd deployed his full aura of command about the $200 Ferragamo, and the scissor-man got it right away and left.

He took the tie off, and when his eyes adjusted he found Andor in a booth beside a redhead bimbo, body by Barbie. Gustav did not appreciate being summoned into a situation where he was out of place and unacknowledged. "Ad, I didn't know you were in town until you called. Please stay in touch."

"Sorry, Gus. It was a spur-of-the-moment thing."

"Honey, would you go powder your nose?" Gustav said.

Barbie drew back. "I don't need to powder my nose."

"Do it anyway."

She caught on, like the tie-cutter. "Sure, sure. Please don't just leave me here, Mr. Walker."

Gustav sat down in the booth, and they waited until she was well gone. "Walker?"

Andor shrugged. "That lawyer from the land of fairies is pissed about the South African speaker we sent him. He called me and threatened."

"*Threatened?*" That perked Gustav up.

"Sort of. Says the cops there are harassing him." Andor smiled. "We did fuck him over a bit, Gus, sending that colossal asshole."

He was in no mood for this. Their Iran-bound freighter had been boarded outside the Straits of Hormuz—ironically enough by the destroyer USS John S. McCain, named for a man who'd uselessly absorbed many millions of their political dollars. "People who want to ride with us better ride happy. I've already instructed Bernie to drop him. But did he make a direct threat?" Gustav Reik hated the vagueness that crept over his brother so often.

"He said something about friends in the press."

"He's history. I'll deep-six his whole district if I have to."

"You sure about this?"

"My generous period is over. I had to write off our cargo today—sixty million. Okay, it's not even real money. But we've got to stay on top of events; domestic politics is the key to our future."

Andor sipped at a reddish drink that this horrible place had put in a proper martini glass. "Bro, I've been getting nervous about things since the *New Yorker* and *Atlantic* started following me around. Don't you think it would be better to keep a low profile on this lawyer thing?"

"If you want to keep eating at the big table, Ad, indicate by saying yes."

"Settle down. Have a drink."

"Not now. I'll handle Mr. California. And you can go powder Barbie's nose."

*

The only Joshua tree within miles was a hundred yards up the road, and he found her sitting on a small suitcase, sort of behind it. Not exactly hidden.

"Oh, thank you," she said, lunging inside his pickup. "Go!"

"Was he holding you?"

"Not exactly. Have you ever been caught up in something that made you need a knock upside the head to wake up?"

He thought of Tien, of course. "I get it. The guy's compelling."

"He's a mile wide and I couldn't get around him. Just when you start thinking he's intolerable, he does something sweet. He's a bit off the track, too. Probably Asperger's."

"You came here to profile him?"

She made a sour face. "I screwed that up, didn't I? I hit the big time for a journalist, but I'm still just a farm girl from Iowa. When you get out of control, how can you know if it's just temporary?"

"Things aren't necessarily better when they're more intense," he offered.

She looked behind quickly to see if any cars were following.

"You're safe with me, ma'am. Megan? I won't even ask for your hat."

"Or the blowjob?"

"My life is complicated enough. And I used up most of my playground bluff on that big guy."

Twilight was just falling. "I'm glad you don't have to get hurt to prove some macho point to yourself."

"Me, too. Where do you want me to take you?"

"Any airport, thank you. Can I call you Jack?"

"Of course. Talk to me. Get the poison out of your system."

She stared hard at him. "Hardi's right. How did I blunder into such a saint?"

He shook his head. "You know what really makes a saint? A point of view from so high up that you can't make out the people down there. That way you can love them all."

She smiled. "I was such a dope, Jack. I've met a lot of men who fake a kind of stony, commanding presence. Gary Cooper, you know. I thought I loathed it all; I resented the servility of emotions they took for granted in me. But Hardi just walked up and blew all my resistance away."

"Why don't you try imagining him nude in fancy cowboy boots."

She stared hard at him. "I take it you're not available."

"You may not be able to see it, Megan, but I'm a bigger mess than you are. You prefer Linbergh Field in San Diego or LAX?"

*

Ellen hunkered down behind a trash dumpster in the doorway alcove of the Sweet Blanket Beauty Salon that was just across a shiny wet street from the Commando clubhouse. She'd seen Beef go in ten minutes earlier.

Waiting, she felt a pang of regret that her last encounter with Sabby had been a spat. "'Before we can forgive one another, we have to understand one another,'" Ellen had quoted Emma Goldman to her. And Sabby had gone off on her usual mania: "Not with Nazis, never!"

Ellen heard a *scritch-scritch* coming along the sidewalk. A weak streetlamp lit the drizzle that drifted into her alcove. Thunder rumbled in the mountains. Scritch. Scritch.

Eventually a shopping cart nosed into sight, full of trash and hung with plastic bags of cans and bottles. A grizzled black man in bib overalls came into view behind it. He'd almost passed by when he halted and glared straight at her like someone in a nightmare.

"Who dat debbil?"

She peered around the wheeled trash bin, the worst possible hiding place to avoid a scavenger.

"You wid de almon' eye dere!"

"I'm nobody. You can have everything in this can, sir."

"You tempt me into de dark? You for sure de debbil."

"I'm just a girl, sir." She dug in her jeans pocket and waved a twenty around the side of the bin. "This is for you." She scuttled out, set it down, and hurried back. "Please."

"I know your tricks!" he shouted. "Cotch up the next soul, debbil!"

From the depths of his cart he dug up a rock about the size of a baseball. He backed off and kicked a straight leg high as if a pitcher's moves were imprinted in his muscle memory. He fastballed the rock toward her, and she felt it skip hard off the lid of the trash bin. Then the glass door behind her shattered. An earsplitting alarm tore open the night.

*

Beef and Marly Tom and Sailor Boy Sallis had been trading turns at the foosball table. They missed Zook, but he hadn't been responding to his cell, and they were worried.

"Where you think Zook's off to?" Tom asked.

"We can kill one evening without the great Zook," Sailor Boy said.

"I have some 4-1-1," Tom said reluctantly.

"Go on," Sailor Boy said. "You're the only guy here who reads books that ain't got pictures in them."

Beef gave a resonant fart sound by flapping his underarm on his hand.

"The slope cunt that's been following us around and panting like a teacup dog—she went and got herself gone."

"Who cares?" Beef said.

"Manny told me the cops think somebody had his fun with her and killed her. They're looking hard at Zooker. We know Zook doesn't do shit like that so I say we got to prove him innocent."

"How?"

"I got a list of child molesters and weenie-waggers in town. We gotta find if any of these guys did the deed."

They heard a ruckus outside, a man yelling, and they cocked their ears. After a silence, glass shattered and a burglar alarm went off nearby. Beef sprinted straight out the clubhouse door before anybody else could move.

*

Ellen dodged and danced, confronting the fierce black man who'd decided to block her into the alcove. He countered every feint, his arms wagging.

"Oh, debbil, I got you in lockdown!"

"I'm not the devil, you idiot!"

She heard a door slap open across the street and the nightmare went into overdrive as Captain Beef himself emerged into the street.

She darted past the shopping cart and the man ripped off the do-rag covering her blue hair.

"Debbil!" he yelled.

"Stop there, Chinkie!" a baritone voice shouted.

She knew her town as well as anyone, and ran hard to the right, then darted into the East Pacific Bank parking lot and made for a far retaining wall. If she could get into the back streets, she knew every alley and hedge. She heard shouts and steps behind her, and the baritone seemed to be gaining.

She struggled over the wall and leaped down into a gated alleyway that opened on three apartment buildings with parking underneath. She ran for the electric gate at the side, but no one was entering. Voices cried out behind her.

The only possibility now was a constricted passage between two stucco buildings that she hadn't used since she was twelve. She made for it now.

"We got you, bitch!"

"Give up and we won't dance a party on your butt!"

She threw herself into the gap, so tight that she had to turn her head sideways and shove her body along, foot by foot, scraping dimples off the stucco. Claustrophobia sent a warning straight to some inner animal. If she freaked now, she thought, the fire department would have to demolish the buildings to drag her dead body out.

A shadow filled the slot behind her, a voice purring, "We could shoot you now, rice girl. But we get you coming out."

She pushed and pushed but wasn't even a quarter of the way through the slot. When the shadow behind disappeared and the taunts died away, she thought of reversing course. They'd never expect her to go back. The decision was helped along by gathering panic.

It seemed harder heading back, but she thrust with all her might, pressing her hands against the stucco.

"Dude, can you see her?"

"It's dark. Maybe she's stuck."

"Let's just shoot in there to make sure."

What on earth had got her trapped in this place, of all places? Following Comrade Sabby on her absurd crusade against these jackasses, of course. In the real universe, these jackasses didn't even count as compost.

She tried to calm herself by not thinking at all as she shoved herself along foot by foot. Then she tumbled out into cool air, gasping at what seemed a whole lot more oxygen. No pursuers were visible. She backed into shadows and then sprinted toward the electric gate as headlights approached.

SIXTEEN
Goods of Desire

It was a Hong Kong–style restaurant on the roof of a Chinese mall. The linen-table ballroom was half a football field long and deafening with the persistent rain, plus Chinese families yakking and laughing.

Jack Liffey and Walt Roski had been hit by a furious downpour just as they arrived between the curly-haired guard lions outside, clutching newspapers over their heads.

"So many worlds," Jack Liffey said at full volume as they were seated. "A few miles from here you can eat *pupusa*s and hear nothing but Salvadoran Spanish."

"*Sí*," Roski said gloomily. "What I notice is that these worlds don't mix much at street level. When I visited New York, it was different. Those kids who jump onto the subways to break dance for money, they were always Black, Puerto Rican, and Italian, one of each."

"Maybe it's cars that keep us apart."

"Maybe people just don't like each other very much," Roski said.

It appeared that the owner himself was approaching to serve the only white guys. He offered a menu the size of the Guttenberg Bible.

Roski ordered vegetables with elm and yellow fungus.

"Vegetarian?" Jack Liffey asked.

"My cardiologist told me it's heads-up time."

The man bowed away.

"You said something was up."

"Edgar Hoovers are in town in force. The handcuffs I found, you know. Kidnapping is an FBI matter."

Jack Liffey thought of the set of handcuffs he'd seen dangling
from a woman's ankle. He'd dropped poor, befuddled Megan Saxton
at LAX earlier.

"I've worked with the suits before, and sometimes it's hard to
believe they're human beings. Black fabric, shiny shoes, grim faces.
Fixed ideas and a mean cunning."

Jack Liffey sipped the dishwater tea. "Please explain."

Roski grimaced. "The Bureau's decided that eco-terrorists set
the Sheepshead Fire. That's their flavor of the month. Earth First! It
doesn't matter that it doesn't make a bit of sense. I tell them the fire
killed a Lefty girl. They say maybe she was setting it. With *handcuffs*
on? They wind them up in D.C. and plant an idea. The mouth just
moves on and on." He slapped his thumb against his fingers. "But
the ears don't work."

"Piquant," Jack Liffey said. "You seem to be taking this personally."

Roski made a crumpled-up face like a fist in a sock puppet.

"My wife used to watch Fox News all day, and buy these strange
publications they push. I come home and want to unwind and she
tells me somebody is flooding us with Masonic symbols on our
cereal boxes. Jesus, the judge gave her the kids. They're going to
end up wearing tinfoil hats."

"I'm sorry, man."

"Oh, they're smart kids—but what happens when they realize
their mom is a flake?"

The waiter brought their meals.

"You want me to find out where your wife went?" Jack Liffey
asked.

"Would you do that for me?"

"It's what I do," Jack Liffey said.

"You know, this case is up to us now. Nobody else gives a damn.
The girl was a Chinese radical, so fuck her."

*

Paula Green saw the two men coming out between the curly-haired
stone lions with the rain still battering hard. They paused at the edge
of the canopy, shook hands, and spoke briefly. One was Jack Liffey.

The other man she didn't know. Hard to follow somebody by herself in a messy storm, but she figured she'd try anyway.

The men went different directions and she had to choose. I must stand out like a unicorn in church, she thought. The large African American woman scurried across the roof in Chinese Beverly Hills.

*

Near the bar, two bearded guys about Jack Liffey's age had just jumped to their feet from easy chairs. They wore pricey polo shirts and were so tipsy they messed up a complex 'Nam-era shake-tug-and-hammer. They followed that with shoulder bumps like football players in heat.

Jack Liffey moved as far away as he could, carrying his Coke to the far side of the Tap Room of the Pasadena Langham, once the legendary Huntington Hotel. Tien had demanded he meet her here. Nobody else he knew could even afford the drinks.

"Oh, I don't know—your *left*!"

The bearded guys began stationary marching.

"But I been told

Eskimo pussy

Is mighty cold.

Your *left*!"

They seemed to run out of steam and settled again, and the worried-looking bartender relaxed.

The scene dredged back a memory he'd as soon have stayed wherever it had been stuffed.

Don't...you...smile, Liffey! I'll unscrew your head and shit down your neck!

Drill Sergeant Harrison in basic. Fuck you sideways, Sergeant. Bullying is just bullying, and it's not funny. Something was stirring up his psyche. Tien?

He watched gas flames lick over ceramic logs. No, it wasn't just Tien. For some time now he'd been avoiding something profoundly disheartening inside him. Maybe just drifting toward the final acts of his life, not sure he wanted to play out the remainder the way things had been going.

Whoa. Tien strode in, glorious in a black silk slit-up-the-side *ao dai*. No trousers under it. He'd never seen her wear one.

One of the drunks stood up. "Boom-boom time! You make ficky-fick?"

Jack Liffey got to his feet angrily, but Tien calmly presented the drunks her middle finger and strode past. Still, he continued toward them. She tried to stop him halfway, unsuccessfully. The honorable life required a little venom in the blood.

"*In*coming," the sitting polo shirt declared.

Jack Liffey arrived at their small coffee table with second thoughts about his rage. He'd almost driven his knee into the one who'd insulted Tien.

"Stand down, pal," Jack Liffey ordered.

"A fucking new guy checks in!"

"You can insult me all you want, but that was not acceptable."

The standee was so drunk he lost his balance and sat on his own. "Got it now, the slope's your wet spot. *Didi mau.*"

Incountry, you'd only said *fuck off* to dogs or Vietnamese, and only if you were an asshole.

The calmer one slapped the other backhand in the chest. "Sir, he doesn't mean anything. He lost a friend yesterday. We were just boots, three-stripers. All is respect. What were you?"

"Never mind what I was." Jack Liffey walked back toward Tien, who had found his lonely Coke by the fireplace.

"Oh, Jack, you so valiant. My honor very delicate. Those *hombres* just drunks. That not even got Alligator shirt. Bad copy."

He felt himself still breathing hard, and his chest ached with it. Indigestion? "What're you doing here, Tien?" he asked.

She lifted an eyebrow. "Business in Pasadena. Maybe I buy the city, maybe just half. This old hotel mighty good place for tryst, huh?"

He made a face.

"I got President Suite. Teddy Roosevelt stay. Come look at the view. Come play with me. I see you got tight windup tonight. Come relaxate."

"I don't think it's a good idea, Tien."

"It *my* idea. All my idea good idea. Time to celebrate."

"Celebrate what?"

"Big strong Jack and weak Tien. Perfect team. Hey, I got nothing under this *ao dai* but me."

He never had figured out whether she'd been a top-of-the-line hooker in Saigon to buy her way out, as she'd once hinted. His imagination was feeling her body beneath the silk.

"I know what you need." She reached across him and discreetly tapped his erection through his slacks. "We go up in lift now. Whole world is easy."

*

Ellen lay terrified on the metal floor of the windowless panel van that was hammering her hip. Her wrists were handcuffed behind her back, her ankles duct-taped together, and her mouth thoroughly muffled with duct tape that circled her head twice. The primeval feeling of helplessness pushed away any rational calculation. She'd started out trying to memorize the turns and straight stretches, from the spot on Baltimore Avenue where Beef had grabbed her, but her reckoning had quickly fallen apart.

The van slammed to a stop and she slid forward so her shoulder rammed a seat. A gust of wet wind blew in as Beef stepped out. He hadn't blindfolded her, but she couldn't sit up to see a thing. All she heard was drumming rain osn asphalt and the idling truck engine. Concentrate, girl. For all that white noise, the world was far too quiet—no traffic, no wind against houses.

The van rocked a little and the door slammed. "Stay still. Fun later."

He drove onto a much rougher surface and got out again. A squeal of metal. Closing a gate, she thought. A fire trail! Oh no!

"Stop squirming back there or I'll come back and paddle your ba-dink-a-dink."

She would have to gather all her wits to survive this. Ellen shifted around to resist being thrown back and forth.

The van slowed. "I said stop squirming. Am I making a mistake being kind to you?"

She bleated through the gag, hoping it would seem compliance.

After several more minutes of rough driving, he hit the brakes hard. "Fucking shit."

He sounded like a child balked. She heard a few thumps, maybe his hand pounding the steering wheel angrily.

"Zook, you ain't supposed to *be* here!"

He was silent for a long time, then got out.

"Sit and wait, girl."

She gave another mild bleat to appease the gods of the insane.

"Don't wander away." He leaned over the seat quickly and snapped her picture with his cell phone. He followed this by emitting a very male braying. It was profoundly disturbing but was probably meant to be a laugh.

*

She sat on a pillow and waited. Why was she doing this? She had a perfectly satisfactory inner life, she had her painting--and she had at least a semester before UCLA and her dad caught on that she was AWOL from most of her studies.

The swami's assistant brought a bottle of Amstel. "Enjoy. Evolve."

"Have you evolved?" she asked.

"It would be immodest to say."

"Does the swami like boys, too?" she asked.

His smile collapsed and he fled. The swami entered from too far away for him to have heard her impertinence.

"Are you comfortable? An ordinary Western chair can be brought. Minor things like that are insignificant."

"I'm a minor thing, too."

He made a palms-almost-together gesture of reverence, bowed slightly, and settled onto the floor. "Please relax. Open the direct passage from your ears to your core being."

*

Tien Joubert hadn't spent a lot of time showing him the view in the Presidential Suite.

"Just like that, Jackie! Higher now. You the best, the best, the best!" She emitted that amazing cry, a small, wild animal, and then bucked hard against him, almost chipping his tooth. He ended up on the floor, rubbing a cramp in his shoulder.

"Recharge battery now," she said. "Not so long, though."

There was a tangle of bed linen off the cushy bigger-than-king bed. There was also a .38 snub-nosed revolver within her reach on the head table—a first for the Presidential Suite? *Nothing*, she'd said. *Just protect from business that maybe go a little southern.* Her meeting was with representatives of a Hong Kong triad, he'd discovered. Jesus Christ.

But he'd been hibernating a long time deep in an emotional cave, and she sure could pep him up.

*

Paula Green ordered another diet Coke and sat back down in the isolated chair in the Tap Room. The ritzy place was jumping. She'd been hit on by two white-shoes hopefuls and sent them packing, and she'd had to badge a hard-eyed ex-cop from Long Beach who was part of the hotel's "security matrix," as he'd put it. It might even be flattering that they'd all assumed she was a trolling hooker.

She conned the desk into telling her that Jack had gone up to the Presidential Suite with a very rich Asian woman. Everyone refused to reveal the name, but Paula would find it out before she left.

It was possible Jack had taken Gloria literally about a fling, but Paula gave him the benefit of the doubt. He might be on the job here.

The Tap Room was filling up with affluent-looking couples, dressed down for an L.A. evening with their carefully laundered, torn-knee jeans, rock-n-roll tour t-shirts, and Prada tennis shoes. Bring it on, white folks. Me and mine dress up for real on weekends and dance to jazz and blues.

*

"Zook, man. We missed you."

"What you doing at the cabin, Beef?" Zook said.

The big man stood blinking in the blast of hot air coming out the door.

"Jeez, man. I thought we shared. All for one and all on one. I need the cabin for a date."

"Last time you had a date, you were waving your kielbasa at a room full of college girls."

"Don't be mean, Z. I got my date with me."

"I ain't going to no motel tonight."

"Zooker! I *need* the place."

"Good for you. This is my family's cabin. I need it for me. Ah, shit—you really got some cooze, take her in the back and close the door."

"Thanks, Zookiesticks. You're my hero." Beef hurried back toward his van.

A thinking man looked out for the ones who were a few marbles short, Zook thought. But his refuge had been wrecked for the night. He settled back in his swing chair and set aside the book Jack Liffey had given him, still fighting with the section on women. He wondered what sort of date Anthony Buffano could have mustered up.

Who would want Beef? Honestly. Zook was expecting a gap-toothed old skank who'd make him want to wipe down every surface she'd touched. But the date Beef carried into the cabin under one arm was a terrified young Asian with short blue hair, gagged with duct tape and handcuffed.

"Fuckin'-*A*!" Ed Zukovich leapt to his feet as Beef slammed the door. The big man was also dangling a persuasive-looking .357 revolver. "What the fuck are you *doing*?" Zook said.

"Mind your own beeze. And stay out of my grill tonight. You can have a turn later, you want."

"Not in this life, man. That ain't no date. You don't handcuff a date."

The girl squealed urgently.

"It's all part of the game. Don't be no slope-lover, dawg. I gotta do what I gotta do here. This the bitch been following me around wantin' it."

Zukovich knew he couldn't face Beef down, not when the guy had his hormones up. Just hit the road in the Studebaker now, Zook, and don't come back no more no more. The big guy had always been damaged goods. They'd known it all the way back to Macy

Intermediate, when they'd saved him time and again from his worst self—flashing the little girls, torturing pets.

An inner voice reminded him: You're a serious man, Ed Z. If you walk away from a defenseless girl, you're on the way to becoming an expendable fart on this planet. The serious man has to stand up.

"Girl, just hold on," Zook said softly, with more authority than he felt. "It ain't gonna be." This is maybe the fight you got to ride until the wheels fall off, he thought.

Beef kept redirecting the pistol in small increments, staring at it blankly then at other things in the room, no particular target in mind as far as Zook could determine.

*

Tien snored loudly, aflop beside him. He was pleased to have worn her out, but he had very little energy reserve himself. There was a burning in his chest under the sternum and Jack Liffey lay very still willing it to subside. Probably the French onion soup.

He rolled to his side and looked out the curtainless window. The rain was on pause, and southeast a million crystal-sharp points of light stretched away for miles. Pinholes through the skin of the city to the white-hot reality underneath.

Tien's sleep t-shirt hung over a chair. A monogram said G.O.D. He'd asked about it, expecting a religious joke, but then wished he hadn't asked. Goods-of-Desire—an import company she owned, but really it was Hong Kong slang for the massive Chinese industry of counterfeiting Western luxury goods. Fendi, Louboutin, Balenciaga. Corrupt army officers ran the plants, but the triads ran the export. Tien had said she hoped to be their outlet for much of North America.

She'd told him she wanted to become the world's first Vietnamese billionaire. But if she put her foot wrong, she might end up a cardboard box of truculent ashes.

*

The swami's mesmerizing voice was well into his spiel and Maeve followed his instructions—closing her eyes, letting her mind drift.

"The reconstruction of memory happens faster than thought, faster than reality even formed the memory."

Maeve's mind drifted away to worry about Gloria and her dad. You could only stay focused so long.

Suddenly his hand rested high on her thigh and she was back in the mundane present.

"Are you comfortable, Maeve?"

"Tell me what to do to become comfortable." This was the test. Bunny had warned her about.

"Your jeans are far too tight to sit like that. Loosen the top button."

She popped the button, and then undid a button of her blouse, too. How absolutely crass.

"If you're warm, you should take off your shirt," he said mildly.

She opened her eyes and saw him staring hard at her breasts. "Sir, you can help me evolve or you can play with those. It's your choice."

*

Paula Green had a clear view of the elevators from the bar. It was approaching midnight and she felt her stakeout determination weakening. She'd be thrown out of the bar at two a.m., and she wasn't going to spend the wee hours in a rain-drenched bush.

Abruptly an elevator slid open to disgorge Jack Liffey. Don't stop for a nightcap, please. There were only two others in the bar.

Disheveled, he hurried right past the Tap Room. She was astonished to see he was weeping like a child.

SEVENTEEN
Danger is Simpler than Life

Ellen drew her body into a fetal position on the cabin floor. It was the thunderous gunshot nearby that had prodded her. The dogboys had been snapping and barking at one another, testosterone overload, when it happened. Upward she saw a ragged hole in the roof the size of a fist. Rainwater was coursing through the gap to splash the floor near her.

This was a hell of a cloudburst, a real storm-of-the-century, she thought, trying to find something she could concentrate on to calm herself. The trembly panic was impossible to control.

Ellen wriggled around to watch the big guy. That type seemed to be all over the landscape in America, big-boned and red-faced, with cold, piggy eyes. They had no inner reflection, and they always hated women.

"Shut up, Zook! Just shut up!"

"Look wat'cha done to the roof! You never had any sense! All the way back when you was on double Ritalin."

"Zookers! You're my only friend!"

"Give me the gun. I'll trade you for a beer."

"I got to protect me tonight. They're after me!"

"*They* is…?"

"I seen cops looking at me."

"Everybody looks at you, dude. You're a guy people look at."

"Well, let Miss Kung-fu look at this."

Ellen heard a zipper and screwed her eyes tight. Oh, no.

"Beefer, mellow out!"

She felt a kick in the back and gave a muffled yelp. "Open them slant eyes, fortune cookie. You ain't never seen this on no bamboo guy, I promise. Open or I kick your head."

Rather than get kicked again, she opened her eyes. Antonio Buffano stood astraddle her, waving something out his fly like a foot and a half of limp pink fire hose. No wonder he had a rep. It just wasn't possible for a human penis; it was some freak of nature, a repulsive mutation.

He haw-hawed away. "She can't believe she gonna get the big beef injection."

"Later for sure. Here's a beer, B. Give me the damn gun and climb off your horse."

"Back off, man!"

She heard another earsplitting gunshot and clamped her eyes tighter, hoping against hope that the smaller one hadn't been shot. A scream of pain disabused her.

*

Seth Brinkerhoff, wearing silk pajamas, stood dazed in the downpour in front of his house. His wrists were manacled behind him, his bare feet freezing. "Look, I'm an attorney. I want to see the warrant again."

"You saw it, *puto*. You have the right to remain silent. Use it."

Four officers from the San Marino Police Department in rain overcoats had forced his gate and then burst into his big Spanish Revival home, while two others shoved him outside into the rain. He was soaked and very annoyed.

Seth had looked first for the judge's name. David Corbett, okay, and the signature looked legit. He'd read as far as: *Affidavits having been made before me by*—some name he didn't know—*who has reason to believe that on the properties*—when they'd yanked it away.

"You're messing up, Sergeant. This'll be thrown out as illegal search if I can't see the warrant."

The cop with the flat nose reluctantly unfolded the warrant from his coat pocket. But they were interrupted by an officer hanging out the front door.

"We got it, Sarge. Cowabunga. Bring the suspect in. Let's make him step in his own shit."

They all trooped to his study, where a semicircle of cops were tutting and ogling his computer screen. It took him only a few moments of shock, staring at unspeakable photos of child pornography, to realize what was happening to him.

"That's planted," he said evenly. The only question was whether they'd planted it themselves, just now from a thumb drive. Or maybe it had been insinuated into his cloud account by a good hacker.

"Sure," Flat Nose said. "Every swinging dick in prison is innocent. You're the worst kind of scum. Everybody hates a short-eyes. Where you're going, don't bend over for no soap."

There was going to be a lot more humiliation like this ahead, Seth realized. Insinuations about being single, the contentious divorce, maybe even the black hooker he'd picked up five years ago.

"I want a lawyer. I'll call him now."

"Not from here. Don't touch a damn thing."

They frog-marched him outside. Of course he realized who had set him up—and if so, it was all going to be watertight. It was virtually impossible to fight the fifth and sixth richest men in the United States.

*

Jack Liffey sat on the glide on his porch, after a half hour sitting disconsolately in his car in the driveway. A sheet waterfall streamed off the roof onto the scraggly grass to flow down to Greenwood. He'd had to drive home cautiously through the swamped streets even with his high clearance.

Sweep me into the L.A. River and then out to sea, he challenged the gods. What would he say to Gloria when he finally went into the house?

Remorse does strange things to you, he knew.

Okay, let's go. He unlocked the front door. "Glor, I'm home!" And I sure got a lotta 'splainin' to do. She was usually up till three or four, but he heard nothing from upstairs.

"Gloria!"

Still nothing. Okay, she was pissed.

He mounted to the second floor just as lightning flashed outside and then rumbled. Loco charged past him, heading for some deep refuge. Abandoning ship, eh, Jack Liffey thought.

He opened the door to the bedroom and saw she had only the nightlight on. Gloria was quite still, a long shadow of mounded-up covers. He knew she wasn't asleep. In sleep, she purred and wheezed at least.

"Glor, I'm here. Do you need anything?"

No reply. There was a faint photoflash through the curtains, far away. Grumble.

"I have something to talk about. It's not a good time for it, but it never is."

He sat gently on the corner of the bed, careful not to touch her shape under the covers. "Are you okay?"

He waited. Nothing.

"All right, it's a rough life."

Pause.

"I'm afraid I have a confession, hon. I won't hem around. I'm sorry—I know you told me to go have an affair, but honestly I started before you said that. It just happened. I guess everybody says that." He winced, waiting for a domestic lightning strike.

Nothing.

"This is such a soap opera situation. I don't know how to escape it. It was that Vietnamese woman I told you about long ago. She's so different from me it unlocks something. Maybe that's what you felt with Sonny. No, I'm not blaming you."

Pause.

"Okay, I know you're pissed. I better say it all. Here's the worst part. The pull is terrible on me and I don't even know if it's over."

Pause.

"Please talk to me, Gloria. This is hard, and I love you very much."

A powerful fizz-bang detonated close by, the flash filling the room briefly. Everything inside him was roiling. Against his better judgment, he reached out to rest his hand on her hip. Inner shock jolted him as he fell through her heaped-up blanket. He hurled the cover back and saw only sheets. Damn. Now he'd have to do it all over again.

He made a cursory search of the house—she wouldn't be hiding in closets, and her little SUV was still immobile at the top of the driveway, one tire almost flat. Had Sonny come to claim her?

At last he found the note on the fridge. The childish block letters weren't Gloria's.

Jack Dont worry Im taking Gloria out for a beer She needs a break Paula

He felt himself deflate, and the release of all that pressure revealed that the indigestion was still with him. Have to find some Tums.

The phone ringing just about sent him off the ground.

"Where the hell are you?"

"Uh-oh." A man's voice. "One problem inserts itself into another," the voice said. It took Jack Liffey a few moments to recognize Walt Roski.

"Walt, it's okay. Really. What's up?" He tried to refocus. They were approaching what they called the hour of the dark night of the soul, the hour of the gun-in-the-mouth. It was 1:15.

"I just got some information about the girl, and I'm afraid the rains are going to erase the heel of the fire forever. Can you help me? We can still get there if we hurry."

"I'm your man," Jack Liffey said wearily, not feeling at all like his man.

"Meet me at the fire gate."

"Twenty minutes at most."

*

"How you doin', hon?" Paula asked.

"The ribs are not happy," Gloria said, dealing with the physical pains of her first car trip in months. "And that other thing's no fun."

Paula had told her about Jack and the Vietnamese woman. They sat in the drumming rain, looking out over the wilds of a park at the edge of the mountains, only one live soldier left in the last six-pack.

"Sorry," Paula said.

"Don't bust on me, girl."

"I ain't, hon," Paula said. "I bet you worried that you told Jack to go do his bone."

"I heard him talk about this woman before. Long gone, so he said. Hah. A hot prick-slayer as rich as two Donald Trumps."

"You the hottest prick-slayer of all time, girl. Stop beatin' yo'self up. I know Jack loves you. But I seen you push him away."

Gloria swigged more beer. "Let it go. I don't know why I do what I do. He says he loves me. It scares me to death."

"Get unscared quick, hon. Jack is swimmin' on the loose, and this Vietnam woman got a big ol' fishhook stuck in him. He came down from the penthouse crying like a baby."

"Can you make it a little less real?"

Paula shook her head. "No, I won't. You need a cold shower. Jack's a good man and you went and runned him around the ol' green devil with yo' own fun. You ain't got no maidenhead left to trade for. I only wish I ran into a Jack for me. I grab him quick."

Paula's cell phone rang in a little hip-hop beat. She answered, "This her. Paula Green, yeah." Her face went through about twenty changes as she listened.

*

For some reason the gate had been standing open in the furious downpour when he arrived. Despite Roski's annoyance at waiting forty-five minutes past the "at most" and Jack Liffey never showing up, he was pleased that at least he didn't have to get out of the Jeep Wrangler to unlock the gate. It had become the sort of bucketing rain that would soak you to the skin in a few seconds.

He yanked the lever for four-wheel and low axle, and then ground up the trail that was running with several inches of water from one side to the other. Even with four-wheel, the car squirted left and right.

True white-knuckles driving in the dark, relying a lot on the rally lights on the rollbar over the cab. Even the wipers were having a hell of a time keeping up in the worst volleys. He couldn't really remember a rain as heavy as this. The media would be full of record blah-blah in the morning. Not seen since blah-blah. Blah-blah people were killed. He hoped not, but people always wound up swept down the storm channels, with firefighters chasing them from bridge to bridge with nets and ropes.

A lightning bolt seemed to hit the mountainside not far to his right, the flash revealing his surroundings. He counted. At thousand-three, the crackle-rumble rolled over the car. Half a mile.

*

"Beef, listen to me. You on angel dust? You got to be yourself." Zook clung to his own right arm where he'd been slightly gunshot, more or less by accident. Beef had sheepishly helped him wrap a t-shirt around it, though it still dribbled blood.

Zook thought of grabbing the gun away, but he couldn't take the chance. There was a dangerous glitter in Beef's eye tonight, and the guy was stubborn as an anvil.

The girl lay at their feet as they argued. Zook had no armament available except the reasoning of a thinking man. He told Beef that women were people just like men, but sort of underdogs in the scheme.

The storm blustered, hitting with bursts of four and five lightning bolts. Now and again they heard a rapid clatter on the roof like golf balls. Hail. One flew in through the hole in the roof and bounced a foot off the floor. Zook went on telling Beef about how men made women look at themselves with male eyes as he kicked a big metal washbasin under the leak.

Beef's eyes seemed slyly confused, and he still flapped the pistol around. Zook knew he had to get the pistol away.

*

The swami was weeping with his forehead chastely on her knee, and she wanted to jump up and flee, but a more generous nature held her back. We're all weak, after all.

"It'll be all right."

The man said something in another language—Hindi? She rested a hand lightly on his hair, but yanked it away at the greasy feel.

A zigzag of lightning out the window burned onto her retinas. L.A. wasn't much prone to thunderstorms.

The man sat up, the mortification in his face so total that she couldn't bear to look at him.

"I thought I'd reached an important juncture, but I may not be there."

"We're all human, sir," she said.

"Higher evolution requires extreme discipline," he gasped out.

Another glow-flash from the mountains far to the east.

"Mahve…"

"*Maeve.*"

"I truly want to teach you, but I find I want your body with equal fervor."

"Let's not spoil things," she said.

His nose began to run and he rubbed it on his sleeve. She began to suspect he was on something like coke.

"At some point in the process you have to surrender everything, even the wonders of your body," he said.

"Surrender to whom?"

"To your own glorious future, my dear." His eyes were fixed on her, but only with his own hunger. She guessed even his chagrin was faked.

"I wonder if this is a moral problem or a scientific one."

"I don't see a problem, only resistance," he said weakly.

"I see bad faith. But I can make it simple." She undid her blouse, thankful she'd worn an opaque white bra. "You can play with my breasts, as I said, or you can choose to guide my evolution."

*

Roski braked as he reached the cars stopped at the cabin. His rally lights showed immediately that the small bridge beyond the cabin had been swept away, and the angry cascade was frothing just below road level. He'd get no farther tonight.

One vehicle in the road was a panel van. Behind it was a beige

Chevy Caprice. The dome light in the Caprice came on and a short, stocky man got out wearing police gear with a transparent longline over it. An acne-scarred face came into the throw of the rally lights as he approached, and Roski felt sympathy immediately. The Zapata moustache hid nothing.

He walked back to Roski. "You look official."

Rolling his passenger window down admitted a spray of rain. Roski didn't feel compelled to identify himself, but he did.

"I'm an arson investigator with County Fire. Walter Roski. Who are you?"

"Sergeant Manuel Acevedo, Monterey Park P.D. Manny to you."

"Climb in, Sergeant. The rain is terrible."

The man shrugged, as if nothing as insignificant as rain bothered him, but he got in. He hadn't shown a badge, but Roski believed him. That deeply entitled police belligerence was hard to fake.

"You're out of your jurisdiction, Sergeant. I take it this is sur-veillance."

"I got reasons. And you're here because of what?"

After months of despondency, part of Roski wanted to get into a dick-waving contest with this absurd character. Any worse and he'd be past caring at all.

"My crime scene is three hundred yards up the road, where a Chinese girl died in the fire. I'm obviously not going to get there tonight. In fact, we're both in danger right here. The burned-over hills up there are pretty iffy in this weather."

He saw the policeman glance at the creek, then the hill and take in his conjecture about landslide. Boiling, dirt-filled water was just below the road, teasing above it with trees and brush. They said it wasn't the height of the water as much as the speed of its rise.

"You think it's gonna let go?" Acevedo asked.

"Who knows? It could take out half of San Marino down there, but if people insist on building houses in the debris zone, screw 'em."

The cop caught his what-the-hell tone and stared. "Most firemen I ever met is goody-two-shoes, but not you. Hear what I'm sayin'?"

"I'm in a bad mood, Sergeant. Can you tell me who your surveil-lance is about?"

The cop gave an odd little shoulder roll like a boxer freeing his joints to fight. "You know who owns the cabin?"

"I've met some of them. Bikers. I had to tell them to hold their parties down."

"So should we warn these skells to get the hell out of here?" Sgt. Acevedo said. "The FBI came to see me today and told me Chinese eco-terrorists are planning to bust a cap on everybody, even Mickey Mouse."

Roski took in a deep, slow breath. And the Earth was flat, resting on four elephants on a giant turtle. What was below that? Turtles all the way down.

"You can forget that, Sergeant. The Chinese girl who died in the fire was planning to become a nun. One of these bikers might even have killed her."

The car was rocked by a squall so intense it felt like an ocean had dumped on them. Acevedo's eyes went to the windshield as if the glass might crack in the downpour. "You got evidence of that or you just winding me up?"

"Nothing for a DA yet. Look, the Feds decided to go after terrorists; that's what they do. If you're a hammer, everybody's a nail."

"That doesn't mean shit to me."

"The Chinese girl was handcuffed and we've got one of her skull bones with a bullet wound. It's possible the whole damn fire was set to cover up the murder. And I think—no proof—that somebody raped her before she was killed. Any guesses?"

The policeman went silent. Where the hell was Jack? Roski wondered. He needed Jack's stability and perspective.

*

"I got to have my fun!" Beef complained.

"Dude, you're my oldest friend, but I gotta tell you, your pro-clivities tonight come as a surprise," Zook said.

"What the fuck's 'proclivities'?"

"What you want to do."

"There it is," Beef said petulantly. He kicked at Zook's books on the floor. "I got my own dealings in life. I don't just do what you tell me."

"What are your plans for the girl?"

Please don't ask! Ellen thought. She saw that the sane one was still bleeding.

"Zook, she's a Chink. Who cares? I caught her watchin' me and I gotta teach her a lesson."

"Attractive in theory. But you know, dawg, kidnapping is a federal crime."

Ellen was attending very closely. Beef didn't even seem to hear this other guy.

"I got my dreams, too, Zooker." He leaned forward to stare down at Ellen, which made her glance away. "I bet this one's real smart, like all the slopes. We know smart girls just love to fight a while and then give it all up."

"I think it's problems of scale that are making your heart go pitta-pat, Beef. Really small openings, so to speak. Orifice disproportion, we say in philosophy. I didn't open the cabin door to lay down my good and let you take us to federal prison."

The discussion grew belligerent again. Ellen wanted to retract into her fetal position, but decided not to budge. She'd been unobtrusively twisting in the handcuffs for some time. Her hands were slim and she had a double-jointed thumb, but she hadn't done much more than chafe her wrist.

"Zookie-man—"

"*No*, Beef. This is mad bait. I'm not going to no jailhouse over this."

The gun started wavering toward him again.

"Gimme the piece, dammit!"

Ellen watched Zook thrust his hand out flat toward the gun. She tugged harder at her wrist and almost yelped with the pain. "I mean it! Don't throw your life away for one night's fun. I'm a serious man, and I'm on your side."

The deafening blast could have been a bolt of lightning, but it wasn't.

"*Asshat*! Jesus Christ, you shot me *again*!"

Ellen watched Zook squat down and mash his hands against his bleeding tennis shoe. One really big tug-and-twist got her wrist an inch toward freedom.

*

By two a.m., nine inches of rain had fallen in the San Gabriel Mountains over twenty-four hours. A mile east of Sheepshead Canyon, where the blaze had started twelve days earlier, angry froth boiled down all the watercourses. The roots of burned-out sagebrush and buckwheat offered little holding power as the sandy, granitic soil became oversaturated. Organic sediments leached away first, leaving only slippery grains of silica.

An undercut cliff gave way a few inches at a budge until the remains of a pointy yucca tumbled into the stream to carry downwater like a spinning ball of razors. A crack yawned open, and a surviving clump of beavertail cactus slouched toward the stream, pushing along the earth below the crack. In the fissure, exposed to the air for the first time in an eon, a boulder the size of a bathtub suddenly broke free and took a ledge of earth into the water with it. The boulder tumbled twice to gain maybe fifteen feet in its million-year march to the sea. An even larger bank nearby began to slump, just as a ragged collection of lumber from a former structure swept by.

A rumble announced something very different upstream, and the water level in the wash began to diminish.

*

Paula's car came to a stop at the open fire gate not far from where they'd been girl-talking. Water flooded out. "Damn, the Chatahoochie in flood! I don't know about this."

The beer overdose had turned her relatively mellow, and Gloria readjusted herself to relieve some of her hip pain and look out. In the headlights, she could see water sheeting out of the fire road into the street, carrying gravel and dirt with it.

"We ain't equipped," Gloria said. Paula was driving a Honda Accord.

"I'm on it." Paula smiled. "Danger a lot simpler than life."

"It's why we're cops. How'd you hear about this place?"

Paula raised her eyebrows. "Good friend in the state bureau. Sorry to tell you, girl, they're camped on your telephone. He say two hours ago Jack got a call from the arson guy and they agreed to meet right here."

"Okay. Jack says so, he'll do it. They must've went up."

"You good to go?"

Gloria pointed up. Paula drove straight into the exit flow of frothy muck and water. The car began wheelspinning and fishtailing as she accelerated and steered madly.

*

Avulsion, the process was called. A seasonal flow had come down the same canyon intermittently for centuries, even millennia. Suddenly it dumped an impenetrable dam of rock and earth across its course. A new lake swelled behind the dam, until somewhere upstream a hunting finger of water would find a new escape from the lake, perhaps a similar watercourse abandoned when the mountains were young. Water would escape down the old/new course.

This creek would soon avulse as water built up against its fresh haphazard dam—mud and stone, a rusted water tank, a crushed cabin, a 1950s Mercury, and a lot of trees. Had a geologist been standing there watching, he'd have noted with alarm what was happening, but he wouldn't have known which way to run.

*

On Red Oak Drive, a quarter mile from the fire trail, Jack Liffey's old Toyota pickup seemed to have drifted into the rear of a parked Mercedes. The Toyota's engine was still running, chugging and rocking as it began to weary.

Jack Liffey sat in the driver's seat, his face frozen into a rictus of pain as his right hand clutched his left shoulder. Eventually he came to life, aware that he'd probably been somewhere else for a while, but not for how long. He opened an eye as the searing pain lifted. What the hell was it? A muscle cramp? Gas pain? This was no time to coddle his useless old body. He took a part-by-part inventory and everything seemed present and working.

He'd promised to meet Walt Roski, so he would meet Walt Roski.

EIGHTEEN
Where's Jack?

"Yo!" A deer hurled itself out of nowhere between the old Studebaker and the cabin.

"A deer in the headlights," Roski smiled. "How many times have we used that cliché?"

Sgt. Acevedo clearly didn't know what he was talking about. He pointed toward the swollen creek that was dropping below its banks after flooding onto the roadway. "What the hell is *that*? You know any science, Arson?"

"Maybe the creek shifted course up above."

The rain seemed to be determined to carry on undiminished for forty days and forty nights.

"What's so important for you at your crime scene?"

"Nothing now," Roski said disconsolately. "It's D-O-D. Down the drain."

Acevedo looked back to the cabin, where the driving rain was tearing away smoke faster than the chimney could pump it out. "I'm going to door-knock and get into the warm. I got some issues here."

"Fine with me." Right now, Roski felt ready to hit somebody, and this might give him more opportunity. He'd been looking forward to talking to Jack. Where the hell was he?

*

The mud and rubble carried out the open firegate dammed itself into long crescents and then water and more mud brimmed over them on the dead-end street. Jack Liffey could only assume Roski had gone up already, so he crunched the pickup slowly toward the open gate and through. Luckily he had a high clearance.

His headlights picked up only a sheet of dark water ahead, but a few weeds marked the shoulders of what should have been the fire road. He coughed in spasms from time to time and wiped sweat from his forehead despite the chill. He tried to reconstruct what he'd eaten down in San Diego to upset him so. Some tough hamburgers he and Megan had grabbed on the way back. Maybe chewing the gristle was why he felt like somebody had punched him in the jaw.

From time to time lightning left an image of the mountains burned on his retina. A day of omens and signs.

*

Bunny was half dozing across the sofa when Maeve arrived and got out two beers immediately. "Thanks for the boob warning," Maeve told her.

Bunny burst into tears of relief. "I was *so* scared of losing you to the swami, Maeve. But I was good, wasn't I? I let you meet him."

"Come here. I think your jeans are too tight."

*

Ellen's initial panic had eased a little. Maybe the insane world was normalizing. Zook's minor bullet wounds were even coming to seem comic. He had his shoe off and Beef was helping him wrap the foot with a dishrag and duct tape. Beef kept the pistol in his waist.

One big tug and her right hand would be out of the cuffs, but she was saving it for a better moment. Don't poke the bear until you can run. A great Chinese aphorism—probably from a fortune cookie.

A heavy pounding rattled the front door. "Police!"

"Get her out of here!" Zook snapped.

"Woodshed," Beef said.

She clenched her fist to make sure the cuff stayed on as Beef lifted her roughly and dragged her like a ragdoll. He lifted a timber out of two angle irons to free the back door.

"No noise, Chinko."

Cold rain swept over them as he dragged her legs through the mud and into a shed nearby.

"Hold on, gentlemen!" Zook called from inside.

"I don't give a damn what you're flushing, Zook," a male voice shouted. "I'm cold and I'm not narco."

"You had me at 'Police,' dude! I'm in the middle of taking a dump."

"Thanks for that report."

*

Roski followed the cop in and the punch of warmth was quite agreeable. A Franklin stove steamed across the room.

"What's all this, Zook? You're bleeding from every fucking part of your body."

Sgt. Acevedo glanced around and noticed Beef waiting at the back door with a big pistol in his waistband. The reaction was instant, almost reflex, his Glock out like Wyatt Earp.

"Lose the piece, Beef! Now!"

"I'm in my own place! Right, Zook?" Beef had drawn his pistol out, but only vaguely waved it about.

"You're about to die where you stand, fat boy."

"Put *your own* gun down." The indecisive sway of the pistol gave way to a vague aim toward the policeman.

The hair was standing up on Roski's neck. "*Gentlemen*, let's be calm—"

"Shut up!" the cop blurted. "Last chance, Beef."

"You're the invaders!"

"Put...the fucking...gun...*down*! I won't say it again. You're dead in five seconds."

"I ain't your pussy!"

"*Stand down!*" Roski bawled. Against his better judgment he stepped into the line of fire. "I'm in charge. First Marines! You—" Roski pointed at the big guy to save Acevedo a little face, and spoke calmly. "Son, set your pistol on the floor. Nobody's going to get shot here."

"I was in my rights."

"We can talk about that later. I'm standing right here and we're all safe."

The other young man spoke up for the first time. "Jesus, Beef! Put your strap down. We know Manny."

Beef concluded some inner struggle and then stooped slowly and set his pistol on the floor. Roski realized how tense he had been. His jaw hurt with it.

The big guy looked him in the eye. "I was in my rights."

"Be glad we don't have to test that theory." Roski collected the long-barrel .357. He motioned discreetly to Acevedo to lower his Glock. Acevedo's pocked face was beet red, his eyes insane with some ancient fury, something left over from the age of killer reptiles.

For some reason Beef pulled out a cell phone and took a photo of Acevedo at his most trembly. He guffawed in an ugly way. Planning a lawsuit?

Roski rested a comforting hand on the policeman's shoulder. "We're on top, Sergeant."

"Have a beer, gentlemen," the one called Zook offered, almost plaintively.

"I'm good," Acevedo said dully. He held out his palm to Roski for the weapon. "First Marines, huh?"

Roski handed him Beef's .357 and the policeman stuck it into his waistband and holstered his own pistol.

"Third of the First," Roski said. "Thundering Third. Haditha Dam."

The policeman nodded. "California 185th armored. Mosul. Fucking IEDs everywhere. And sand niggers."

The phrase annoyed Roski. "You seem to know these two."

"You cut CIs a little slack."

The big one couldn't stay quiet. "We ain't snitches."

Roski looked around the room and figured the worst was over. "You're going to need a doctor," he said to Zook, who was still bleeding.

"It ain't nothing."

Just a lovers' quarrel in the land of the dirtbags, Roski thought. Jack, where are you? I need your sanity.

*

A mile above the cabin, the pressure of water built up at the bottom of a dam that had formed naturally only a half hour ago. Seepage penetrated the soil and the sandy mud approached the condition known as liquefaction—where dirt flowed like water.

Upstream, a boulder the size of a bus tumbled into the current and a small shockwave raced toward the dam. A small plug of mud blew out and the short-lived lake began to eat the dam away to surge back into the wash it had followed for a thousand years.

*

In the pitch-dark shed, Ellen Chen twisted her wrist hard, and her hand came free with a stab of pain. She lay for a minute on what seemed a woodpile. She shook her arms to celebrate the delight of release and unwound the duct tape from her mouth and head. The first tangible benefit of her short hairdo.

Then she freed her ankles. She knew she had to put space between herself and the nutters right away. She felt her way to the door as the woodshed clattered all at once with hail. Great, what more could go wrong? The ordinary doorknob turned easily.

Ellen peered out and saw the lighted windows of the cabin fifty feet away. The ground was littered with dime-sized hail. She found a canvas log carrier left carelessly by the door. It would protect her from the hail. She held it taut above her head. A few hailstones hit her hands as she stepped out, but it worked.

She rejected going down to the fire road because she'd have to pass right by the cabin. Uphill, a deer trail. The night was terribly cold, and she tried to remember if Che had ever made an escape in such conditions.

*

Big, soft hailstones mashed against the windshield and the wipers fought hard to clear the slush.

"Holy—!"

Paula stood on the waterlogged brakes and just managed to halt before ticking a Jeep Wrangler abandoned in the road beside a big neutral-colored Ford. A van was ahead of them.

"What the hell is all this?"

"Folks that sure ain't expecting traffic."

"They gettin' some. If Jack's in there, I bet he's not happy."

"When's he ever happy?" Gloria said.

"Hush, girl. You played your part in that."

"You're a hard woman."

"You want me mellow, shoot me. Can you manage a little walk?"

"I got my cane."

"I'm the primary here, remember that."

"You shoot 'em all, except Jack, and I'll tell you if you done right."

*

Beef sat sullenly in the corner, entertaining himself by looking at what seemed photos on his cell phone. Every once in a while he emitted a guffaw without much humor in it. The big guy seemed to have only two mental states, Roski thought: sulk or a kind of derisive amusement.

Zook launched into some garbled philosophizing about how women were oppressed by their own eyes or maybe men's eyes; Acevedo was rummaging in obvious hiding places for something, and Roski decided on having a beer after all. He needed it. Bending to the cooler, he caught a glance of the big guy's cell phone.

"What's that?"

Beef hid the screen against his chest. "You a Chink-lover, Mr. Marine?"

"I can take 'em or leave 'em."

"Okay. You got to like this, then."

He held his phone toward Roski with the image of a defaced Chinese business sign. Then he punched forward to a photo of one of the racist posters Roski had seen on the street in the valley. "This is get-back."

"Very clever," Roski said lightly. "What else do you have?"

*

The two women were halfway to the cabin, Gloria hobbling badly on her cane, when they heard yet another car approach. They looked back to see Jack Liffey's pickup slide into Paula's Accord with his brakes locked up. *Crump.* Not hard enough to do much damage. The roadblock had obviously caught him by surprise, too.

"That answers one question," Paula said.

"That's my man, all right," Gloria said.

He got out of the pickup, astonished to find them there.

"You know why I like him," Gloria said. "Jack always worries more about what I'm afraid of than what he's afraid of."

"He don't look right, girl," Paula said.

She was right. He staggered toward them, clutching his arm.

*

Roski sampled his beer, and he and Beef both noticed Sgt. Acevedo draw his hand happily out of an old sugar bowl with several joints.

"Hey, dibs," Beef called

"That's my weed," Zook said.

Nothing but the joints seemed to matter just then. Beef thrust his phone into Roski's hand and stood up to inch himself toward the policeman.

The policeman slowly developed a grin as he watched Beef approach. His hand went to his holster, unsnapping the strap over his Glock. "Don't get too close unless you wanna French kiss," Acevedo said.

In the Marines, Roski had taken a course called "Village Entry," where they'd been taught that the minimum personal safety distance was five feet. Any closer and you couldn't react in time. Beef was getting there with Acevedo.

"Don't you trust me, Manny-Wanny?" Beef carried a strange warp in his voice.

But Roski's eyes were drawn irresistibly to the phone in his hand, and he swiped the photos forward. Smoke billowing out an auditorium double-doorway with Chinese people rapidly exiting. A close-up of a slashed tire. A spray-painted smiley face with slant eyes on a shop window. A broken picture window on what looked an expensive house. A girl lying on her side on the ground.

Roski held his finger back with a chill.

"No trust here, big guy," Acevedo said. "Down in Chiapas, my grandparents had a saying: 'Trust is next to God.' But after the drug business came in, it became, 'Forget trust—you can meet God later.'"

It wasn't just any girl in the photograph. An Asian girl with long dark hair. She was handcuffed and her ankles were taped together. She seemed to be lying in a gravel wash. Hello, Sabine, Roski thought. Oh, sonofabitch!

"Haw! You Mexes is great comedians."

"Beef, don't!" Zook called.

Roski couldn't tear his eyes off the phone. There were two more pictures of the girl, one closeup showing a gunshot wound in her forehead. Jack, you're not going to like this.

"Hey!"

"Shit, no!"

Roski heard a scuffling going on, but he couldn't look up. He swiped forward again. The bitter chill retook him, almost as bad as the first one. A lighted cigarette poked out of a cheap bar matchbook that rested on a pile of crumpled newspaper. The next several photographs were all of the early stages of a forest fire. He knew bugs usually stuck around to watch.

The deafening gunshot broke Roski's angry trance, followed by a shrieking like a steam-whistle from Acevedo. He saw Beef's hand on the pistol still in the cop's waistband. Beef yanked the pistol out fast and whirled to aim it at Zook.

Zook's eyes went wide with bewilderment. "Tony, we been besties—"

*

Jack Liffey staggered up to the women. "I can't deal with this. The pain is terrible."

Just then they all heard a gunshot, then another, from the cabin.

"I guess we're going in," Paula Green said, drawing her pistol and glancing at Gloria and Jack.

"I guess we are."

"Just please!" Jack Liffey clutched his left shoulder and toppled into a pool of mud.

"Or maybe not," Gloria said.

"Can you help me lift him?"

"I will, if I can or not."

*

Ellen felt like a wet housecat scrambling up the deer trail, soaked to the skin and freezing. In her mind's eye, the fat one was only a few feet behind her, about to grab her ankle and yank her back. Lord, that monstrous appendage of his!

She emerged from the chaparral into a startlingly denuded fire zone with only stubs of former plants. Off to the left she saw a small shelf of rock far above the creek, and she calmed down enough to go to it and press herself in under the rock shelter, clutching her ankles and breathing deeply.

Down very deep she felt a kind of continuing fear that she'd never felt before—the end of her innocence of terror, she felt—and she wondered if she would ever recover. She knew she'd be reassessing the Orange Berets for the rest of her life, but she refused to repudiate her impulse to justice.

All at once her whole world rumbled, and she pressed a hand to the rock overhead for comfort. A baritone vibration was palpable beneath her. The noise swelled and acquired sharper overtones, clattering and clacking. It was from the ravine. She watched in awe as a flood surge of water and rock and debris fled down the gorge, much of it well above the land. The cliff opposite gave way and slumped into the flood.

A crack opened up below her own shelf as she watched, horrified. She wanted to flee but couldn't move.

*

As the women propped Jack Liffey between them, they heard the terrible rumble begin, like a giant machine turning over deep in the earth.

In Jack Liffey's forgotten headlights, they caught a glimpse of the first destructive wave coming down the gorge. Stones in the flow grated horribly against one another, the kind of sound that you guessed people rarely heard and survived.

"Don't be no scaredy-cat!" Paula said.

"His truck's blocking us," Gloria said.

"Throw him in the back. We'll have to take it."

*

Inside the party cabin, everyone seemed to realize that the terrible noise meant impending death. Roski grabbed the only guy he could get his hands on and hauled Beef out the back door into sheets of sleety rain. He frog-marched him straight across a clearing past a shed and uphill. A surprisingly dead weight, gone into some kind of panicked freeze-up. Roski was incredibly strong from constant weight training—one of his few vanities. But the young man eventually began to resist.

"Help out here or die," Roski said. Beef began to get control of his legs.

Roski heard the rasp of rock on rock, and one glance showed quite large boulders leaping above the watercourse like dolphins. His only cogent idea was to go up and up. Eventually, Beef tore out of Roski's grasp to tumble backward.

"Stay off me, you old fart!" Beef struggled to his feet.

"Look at the water, man. It's going to kill both of us."

"Shit on a stick!" The flow was too much for the gorge, spreading out wide wherever it could. The cabin below had been swept away.

Both men scrambled upward.

"Shit shit shit!"

They flailed through weeds and brush and came out into burn. Beef had little endurance and sat heavily in exhaustion. "Leave me for the Injuns. I'm a no-hope."

Roski considered for a moment, and then came back to squat next to Beef.

"Nobody leaves anybody tonight," Roski said mildly. "Tell me about Sabine Roh.I saw your pictures. We're all guys together."

"That other Chinese cunt?"

Roski nodded serenely. *Other*? he thought.

"What's to know? She was following me around like a dog and driving me nuts; she pretended she liked me. Whatever happened to her, she deserved it."

While he was talking, Beef slowly withdrew a big serrated killing knife from his Red Wing boot. He seemed to think the movement went unnoticed.

"It's too bad you know the name, old man," Beef said.

"Hold on, pal," Roski said equably. "After you took care of the girl, you started the Sheepshead Fire to cover it up? Seriously? I saw the picture of the matchbook, too."

Beef haw-hawed once. "Life is tough titty. I don't ask God for nothing in the bad times, because I don't ask in the good times neither." He brought the K-bar up with a smirk as if to show Roski how he was about to die.

Roski sighed, and without any windup rammed the heel of his right hand very hard into Beef's throat, crushing his larynx. In the Third of the First, they'd been given Israeli Krav Maga training in hand-to-hand combat. The trouble with an extravagantly aggressive martial art was that when you really needed it, all you knew how to do was kill.

Anthony Buffano collapsed like a deflated balloon, gagging and clutching his throat. Roski lifted him by a handful of shirt and dragged the worthless hulk across burned-over hillside to the edge of the ravine and tossed the big sack of crap into the debris flow, watching the body flail end over end as it descended the cataract.

Nobody killed a firefighter on his watch. He knew he'd never tell anyone about this except Jack Liffey.

Jack, where the *hell* are you?

EPILOGUE
The Long Sleep

A light rain was coming down as the skirmish line, wearing bright orange vests and hardhats, made its way across the vast rubble field, poking deep into fresh mud with fiberglass poles. Several dogs ran ahead of them and pawed the ground here and there. Excavating machines waited far down below on Serrano Place. Only a few homes in the neighborhood had survived, teeth in a shattered denture.

"Where the fire trail crossed the creek," Walter Roski said. "If you've got a survey map."

George Maloof, the head of the San Dimas Mountain Rescue team, pointed out what little he could decipher of a slope where no landmarks remained. The landslides had ultimately torn loose a half-mile of mountain and buried two centuries-old canyons, five old cabins, two fire trails, the surrounding slopes, and much of the neighborhood, where another rescue team was working on the debris of houses with a chugging Jaws of Life and prybars.

Maloof studied his handheld GPS, on short loan from the Air Force for the rescue operation. It was more sensitive than the commercial units, using twelve satellites to locate itself within a centimeter.

"Maybe where that German Shepherd is alerting."

"How many people have been found?"

"I don't have a total. Thirty-some dead. A few were alive in the flat, nobody up here."

"Dumb question, sorry," Roski said.

They walked on in gloomy silence for a while, watching the soil as if they could see into it.

"I ran into a religious group once," Maloof said, "who said wanting anything better than you're given after a tragedy is an insult to God."

Roski wondered if this guy was religious and what religion. But the personal was personal.

"*Inshallah*," Maloof said. "When what you want didn't happen, you praise God and learn to want what did."

Barks and human shouts swirled around them. Roski knew he was overwrought, as usual. "The real trouble with catastrophes is that the idiots who survive talk as if they had a special deal with God."

Maloof didn't smile. "Yeah, that's what idiots do."

The dog had given up alerting and moved on, but the spot had a small red flag. A large oval of hardening mud showed a grayer and smoother texture, as indecipherable as a faraway spiral galaxy.

"Yeah," Maloof said. "We're ten meters directly over the cabin."

*

Gloria grabbed at Paula's blouse to hold her back. Paula had parked in the shadow of the 1930s art-deco hulk of L.A. County Hospital, condemned to death after the 1994 earthquake and now just offices. The replacement glass and steel Kleenex boxes looked like every other hospital in the world.

"I know I screwed up with the Bakersfield guy. Haven't you ever been hit by a craving you didn't expect? You think nothing can touch you and then some guy like a hundred other guys hits you with a magic raygun. It's a goddam hostage situation. It's junior high again. And when it's over, you think you're back in your normal world and he drops you a stupid little note—*Can I just have permission to think about you, my darling?* Why do we think love is so great?"

Paula frowned at her. "Girl, the real problem is you got sex stuck up here—" She tapped Gloria's forehead. "—instead of down where it belongs. Come on."

Paula Green badged a couple of post-9/11 security guards at the back door of the hospital to butch around the metal detector on the way to the cardiac ward.

"All I really know about life came from my mom," Paula said

vaguely. "She said it's bad news to whip the slaves."

Gloria laughed.

"Elevators over there." They hunted up Five-West, and Paula barked into the intercom beside the locked doors until it buzzed, and they were into Cardiac Intensive Care.

A semicircle of ten glass cubicles faced a nurse station. Inside the nearest one was a six-foot-long inert object on a bed. The object looked a lot like Jack Liffey, though it was the focus of a small universe of apparatus, with wires and tubes leading to monitors and wheezing machinery. Two women were glaring at one another across the recumbent object—one young, fairly tall, and Maeve. The other was older, petite, and Asian.

"That be her," Paula said grimly.

"Uh-huh." Gloria hip-thrust Paula aside, dug out her own badge, and showed it to the nurse sitting at the *Star Trek* controls.

"Room one. What's the story?" A voice that was not to be delayed or denied.

"Came in with near total coronary blockage. Circling the drain. They did an emergency triple bypass. Unusual case—he only has three coronary arteries. Lucky he lived this far."

The nurse had obviously been through police situations before— County was the biggest trauma unit in the U.S., famous for its weekend knife-and-gun club in the ER—and she summarized fast and well.

"His body came through it, but we have no idea how long his brain may have gone without oxygen. They think he had several myocardial infarctions over a couple of hours, but a massive one toward the end. He must be one tough cookie. Officially, his condition is guarded."

"Those visitors," Gloria snapped.

"We only allow one, if any. The Asian woman said she was his wife. The girl forced her way in a few minutes ago and said she was his daughter. Security is on its way to deal with them."

"Call off the dogs."

Gloria was manifestly in charge now. She used her cane to hobble around the big dashboard to the cubicle, and Paula held back. Tien and Maeve glanced up from their mad-dog glaring.

"You," Gloria said, pointing at Tien. "Outside now to talk. Maeve, stay with Paula."

The Asian woman nodded at Gloria's command. She seemed to know who Gloria was, but Gloria didn't care. All she knew was she needed to win this fight. She slapped the big square switch that opened the doors and led this man-stealer out to the snack room.

*

Ellen Chen lay on her own bed, in her own room in her parents' home, her infant daughter breathing softly in the bassinet. The night before she had hiked down the hill after the worst was over and given herself over to a fire crew. Strangely, no cops had shown up at her home, though she'd told a sympathetic fireman everything, the kidnap and the handcuffing. She'd told them everyone she thought had been in the cabin, then she'd refused a hospital checkup and insisted on being taken home.

"I'm just wet and cold, man."

Ellen plucked out her journal, untouched for weeks. She read her last entry:

We're told "meaning well" is all that matters, that it excuses any consequences. That's the problem with individualism. We are responsible, even if we can't know what will happen. I accept it.

How grandiose I felt only a few weeks before. She pondered for a while. So strong and pure. She found a pen and added:

I must talk to that troubled old man. I bet he knows things I don't.

*

Tien and Gloria squared off in the snack room.

"You the pain-in-ass in Jack's life," Tien snapped. "Another hairy American girl who can't never be nice to her man."

"You got it," Gloria said. "And you're the short time that opened her crack for GIs with five bucks."

The Asian woman paused and seemed to deflate a little. "I start this nuclear missile war, okay. Sorry, sorry. I'm from good family, plenty college, not street trash. There some way to stop this? We both breathe deep. Both two care about Jack."

"That remains to be seen—" Gloria had been about to hit her with a blast of ranting, but she stopped herself. This face-off might be the toughest war she'd ever had—a war for the rest of her life. And winning might not be simply a matter of overpowering the opponent. Who could tell where Jack's head was? She'd certainly given him reason to walk out. "Let's de-escalate. Say your piece, woman."

They stared at one another for a while, breathing deeply. A man in a smock looked in, took fright at the tension in the room, and fled.

"I want to make Jackie happy in his last years. Give him big boat, nice Porsche, Italian suit, Rolex, fine shoe, and make his daughter rich, too. I give her scholarship all her life. What *you* gonna do? Close your knees to him? Get boyfriend?"

"Say *what*?"

"Don't think this come from Jack complain. He never. I got source."

It didn't seem like finicky Jack to grumble to a mistress. "Slow down, woman. I hear you're filthy rich and you want to make Jack rich, too, and all his family for three generations."

"I always want everybody happy. Win-win-win. You go away right now, I give you ten million dollar. Company stock. You want cash money in paper bag, I get it. You want something else, you say."

Gloria was struck dumb. Ten million dollars! Plus leaving Jack and Maeve rich and pampered the rest of their lives. How dare she turn that down on their behalf? Particularly after all the grief she'd given him.

And the money for herself—Jesus. More zeroes than she'd ever thought about. She could be the benefactor of the tiny Paiute reservation outside Lone Pine, replace every shabby trailer with a ranch house.

*

He lay with his eyes closed and his arms wrapped around a small pillow on his chest. Paula Green had been in enough ICUs to know that the glowing numbers seemed fine. Pulse around ninety. No weird spikes in the EKG. Blood pressure was normal. The rest of the equipment was from Mars.

Paula asked Maeve for an account of Jack's condition.

"The nurses say it was lucky you guys got him to the ER when you did."

What Maeve didn't tell Paula was that some fire official had come by in the tiny hours and asked her to pass on a simple message to her dad: *The guy who killed your girl is history.* It had to mean the girl her dad had been looking for. Killed. He would see it as another failure.

"They did a bypass last night. The doctor said he had so much plaque in his arteries he was ready to keel over at any moment."

Gloria came striding back into the cubicle alone, looking like she'd been falling a mile and hadn't quite hit yet.

"What it is?" Paula asked.

It took a few moments for Gloria to shake herself free from some train of thought. "How's Jack?" she snapped.

Paula let Maeve explain what she knew, and Gloria nodded at several points, a little more heartily than she should have. Paula chased away a nurse who looked in to try to shoo them.

"Glor, don't keep us in suspense," Maeve said. "You had it out with that woman."

Gloria's eyes were burning and confused. "She made me an offer I couldn't refuse," she said evenly.

An even more insistent nurse looked in. "I'm sorry, but you all *really* have to leave."

"Tell us," Maeve said to Gloria.

Gloria's eyes settled into their accustomed fierceness. "I made her an offer she couldn't refuse neither."

*

Jack Liffey lay with the world's heaviest brick on his chest, afraid to move at all lest he stir the pain in his chest into something worse.

He heard voices nearby, but his eyelids were far too heavy to open. The voices were comforting nonetheless. He'd taken in that he'd had serious heart surgery—serious enough so he really should have been walking down that glowing tunnel to meet a beloved uncle, but none of that had showed up.

He wondered what had become of the lost young man he'd given the John Berger book to. Zook. Bad companions, as everybody's mom used to say.

Hate the other, the outsider; hate non-whites, hate gays, hate people from the next neighborhood over. These days it seemed to be your range of hatreds that defined who you were.

And it was so often the comfortable who hated. People who had plenty to eat, warm shelter every night, all the toys. He wondered if there was some toxic gas venting from deep in the American psyche.

*

"Hold on, girl!" Gloria yelped into her cell phone. "An eye's opened up!"

She was hovering over Jack Liffey in an instant. It was an ugly room in a nursing home now.

"Jack, are you with us?"

He winked.

"I'll get back to you, Paula. Can you speak, Jack?" She rested her hand on his forehead. Both eyes were open now, squinting. "Make me a sign."

The eyes blinked twice. Then she suggested one blink for yes and two for no and found out that he was genuinely present.

"You been away, my love. It's six weeks you been in a coma." She didn't tell him he'd had a stroke after the heart surgery. And she didn't say she'd refused the Vietnamese woman's entreaty to fly him to Zurich for some super-duper neurologists. She knew absolutely that Jack Liffey wouldn't have wanted anything that an ordinary man couldn't have.

"Maeve's been coming to talk to you all the time, Jack, and a fireman named Roski, and a Chinese girl named Ellen, too. A whole lot of grown-up bad boys from the hood that say you helped them out years ago."

One blink. Maybe an acknowledgment.

"What do you need, my love? Want me to suggest things?"

He closed his eyes and stayed that way for another week.

Maeve was at his bedside when he surfaced again, and she squealed to see his eyes. He coughed to clear his throat.

"Give me eat," Jack Liffey said.

CPSIA inform
Printed in the
LVOW10s234

415848L

22442